## ALSO BY KATE WATTERSON FROM TOM DOHERTY ASSOCIATES

# CRUSHED

## Kate Watterson

**TOR**

A TOM DOHERTY ASSOCIATES BOOK • NEW YORK

This is a work of fiction. All of the characters, organizations, and events portrayed in this novel are either products of the author's imagination or are used fictitiously.

CRUSHED

A Tor Book
Published by Tom Doherty Associates
175 Fifth Avenue
New York, NY 10010

www.tor-forge.com

Tor® is a registered trademark of Macmillan Publishing Group, LLC.

ISBN 978-0-7653-9295-4

Our books may be purchased in bulk for promotional, educational, or business use. Please contact your local bookseller or the Macmillan Corporate and Premium Sales Department at 1-800-221-7945, extension 5442, or by e-mail at MacmillanSpecialMarkets@macmillan.com.

First Edition: February 2018

Printed in the United States of America

0  9  8  7  6  5  4  3  2  1

*For Linda Graybill. A very lovely lady.*

## ACKNOWLEDGMENTS

Many thanks to Bess Cozby.

# CRUSHED

## Chapter 1

*S*he was home.

*He could see the lights, but she'd be at the back, probably in the kitchen at this time of the evening, because no one knew better than he did she worked long hours. He could picture her shining hair, the slight curve of her lips, the smoothness of her fair skin . . .*

*The air smelled like spring, like the lilacs of his childhood, and the cool breeze moved his hair. He edged around the building, pausing when he stepped on an old branch from last year that cracked loudly. He knew full well it was there but had forgotten, and the sound almost startled him out of his fantasy.*

*Almost.*

*He wanted to look in the window but fought the impulse. He'd taken a chance and done it twice before, and she hadn't been aware of him staring through the glass, out there, just watching her.*

*It had occurred to him to give her a gift.*

*He knew just what she'd like.*

* * *

**Jason Santiago walked** up to Detective Ellie MacIntosh's desk without his usual sardonic grin in place. She glanced at him, registered the unhappy expression, clicked a key to save the document she was wrapping up on her computer, and asked bluntly, "What? You have that look on your face."

"Hammett wants to see us in the morgue. Man, I hate that damn place."

That wasn't new information. Her partner started to sweat about two feet inside the door. The same man who could canvas a murder scene and not skip a beat couldn't stomach the sterile quiet.

It wasn't like Ellie was fond of the morgue either, but she handled it better than he did. "We don't even have a case down there right now. What's up?"

He shook his head, and curly blond hair that was about as long as department regulations would allow—and pushing the edge of that envelope—brushed his neck. "No idea."

"She didn't say?"

"Nope. She sounded funny, though."

"Funny is a high-tech remark in law enforcement, right?" She got up, because Santiago was a lot of things, but not an idiot—far from it—so if Dr. Hammett seemed off-key to him, Ellie believed it. As a homicide investigator, what a medical examiner had to say was important.

"Okay, I guess let's go." She checked her phone and shut it off. Hammett did not like interruptions.

They took the stairs. Santiago also didn't like elevators. An elevator to the morgue was the stuff of his nightmares as far as she could tell. Fine with her; she'd been writing reports all morning and could probably use the exercise. Paperwork was not her favorite part of the job.

Dr. Hammett was a composed woman, with a sense of humor that was sometimes hard to catch, and always businesslike. Dark haired and slender, she was professional, efficient, and no-nonsense.

"Detectives. I'd say it was nice to see you, but you don't want to see me either. We rarely meet under pleasant circumstances, so let's just not go there. I called because I have a Jane Doe that might interest you. There was no immediate suspicion of foul play, nothing for homicide to handle on the scene, but I've determined that's not true. Take a look."

Ellie wasn't squeamish—but she wasn't hardened either. It was her private opinion that when you reached that point, maybe you should look for another job. So when the ME pulled back the sheet, she braced herself, and just saw a young woman who looked like she was asleep except for the autopsy scars. She was even still pretty.

It always bothered her more than she let on, because she experienced a startling moment of self-introspection that included her own mortality. If she had to guess, the woman on that cold steel table was about her age and had similar coloring. Ellie dealt with death on a regular basis—in her job that was unavoidable—but ever since her father's sudden heart attack and her mother's battle with cancer began, she'd felt a personal connection with loss that didn't involve justice being done, because sometimes there wasn't any justice.

Immediately, Ellie tried to put the emotional part of it aside and said, "Her nails are done."

"Our victim was also nicely dressed."

"Where was she found?"

"By the lake on a bench, just sitting there. But from the lividity, I'd say she was put there. There was no assault. Toxicology will let me know if she overdosed. I'm still weighing several possibilities for cause of death, but that really isn't what bothered me enough to call you. Look at this."

She then turned over the young woman's wrist.

Written in black ink on the pallid skin was: *What do you think?*

Whatever Ellie expected when she got up that morning, it wasn't a message written on a corpse.

The ME covered the body back up. She didn't mince words, but then she never did. "Any ideas?"

Not a single explanation came to mind. It was . . . for lack of a better word, Ellie thought, macabre.

Santiago scratched his jaw. "That's weird as shit . . ." He hastily amended because he actually tried to behave in front of Hammett, which said something. "I mean hell. Weird as hell."

How he thought one swear word was better than another one was a mystery, but trying to understand his thought processes was something Ellie had found a useless endeavor since the first day they'd met. Santiago grew on you, but she'd come to the conclusion it really took some time.

Hammett was used to him anyway. "It was written postmortem, in my official opinion, and I will put that in my report. As soon as I figure out just how this young woman died, I'll be in touch. For now, I consider it a suspicious death."

Unfortunately, Ellie didn't disagree.

They left—more stairs—and both of them were already thinking out loud. He said, "I have a friend who writes his grocery list on his palm. Says he loses a piece of paper in about five seconds or leaves it behind on the counter at home and doesn't have it when he gets to the store. His hand is always with him. That's his logic. He could get out his phone, but then he'd start checking his messages, and he hates the grocery store in the first place, so his hand works perfectly to make the whole thing simple."

At least one good thing came out of their trips to the "underworld"—she wouldn't have to go to the gym later. Santiago's elevator phobia was good for her thighs and cardio health. "The most astonishing thing about that revelation is that you actually have a friend."

He gave her a look she might have deserved for that remark, but Santiago, while he had his good traits, wasn't everyone's cup o' tea, as her grandmother would say. Good-looking but abrasive, and smart enough to know he should tone it down, but just not of the mindset to do so. He was a bad-boy cop, not corrupt in any way, but he had a tendency to think regulations were suggestions. She'd been grateful for that a time or two during their association, but it would help his career a lot if he could dial it back sometimes. He was often blunt to a fault.

He opened the door at the top of the stairwell for her. "My point is that maybe the victim wrote it herself."

Possible. But it bothered her—a lot—that the ME thought it was postmortem. "You're already calling her a victim."

"What are you thinking?"

The same thing. Hands down.

"I'm thinking we are about to have a close encounter with missing person reports."

"Yeah." He narrowed his eyes. "What if she was at a bar or somewhere, anywhere, and met a guy or was introduced to him, and she was with a friend and the friend wrote that on her wrist? It is at least plausible."

It was except for one thing. "Postmortem? I think I saw a horror movie like that once."

"Hammett said she just *thinks* so."

"Someone moved the body. How blood pools does not lie."

"There's that," he conceded as they walked down the hall. Things were busy, phones ringing, and Santiago nodded at another detective who passed by. "I'd define it as a possible homicide to probable homicide."

Ellie didn't disagree, haunted by the vision of the young woman's face.

She wasn't a doctor, but Ellie guessed if the writing happened right after the victim died, it would be hard to tell. "Obviously she's not a homeless person no one will miss. Her hair was nicely cut and clean and the nails said it all. She's someone that will be reported."

"I think so too."

They agreed at times, and really didn't at others, but this was one where they saw eye to eye. "*He* moved her. Had to be a he, because though she wasn't big, I doubt a woman could do that. Not dead weight."

"Dead weight? Nice way of phrasing it." Ellie eyed him. He loved challenging cases like this and was already getting geared up. The ordinary didn't interest him nearly as much. "He drugged her somewhere and set her there? That's what you're thinking?"

"I'm not sure. There was no sexual assault. We both

agree opportunity is more important than motive usually, at least when it comes down to solving a case. It could have been two people."

She wasn't convinced. "Or an accident. What if she was at a party and simply overdosed and they panicked and put her body in the park? I want the tox report first."

Her partner said, "I don't disagree with that, but this doesn't look like an accident to me. I'm interested."

Dryly, Ellie observed, "And tired of catching up on paperwork."

Santiago was Santiago. His grin was unrepentant. No denial or apology. Neither of those were his style. "Exactly. Hey, I didn't wish her dead, but now that she is, I'd like figuring out how, why, and who; a lot better than filling out those damn forms. I bet she'd appreciate that."

**The report came** directly to him, which was the one perk he had of seniority over Ellie MacIntosh. Jason had been in homicide longer. She'd started out working for a small county sheriff's department in northern Wisconsin before drawing national attention by solving a series of brutal murders and getting the job offer in Milwaukee. But it wasn't all sunshine and roses. She'd been stuck with him, and he'd been stuck with a virtual rookie.

Instant dislike on both sides.

Not a match made in heaven, except they'd saved each other's lives a couple of times now. The dislike had changed to the conclusion that maybe he was with the right partner who might not like everything about him, but at least understood how he operated.

His problem was *he* liked her more than he should, and there was just not a damn thing he could do about the sexual attraction. It was there, it existed, and he just tried to funnel his energy in other directions.

Hammett's report was a good example.

The toxicology was clean for drugs, but the blood alcohol level was very high. Cause of death was listed as asphyxiation unrelated to the drinking.

Manner of death?

Hammett agreed with him on this one. Probable homicide was her decision.

He printed it out and slapped it down in front of Ellie at her desk. She was sipping coffee out of a cup with a Badgers logo and looking no happier than he was about doing the backlog of reports. He stated, "Looks like my bar theory might be a pretty good guess. Odds on the chief handing it to us?"

"I'll take that bet. Everyone else has cases right now." She looped her blond hair over her ear as she read it, and he was used to that mannerism. "This is disturbing. All of it. So she drank too much and some-one *suffocated* her?" She tapped the paper with an accusing finger. "No marks on her throat. They just waited for her to pass out?"

"Looks like it. We need to find out who she is first of all." He dropped into a chair in a careless sprawl. Too much beer and ESPN last night. He had his vices, and hey, it was still pro basketball season.

She frowned. "I'm not having any luck so far. No one that looks like her has been reported."

Of course she'd been at work on it. That's who she was. Focused and determined. Everything was about the job. He was guilty of that as well. Maybe that was why every relationship he'd ever had had gone south.

"Let's go interview the person that found her. Maybe look around for more witnesses."

"We haven't even been assigned to the case yet."

"Well, here we go."

As if on cue, Chief Joe Metzger, big and burly, an ex-military man who took succinct to a whole new level, walked up. He pointed at them. "Jane Doe is yours."

Jason watched him walk away. "That is a man of few words."

"If those were your words, they'd all be profanity. I actually prefer it when he doesn't talk to me that much." Ellie got up and reached for her coat. "I can't believe it's snowing. Whatever happened to spring?"

"I think it took a vacation on a tropical beach with a bunch of college students and is wearing a bikini and sipping a beer." He slung his coat over his shoulder with one finger. "Let's go."

"Where, precisely?"

"I want to see where he put her."

She didn't disagree. "He was making a point. Sure he was."

"Had to be familiar territory."

And that was Jason's one gift. He always felt it. He was a dedicated detective, he knew that, but his calling really was that he could tell a bad case from minute one when the investigation started.

He said to Ellie, "I think we have real trouble."

# Chapter 2

He'd hated school.

Maybe it was a rebellion against authority. People telling him what to do really dug under his skin. She'd never said it out loud, but as he got older he was fairly sure his mother grew more and more quietly afraid of him. It was a subtle shift in power, but the dynamic was there. When he was sixteen she'd told him to clean his room for the third time, and instead he'd taken the family cat and driven it about thirty miles away and dropped it off by the side of the road.

To his credit, he hadn't killed it, but it had occurred to him. She'd waited for that feline to return for days, standing at the back door and calling, but maybe it was something in his expression when she asked him to go look around for Mittens that made her start to wonder if he was involved.

She let up about his room.

He had a much younger brother and younger sister. It was a good call on her part.

* * *

**The bench looked** lonely, dusted with a light covering of white flakes. Someone had left a crumpled fast food bag there rather than walking the five steps over to the nearest trash receptacle.

"Lazy bastards," Santiago muttered, and took care of it since the scene had been processed already and the bag was hardly evidence. "I personally think littering should be made a felony. Who gives anyone the right to think they can fuck up the landscape for everyone else?"

Ellie agreed on principle, though as usual, his brand of eloquence was questionable. "This is a pretty ordinary city park and not close to the downtown district or any of the trendy bars by the lake. We've already figured out she was probably killed somewhere else, and that she had to be carried a fair distance. Rigor sets in and that's pretty hard to do. The killer kept the body in the trunk of his car, I'd guess. When it was dark and no one would most likely be here, brought her to the park."

"So maybe he lives nearby." Santiago hunched his shoulders under his coat, his expression thoughtful. "Knows the pattern of the place."

He was good at that. Noticing what Ellie might not register because he'd had a rougher upbringing, so pattern of the place apparently meant something to him.

"Or," she countered, "he drove around and found this park and just decided to dump the body."

"Hauling a dead woman out of your trunk is a big risk. This is Wisconsin. Get the hell out of Milwaukee and put her in the woods somewhere. We have a lot of trees, not to mention lakes. That would be a lot safer. I believe you know, of all people, it's been done."

He had a point and was referring to the elusive Northwoods Killer she'd finally tracked down. "This person is making a statement."

"I sure think so."

"Wrote on her arm, positioned the body in a public place while taking some serious chances . . ."

"A statement, I agree. He wanted her found. We really need someone to call in and say, guess who is missing, not coming for Sunday dinner, skipping out on work and not answering her phone, etc."

"Well, I suppose we should go talk to the lucky people who had to report a dead body."

They were an older couple who lived in a ground-floor apartment nearby on a quiet residential street, not run down but not upscale either, with dated homes and scattered brick complexes from the fifties. The husband answered the door and explained his wife was working, but he was retired, and yes, he would definitely be willing to answer any questions.

Tall and thin with gray hair, Mr. Morris tried to be helpful. He led them into a living room that had furnishings to match the place and quickly used a remote to switch off the television. "I don't know why I watch the news. So darned depressing, or most of it is anyway."

Mr. Morris settled back into a worn recliner, and Ellie and Santiago had no choice but to sit on a plaid couch that had seen better days.

"We've taken to walking in the mornings." The man looked almost apologetic. "We thought the exercise would do us good. That young woman looked like she was napping, but then again, she wasn't moving and it was chilly out. We were worried. She was just wearing that thin blouse and a skirt. I had on a coat and a hat. She only had on one shoe and I didn't see the other one anywhere. I honestly didn't want to look closer, but in good conscience, I had to. I think we both realized pretty quickly she was dead. My wife started crying. I know this is ridiculous, but I took off my jacket and put it over that poor girl. She looked so cold."

That was hardly good news from a forensics standpoint, but he had been trying to be nice. Ellie wasn't very happy but kept it to herself. "You didn't see anyone? Nothing at all?"

He considered the question. "A few joggers are usually out, but it was early. We don't jog because we're a little old for that. We do walk. It's good for your heart."

She'd already taken him off the suspect list. "I'm sure it was upsetting to find her. Nothing else caught your attention? No one was around?"

The man's eyes went unfocused and then he said, "Well, maybe. One runner. Not as tall as Detective Santiago here, but close. He stopped, running in place, and asked us if we needed help. I'd called 911 by then, so I told him no. We could see there was nothing we could do."

Ellie and Santiago exchanged a glance.

"Describe him." Santiago had out his phone, ready to take notes.

"I'll try. I was pretty rattled. Let's see . . . brown hair, I remember that much."

"Young? Race?"

"Young? To me, yes. Maybe he was in his late

twenties or so. Could have been older, but not by much. I tend to think everyone is young. Just wait until you get to be my age. White, I'd say. Not black or Hispanic or Asian. Is he important?"

She could explain that some killers liked to hang around their victims so they could get some sort of rush when the body was discovered, just like the arsonist will join the crowd after he'd set a fire, but chose not to mention it. If this nice old man found that the news was upsetting, knowing he might have come face to face with a killer wouldn't make his day brighter. "We'd like to talk to him to find out if he saw anything. What was he wearing? Did you see any tattoos or anything like that?"

Mr. Morris frowned. "Jogging clothes . . . black pants and sneakers. I don't remember a tattoo."

Santiago rose and fished out a card. "Call if anything else comes to mind. We'd appreciate it."

When they walked out to his truck, her partner said with resignation, "Put his coat on her? Oh great, there go any fibers that forensics might find on her clothes. I suppose at least we know now they could be from his jacket. Brown hair isn't all that helpful either. I bet there's hardly any Caucasian males in this city with brown hair."

She beat him to it and opened her own door. "We don't know that person wasn't just a passerby."

"No, but that's about the only lead we have right now and it's damn thin."

He was unfortunately right.

"If you have any other ideas, I'd love to hear them. Otherwise, we're going to have to wait until we find out who she is."

He slammed his door after he got in and started his

truck. "I wish we had even the vaguest flippin' idea of where she went to down those drinks. That dropped shoe is evidence. Maybe it's in the back of his car, but maybe it's in a parking lot somewhere that could lead us back to where she was before she ended up right here."

Ellie agreed, but talk about a long shot. "No one is going to report a lost shoe. Ever seen one lying by the side of the road and wondered how it got there? I have. I think I've had nightmares about shoes on the side of the road, wondering about the story behind it."

"You've got too much imagination, MacIntosh. Hey, you should tip Grantham off that there's a lost shoe story waiting to be written."

Ellie wasn't interested in Santiago's caustic comments about her failed relationship with Bryce Grantham, who had moved to New York and seemed to be having some decent success in his career as an author. Bryce wasn't a mistake, he was just a complicated man, and their romance had no doubt been doomed from the beginning because they were nothing alike.

None of Santiago's business, but he brought it up now and then anyway.

"I think he can come up with his own plot ideas."

He surprisingly let it go. "I understand about the nightmares. We're obsessive about our jobs, which isn't good for the mental health of any person. I don't know about you, but I heard as a kid there was no such thing as monsters, and you and I know that's not true. Last but not least, we spend too much time looking at dead people. That's a fast ticket to Nightmare City, right there."

The sky had turned a brilliant blue—spring was a fickle mistress. Ellie agreed. "I wish now and then I could turn it all off, but my subconscious tends to win the day."

"Yeah, but look at the bright side, now and again we remove the monsters from the picture."

That last point was valid.

**Jason knew he** had a darker side that reminded him of his father. Not the parent who had contributed to his existence on this earth, but the one who had raised him. His biological father was a career criminal, but the man he'd lived with as a child was his mother's second husband and had been a drunk who hadn't been shy about using his fists. That meant Jason had a real problem with happiness because he always felt like it was something for other people.

He didn't embrace this knowledge, he just knew it existed. He'd been that scared kid, walking on eggshells, and then he'd turned into that tough kid, who secretly wished someone was baking him cookies and making his bed but would never admit it.

His tendency to brood didn't do him any favors, and he was doing it now, feet up on a table that had never been used for coffee—he'd bought it at a flea market for five dollars just so he could put his feet on it—beer in hand. The beverage wasn't even cold, but that was his fault for not putting any in the refrigerator. In the state of Wisconsin it was not a crime to drink cheap beer lukewarm.

But some things certainly *were* a crime. Like murder.

So what point was there in getting a young woman drunk and then killing her by putting a pillow or something like that over her face? Yes, she'd been robbed to the extent she didn't have a purse with her identification, but that could be just so there was a bigger time lapse between the murder and the investigation.

He wrote down longhand on the back of his electric bill envelope: *Smart killer or opportunist? Was he just in the bar and followed her, or was this planned?*

Good question.

*Did he keep the shoe on purpose or did it just fall off?*

It could be he'd kept it. Since the brain of a psychopath was hard to dissect, Jason didn't understand it, but sometimes criminals kept trophies.

*Who is she?*

No one had yet reported her missing. *Single.*

Fairly young and well dressed. *Professional.*

He was mulling it all over when his cell phone rang. "Detective Santiago? This is Thomas Morris. I hope it isn't too late to call."

It was eight o'clock. He was thinking of ordering a pizza or some Thai delivery because all he had in the cabinet was canned soup. Jason sat up abruptly and took his feet off the coffee table. "No, not at all."

"I was talking to my wife and she remembered something about that jogger."

"I am all ears."

"He was wearing a sweatshirt that had a square shape on it. She thinks maybe a company logo was printed in the middle."

He was scribbling on the envelope again. "Any chance she caught what logo that could be and could describe it?"

"Something with wings. I did ask her, but she was

upset at the time, and, well . . . that's all she really remembers. She does think she'd recognize his face. Despite our age, she has a very good memory usually."

Talk about a deflated balloon. It was such a long
shot anyway he just took in a breath, because this was
how it went. Hammett examined bodies and he examined crimes. Most people had poor memories when it
came to a scene if they weren't thinking about paying
attention because they were shaken up. "I appreciate
you calling, sir."

"He also had an earring. My wife thinks that is just
wrong on men, so she remembered it."

None of that would help them find the person who
probably couldn't help anyway, but it was always nice
when someone cared enough to go out of their way
to be helpful. "Thanks very much."

He called Ellie right away. "Our dead end skidded
up to the cemetery and dumped into an open grave.
Have you eaten yet?"

"Actually, no, but there's a way to get a girl's attention. Open grave? What are you talking about?"

"It depends on the girl, right? I have yours now.
One tidbit of information that probably means absolutely nothing is the bait. How about Thai food? I
could order some curry chicken and that noodle thing
you like."

She was at loose ends since splitting with Grantham
and he knew it. Jason was not above shameless ex-
ploitation. What he really wanted was to see her, and
it got old sitting and eating alone anyway.

"At your place?"

"Morris called my cell. I've had a couple of beers. I
don't want to drive anywhere, but if you want to

come over so we can talk about it, you're invited for dinner and in luck, since I'm not cooking."

She hesitated, but then agreed. "Good call on the not driving. I'll come over."

"You want the spicy stuff?"

"Sure do. I could pick it up."

"Are you kidding? That's damn selfish. The delivery guy won't be able to put his kids through college then. I'm on a first-name basis with every delivery person in a ten-mile radius. If I called in for carryout, everyone in the kitchen would faint and then we wouldn't get our food."

She was at least laughing when she hung up the phone.

Ellie arrived right before the food, wearing a soft pink blouse and jeans. She didn't look like Detective MacIntosh, but more like a college student, and that alone was worth the tip he gave the guy who handed him the bags.

He had only three dinner plates, but luckily, two were clean. He got them out of the cabinet, told himself maybe buying a real set of dishes wouldn't hurt, though he wasn't going to host a dinner party anytime soon. Or ever. Social events were not his specialty. He'd grown up eating off paper plates and using plastic forks, and then gone into the military where the ambience wasn't much better. His ex-live-in girlfriend had helped smooth some of the rough edges, but then again, Kate had also left him after carefully explaining his level of emotional detachment was more than she could take. He vowed to himself then and there that it was off his list to ever date a graduate psychology student again.

But, thanks to her, he actually had some place mats she'd forgotten to pack up. The relationship hadn't been a total loss. He wished they didn't have flowers all over them, but what the hell, they were a gesture at being civilized.

He caught Ellie's amused expression as he set them down and explained with one word: "Kate."

"I wondered. I was picturing you in the household goods aisle and picking out violets and it wasn't flying. You'd be more likely to choose gorillas or lions eating a gazelle."

"Do they make place mats like that? I'll have to pick some up. There are matching violet napkins in this set, but I draw the line at some point. You'll be stuck with those paper ones that came with the food. While we eat, I'll tell you about the phone call."

She sat down at his small table and opened a container. "That's why I'm here."

No, not entirely, and he had a feeling she knew that. He plunked down and reached for the curry. "Morris called to say his wife remembered that the jogger had a sweatshirt on with a logo and he also had an earring. She was all worked up, so she can't remember more than that. Maybe she will after thinking about it. He did say she might be able to pick him out from a lineup."

Ellie took a bite, and after she swallowed said, "Since when did you change into Santiago the Optimist? We've still got nothing."

"Not so." The curry was hot, and sitting at the table was nice—he ate in front of the television way too much. "If we could get a line on a suspect, she could help us out. Her husband thinks she'd recognize him."

"It's better than nothing," Ellie agreed, but looked skeptical. "Maybe he saw something."

"I just have this feeling he's important. Maybe he was just a runner, but maybe not."

"I usually trust your gut instincts . . . so go on."

He would have. Gladly. But he didn't really want to talk about the case. He didn't do sensitive well, but he was good at honest. What he was about to say was more for his own sake than for hers. Getting it off his chest would just be a relief.

"We have other problems." He said it with an edginess he wished didn't exist, but it did. "You're my partner. I'm in love with you. What the hell are we supposed to do about *that*?"

## Chapter 3

*He was a novice.*

*He'd always known he'd wanted to learn what it would be like. It had been there all along following him like a dark shadow. He was an analytical person, or so he thought.*

*Why?*

*That was more difficult.*

*Attention? It could be. The growing obsession was eating up a lot of his time. There was some measure of resentment no one noticed and that also annoyed him. It was the story of his life. No one cared. At times he felt insignificant and slighted.*

*The first time he'd seen her had been just a photo in an article. But she'd haunted him in a tantalizing way.*

*He was determined to have Ellie MacIntosh wake up and realize he was there.*

**There was no** note with the vase of tulips on her desk.

Good. The very last thing she needed was some poetic card. The cheery brilliance of pinks, reds, and bright yellow were beautiful, but not something to handle before she had a second cup of coffee. She was still processing Santiago's very frank declaration.

He shouldn't send her flowers. Especially not at work.

Ellie dumped in sugar and some nondairy creamer—what was in that substance anyway? No, wait, she didn't want to know—and went to sit down with an inner sigh.

"Secret admirer, MacIntosh?" Lieutenant Carl Grasso walked up, and she wished she could say yes. No longer a secret to her. It wasn't as if she didn't think things were headed that direction, but Jason Santiago had *said* it.

*I'm in love with you.*

"No comment."

It had better be a secret to everyone else, she thought darkly, but then wondered if she wasn't just dreaming. Damn him. Maybe she was more upset over that than anything else. Secret was acceptable. The blunt approach was not, but he wasn't hard to read, and truth be told she had some pretty mixed feelings about him just saying it out loud. Maybe it was best to just get the tension off the table. "What's up?"

Grasso, older and well dressed as always, leaned a hand on her desk, his silver eyes holding false sympathy. "I think you're about to get real busy. Just a heads up as a token of my affection. I was in a meeting with Metzger when he got the call."

"What call? Why?"

"You are about to find out. Just my luck. All I have is a shooting over on Lincoln that I promise you is gang related. My chances of solving that one are in

the null-and-void set. Those people are not coopera-
tive. I've worked these before."

He walked away and she spotted Santiago coming
toward her desk. As usual, his contrast to Grasso's
perfect suit made her want to shake her head. He
looked like maybe he'd just gotten back from an all-
night rock concert.

She didn't wait but gestured at the vase. "Don't do
that again. Not here at work. But thank you, they're
lovely."

He frowned. "Those flowers? Give me some credit.
I *wouldn't* do that here at work."

That was probably true now that he pointed it out.
If he ever had sent flowers in his life it would be a
surprise, and certainly not tulips.

Her partner didn't look happy to see them. He
plucked one out and twirled it in his fingers. "My guess
is Grantham isn't as convinced it's as over as you are.
I hate to break it to you, but thoughtful romantic ges-
tures are not in my skill set. You won't find me singing under your balcony either, but that *is* a thoughtful
gesture if you've heard me sing. A frog croaking is
more on key. Forget the flowers, we need to get going.
We have another visit to make to that very same park
bench. It has a new occupant."

Second victim?

No wonder Grasso thought they were going to get
busy.

Ellie reached for her jacket, immediately distracted
and dismayed. "Are you serious?"

"This guy has some balls putting another body in
the same place."

If she wasn't used to it by now, Ellie might have said
something about his choice of words, but she'd given

up a long time ago. "I agree he's taking chances. Who's driving?"

"You. I left my gym bag in my truck accidentally a few days ago. It has a certain funky odor even I noticed."

"Enough said," she agreed as they exited the building.

They drove to the scene without mentioning the flowers again. Ellie could tell he was tense about it, and she was as well. The last thing she needed was Bryce deciding to try to resume their relationship at this point. She was past it now, but it had taken some effort. Those tulips had not been a bonus to her day. Beautiful but unwanted.

The park was once again taped off, a small crowd gathered, and the uniformed officers looked relieved to see them arrive. It was, with the typical vagaries of a spring in Wisconsin, a beautiful day, but the park wasn't as pretty as it should be.

By a long shot.

This murder was quite different from the last one.

"Deputy ME is on his way," Owens, a tall, lanky man evidently in charge of the scene, an officer she'd met before, informed them. "I handled the last call to this park too. I would have a problem now sitting down on that bench and eating a sandwich even though it is a pretty spot. I don't know what's going on, but I'll be happy when they take the body away."

Ellie instantly understood why. This was not some pretty young woman who looked asleep. This was a man who had been strangled with a thin wire, sitting on the bench in the exact spot. There was a dark spot extending down his temple to his cheekbone that suggested maybe he'd been knocked out before he was strangled, but she'd let the autopsy results determine if that was a correct guess.

She had no idea what was going on either.

Santiago, of course, summed it up in his unique way, but his blue eyes were troubled. "Well, son of a bitch. He isn't following a pattern. I don't think we need an ME to tell us cause of death or manner of death."

"In some ways the perp might be following a pattern. No wallet. We don't have an ID." Police officer Owens didn't look happy either. "Good luck. How's the other case going?"

Nowhere.

Ellie told him just that. "Let's put it this way, we need some luck getting a handle on it."

"Better you than me."

When he walked away, Jason shoved his hands into his pockets. "Let's go talk to anyone and everyone while we wait for the troops to arrive. I really hate interviewing witnesses, but we need to do it."

"Give me a second."

She didn't like the process either, but it was her job to find out who might have killed the current victim.

She pulled on gloves. "Just a hunch." Very carefully, she kneeled to lean over to look at the inside of the man's right wrist. Sure enough, she could see writing on it and definitely felt a chill that was in direct contrast to the sun and clear sky. "Well, he left us another message."

Her partner ran his hand through his hair, puffed out a breath, and squatted down to look it over. "You know, I told you this was going to be a bad case. Admit I was right. What does it say?"

If there was nothing else she could say, he did have spot-on instincts. "I can't tell without moving the body because rigor has set in and Hammett would have my head on a platter. I can see the writing, though."

"Great. He's a real piece of work. I'm not getting our bad guy right away and I don't like it."

Neither did she.

Ellie stood and shook her head. "I have no idea. Unfortunately, being a pretty young woman might make you a target for a certain kind of killer, but this newest victim is a middle-aged man. What's the connection between the two of them?"

"There has to be one. Let's go see if any of the gawkers can help us out."

She was very happy—for their sake—the Morris couple wasn't involved in finding the body, but she suspected they'd decided to walk elsewhere from now on anyway. The person who had called it in was a maintenance worker for the city who was emptying the trash cans and caught sight of the body.

Slightly overweight and rattled, he was perspiring obviously at just having to talk to them. "I thought he was a vagrant, just sitting there. Got the jolt of a lifetime when I realized . . . well, that he was dead. When you got close that was obvious. Jesus."

Ellie was convinced no one connected to a higher power had anything to do with that and went through the usual drill. "No one was around?"

"I didn't see anyone except the dead guy. I was flipping out, you know."

She did, and it was what she dealt with all the time. Patiently, she said, "I do know, but keep this in mind, the slightest small thing, even a single detail, can help us. You might not think it matters, but it could. If there was a gum wrapper on the ground it could help us."

The man didn't remember anything at all useful, but just repeated about six times, "I can't believe I found a dead guy."

"Buddy, I'd ask for a raise." Santiago nudged her. "Let's go do the fun part."


**What a bust.**

He'd been stymied on cases before, but this was different.

Since operating on motive was never productive, Jason didn't approach anything that way. He didn't understand why anyone would kill someone they didn't know or dislike on a personal basis, but it happened.

It was why he had a job.

When he was an MP in the military he'd even dealt with people trained to kill people. The maniacs were better at it as far as he was concerned. If you had the slightest conscience you were at a disadvantage. Trained killers were meticulous, but they had a reason.

*What do you think now?*

That had been the message inked on the wrist of the victim.

"No one saw a thing and the scene is clear of evidence. Killed him somewhere else and brought him here." Ellie walked next to him, her lightweight jacket unzipped, the wind ruffling her fair hair. "A park is a pretty good choice when you think it over. People are coming and going, so a footprint or a fingerprint could belong to anyone. I'd like to know how our killer gets the bodies here without anyone seeing anything."

"In the middle of the night it's still cold enough this time of year that no one is out running, very few people on the streets, and if you had the body wrapped up, you could use the park's lot and be pretty much invisible. Lots of trees and a public place to make sure your work is found and admired." Jason could see it.

"Admired?"

"I think he wants us to know he's smarter than the homicide division of the Milwaukee Police Department."

"You do realize you're a die-hard cynic, right?"

"Oh, and you're not?" He resisted the urge to point out he was the one who lived in an apartment building full of families with small children, while she'd rented a generic condo when she moved out of Grantham's house. It was his opinion it was impossible to do their job and live a completely normal life. His insomnia at times was so acute that if he slept three hours he counted it a good night. Eventually he crashed and burned one day and woke up on the couch with a dry mouth and no idea what time it was, the victim of some dreams he hoped he would never remember, but at least he'd caught up on his sleep. Eight hours was a gift.

"In some ways maybe," she admitted.

He tried hard also to not think about how much he wanted to touch her hair, currently blowing around her shoulders. His focus was askew and Metzger would just plain have his ass in a sling if he realized it. Well, maybe his boss did realize it, and that was bad all the way around. He'd been threatened with reassignment before. The only thing in his favor was that there was no argument he and MacIntosh had a solid record of solving crimes together.

"We're being taunted. He could kill them and leave them, and get away with it, but he's taking us on. Two bodies in the same location isn't quite usual in the first place, but the writing on the wrist . . . that's his dare right there."

She didn't disagree. "I'm sure he's aware now that we'll put up surveillance cameras and have extra officers in the area."

Jason paused by the car, waiting for her to unlock it. "I'm not positive yet if he's smart or just lucky so far, but I'm voting for smart."

His phone rang before she even replied, and he answered it immediately, because if the chief detective, Fergusson, called, he knew it was either bad news or good news, and he might as well get the first over with or embrace the second option. He'd been the recipient of both.

"This is Santiago."

"In light of where you are right now, we have a missing person report you and MacIntosh might want to check into because it fits the timeline of the other case."

Good news. That was a relief anyway.

"I'll text you the details. I looked at the report from Hammett and the description seems to match. Her sister hasn't heard from her and they usually talk every day, she isn't answering her phone, and missed work. The sister lives over by the lake, and I warn you, she's pretty frantic. Let MacIntosh do the talking."

"You say that every time. I might as well have my vocal cords removed."

Dryly, Fergusson responded, "I think we all in the

MPD might appreciate that. Silent Santiago has a nice ring to it. I'll send the address."

Jason told Ellie as they climbed into the car, "That was Fergusson. Change of plans. Maybe we just caught a break, but now we have to go invite a family member down to the Underworld for what might not be the most pleasant experience of her lifetime. I hate this part of the job."

She looked somber too. "None of us like it. Look at the bright side. You don't have to talk."

"You heard that, huh?"

"Didn't need to hear it. The chief told me the day we were assigned together I needed to do the interviews."

"Well, damn, I feel loved." Jason muttered the words, automatically fastening his seat belt. "That's just so flattering."

"You never skim around a point. You're too direct, and sensitivity is not your strong suit."

"Why would I be sensitive about a murder investigation?"

"See, your general attitude is the problem."

That was entirely possible. "I have a lot of problems. One of them is two bodies left in the same spot and no motive, but they have to be connected somehow. Same killer. He didn't leave a signature as a metaphor for his method of killing, he left a real one. I'm here to help the families, by the way."

Ellie raised her brows slightly at the use of metaphor, but didn't comment. He had to admit he didn't use highbrow language often. She said, "Well, maybe he hasn't heard of the FBI's handwriting analysis experts."

"I bet he has." There was no doubt in his mind that they were dealing with someone intellectual. "He's just confident we won't ever suspect him, so he isn't worried about it. And don't ask me why I'm sure, because every homicide detective has asked themselves how we catch them, and the disturbing answer is that we understand how they think."

"That's cheerful."

"You aren't shopping at the cheerful store here. Wake up."

The address ended up being a very nice house in a neighborhood of upscale houses. On his salary, Jason could maybe have afforded the front porch. The woman who answered the door was a housekeeper, and they were led through a grand foyer to certainly the nicest kitchen he'd ever seen in person, with fancy quartz countertops—when he was really bored at home he sometimes switched off sports for home improvement shows just to broaden his horizons at least a little because one day he wanted to be a grown-up and buy a house—and cherry cabinets. A woman was taking a baking sheet full of cookies out of the oven. She set it on the counter and then wiped her hands on a towel.

"Mrs. Turner? I'm Detective MacIntosh and this is Detective Santiago."

Ellie showed her badge and the woman smiled tremulously. "When I'm anxious, I bake. If the kids ever figure it out, they'll get in trouble on purpose just to have cupcakes. Is this about Karen? Have you found her?"

He was afraid they had. This woman looked a lot like her dead sister.

## Chapter 4

*S*he didn't bring the flowers home.

He wasn't sure whether to be insulted or flattered that they were likely still on Ellie MacIntosh's desk. Maybe she hadn't connected the dots, but he was fairly sure by now she had.

They were playing a game.

He was in the lead right now and she had no idea by how much.

The tall blond cop was with her. Maybe they'd argued over something, because their body language had screamed dissention as she'd deactivated the alarm and unlocked the door. Neither one of them even noticed him.

He assumed maybe they might have some level of emotional or sexual involvement, but that was going to end.

He'd take care of it.

\* \* \*

**It was out** of character for her to use avoidance, but then again, she was human. Dr. Georgia Lukens didn't answer the call and let it go to voice mail. Instead she considered the display of glossy dark purple eggplant and reminded herself she didn't actually like eggplant. It looked good, but she didn't have the knack to prepare it properly, or else everyone who loved it liked bitter mush, and she doubted that was the case.

Heirloom tomatoes were much more her style. She picked out a couple and put them into the basket. She could make a salad with the best of them, and her blue cheese dressing with garlic did get rave reviews.

It had been awhile, but she had a date.

Yes, she went out to dinner with one of her male colleagues now and then, but the relationship was basically platonic, though she knew he wanted to take it to a different level. This was a *date* date. With someone else entirely, and if she wasn't a clinical psychologist— but she was—she would just think the slight case of butterflies in her stomach was girlish nerves.

She headed for the dairy aisle, thinking she hadn't been a girl in quite some time and was almost amused with herself. She picked up cream for the Alfredo with asparagus, and was in the checkout lane when Ellie called her. That ring she always took, so she smiled apologetically at the clerk and swiped her credit card.

"Dr. Lukens."

"Do you have time for a short meeting tonight?"

MacIntosh only asked for that on a work-related basis. "Case?"

"Yes."

She glanced at the time on her phone. She'd consulted for the Milwaukee Police Department before. "I have company coming for dinner, but could give you about half an hour. Come over to the condo for a glass of wine."

Their friendship was built on mutual experiences— not all of them were good. On the upside, those same shared experiences had forged an unusual relationship and professional respect on both sides.

MacIntosh accepted. "I might need one. The expensive stuff, please. I deserve it as a public servant."

Georgia grabbed her bag and headed for the door. "Of course. I won't cart out the boxed swill."

"I just need some insight."

"Expensive wine takes care of that?"

Ellie laughed, but there wasn't any mirth in it. "It helps. Is twenty minutes okay?"

"Should be fine."

Normally they saw each other only at Georgia's office, but she didn't have the time to drive there and then back to make dinner. She made it only in time to carry in the groceries before the buzzer went off indicating she had a visitor. She hit the accept button, uncorked the wine, and a few minutes later let Ellie through the door.

Detective MacIntosh looked put together in dark slacks, a light pink blouse, and her usual minimal makeup but she didn't need more, which Georgia envied. She glanced around, always observant. "I like the new lamp."

"It cost a small fortune, but I like it too. I can't believe you noticed. Remind me to not commit a crime and have you investigate it." She poured merlot into a glass.

Predictably, MacIntosh was direct as she slid onto a stool. "Too late for that. Let's talk about crime for a few minutes. That's why I'm here after all."

"You sit at the island and talk, and I will prep for dinner if you don't mind. I have a guest on his way soon."

"Is that right? *His* way . . . hmm. Hot date?"

The table was set and crystal wineglasses and table linens were involved. Georgia responded, "Who knows? First date. Now tell me, what kind of conversation are we having, Detective?"

"Santiago has a theory."

"I'm frightened already. By the way, I don't know if you've noticed this or not, but when we talk about a case he's Santiago. Otherwise, he's Jason. You are trying to put your feelings in neat little compartments. I wish I could tell you that worked."

"I know." Ellie took a sip from her glass. "We're good friends that also interact professionally. Does that work? Very nice wine, by the way."

"French. Glad you like it." Georgia got out her favorite slicing knife and started to wash the tomatoes. She said over her shoulder, "It works sometimes. Santiago is the detective and Jason is the man. I'm not positive you can keep them separate, but you are definitely trying. Tell me about this case."

"Cases. We have two murders. Both bodies have been left in the same spot, both victims died of asphyxiation but not by the same method. We have no doubt it's the same killer. He leaves a signature, and I mean literally. He leaves a note directly written on the body."

From a psychological viewpoint that was interesting. She put the tomatoes on the cutting board, thinking it over, and took out an antique plate. "He or she wants you to know they are out there."

Ellie fingered the delicate stem of her glass. "It's

probably a he, because the bodies had to be carried. Santiago thinks this lovely individual is taunting us, taking us on. We just identified the first victim and she was a graduate student from an affluent family, maybe a bit of a party girl, but the second victim is a middle-aged man named Calvin Hanes who worked for a warehouse unloading trucks. If there's a connection between them, we can't find it yet."

Georgia considered it for a moment, knife in hand. "So maybe you have an opportunistic killer. The act is his thrill."

Ellie's hazel eyes were troubled. "I'm not sure what's going on. Killing two very different victims is one thing, but making sure the police know you are the same killer seems strange to me. Killing anyone is strange to me."

"He thinks he can outsmart you."

"You tell me, you're the psychologist."

Georgia said dryly, "I never planned on being a criminal psychologist, but I am always willing to help if I can. I usually counsel little old ladies to help their anxiety about walking their small dog in this wicked world. Look, let's face it: You and Jason Santiago have worked some very high profile cases that have been all over the news."

"You think we're specifically his enemy number one?" Ellie objected. "He can't possibly know we'd even be assigned the case. There are other very competent homicide detectives that work for this city."

"You had a lot of press with some of your cases. And I'm not saying it is you and Detective Santiago specifically, but perhaps just law enforcement in general."

She considered. "Possible. But then why did he send me flowers?"

That stopped Georgia in her tracks. "What? Why do you think so?"

Ellie took another sip of wine before she explained. "Someone did. It wasn't Santiago, because you know him, he wouldn't deny it, and it wasn't Bryce, because I called him and asked directly. No card, but a gorgeous bouquet of tulips that had to have cost a small fortune. They arrived just before we found the second body. Can I emphasize again, no card."

Georgia didn't like that at all. "Can you trace the florist?"

"The young man that delivered them did it when I wasn't at my desk. A few people saw him pass by, but you know how that is, they were looking at the flowers. I pulled up the security tape and you can't really see his face because of the bouquet, and it is very possible that he held it up deliberately just to make sure he couldn't be identified. He wasn't wearing a uniform of any kind and must have parked somewhere else and walked to the building. He did have brown hair and we have a witness from the first case that saw a man with brown hair pass by right after the body was discovered."

"That's hardly conclusive."

"You're telling me."

"It could be that someone else sent the flowers but the card was lost somehow."

"True enough. I just think the timing is suspicious."

Georgia considered her friend and patient. "Ellie, you are a very pretty young woman. The admirer could just be shy."

"Or maybe a killer walked right into the police station and put flowers on my desk." Ellie finished her wine. "I don't usually operate on hunches, but I don't ignore them either. I think he knew I would wonder if those flowers were from him."

Those intuitive instincts no doubt were part of what made her such a good cop. "I certainly wouldn't ignore it if you have a bad feeling about it," Georgia said evenly, since she had a bad feeling about it all as well. "Even animals like dogs or cats will take a dislike to someone they don't even know. I believe firmly that while we function as intellectuals, under the surface we also operate that way. Studies have proved that infants and toddlers respond well to certain people, and will show instant aversion to others. They aren't really thinking it over and analyzing a particular behavior at that age; it is how they feel. How do *you* feel?"

Ellie looked away, apparently studying the wall. "Like I wish it *was* a ridiculous gesture from Jason, but like he pointed out when I accused him of it, he really wouldn't do that at work. He can be irritating, but he takes the job very seriously. I completely believe him. As it stands, I look at those beautiful flowers and just think about two murdered people. If they are from that lunatic, will I ever be able to look at tulips again and not think of him?"

Ever since they'd first met, Georgia had tried to decide if Ellie was too sensitive for her job. Just being intelligent and dedicated was probably a perfect combination, but separating emotion from it was probably healthier. Ellie didn't—she couldn't it seemed—and while it was best to have compassionate professionals protecting our streets, Georgia had always wondered about the personal toll it took on those individuals.

She decided to weigh her words. "I believe that

when you arrest him, and he goes on trial for murder, you will look at tulips and see justice."

"Thanks for the free session. I'll be in touch." Ellie rose, but paused halfway to the door to ask with a twitch of a smile, "Have you decided what you're going to wear yet?"

Georgia had been keeping an eye on the clock and said ruefully, "No, and I have maybe five minutes."

"I'm out of here. First date. Go feminine. Floral dress and some lip gloss. I hope you have a fun evening."

Probably good advice, and Georgia was someone who gave advice for a living.

**Carl Grasso adjusted** his tie, then decided against it altogether, stripped it off, and did the unthinkable and just tossed it onto the bed. He was tidy by nature, but running late.

The gang-related murder was about as impossible as predicted and the lack of cooperation as anticipated. The bereft mother demanded an explanation and he didn't blame her, but gang culture had a life of its own. They made their own laws and very few were based on the Constitution of the United States of America or state regulations.

As he walked into the garage and carefully punched in the alarm system code, he thought that he'd had his fill of belligerent teens with more swagger than sense for the day. He wasn't the enemy—at least in his mind—but even the ones with a fallen comrade didn't care enough to cooperate, so the fallout was going to be self-inflicted. It was more than a little difficult to investigate with nothing but sullen silence from possible witnesses.

He was going to put it out of his mind for the evening.

It was a lovely one too, he saw as he backed out the car, with a hint of indigo in the darkening sky. Normally he would spend it alone, sipping scotch in a chair by the pool when it was warm enough, or else inside in the room that had used to be his father's study, sitting in an old leather chair he should probably replace but knew he wouldn't, feet up on the worn ottoman. Relaxation was an art form he'd discovered, and he was not a master at it.

Practice hadn't helped much.

The address he arrived at was pricey, but that didn't surprise him. The building had a sleek lobby, and he noted the security system with a practiced eye before being promptly buzzed up when he pressed the button.

Georgia Lukens answered the door wearing a gauzy skirt and pale blue blouse, her hair in a much more casual style than when he'd seen her at her office, softening her face. She was one of those women who wasn't classically beautiful but managed to be strikingly attractive anyway. He'd met her on a case when MacIntosh had been injured and off the job so he'd stepped in, and out of the blue decided to call Dr. Lukens and ask her to dinner. No one was more surprised than he was. Impulsive was not his style.

Essentially, Georgia was the one to apprehend the murderer in that case, so they'd spent some time together when she was detained for questioning. He'd had to do most of it, and it was an interesting way to start a possible relationship.

"Lieutenant. Please come in." She stood back.

The space was comfortable and he could see her choosing the furnishings with an eye to function, and

yet her style was reflected as well. Soothing, but underneath there was sophistication and quiet drama. A
cream-colored couch, but a painting above that reflected a sunset in vibrant colors over a tranquil ocean.
A glass coffee table, but warm walnut shelves holding
books on the walls. The contrast was effective.

"A glass of wine, or do you prefer something else?"
She had two glasses set out and the wine was breathing.

"Wine is fine." He admired the graceful column of
her neck. "Thank you for suggesting dinner here and
taking the trouble to make it. I don't cook a lot for
myself. It is on my self-improvement list, but it's been
there for quite a while, right along with training for a
marathon and painting the hallway. I might have up-
dated that list about fifteen years ago."

She laughed. "Most restaurants are too loud. This
way we can talk to each other."

It was what she did for a living . . . talking to people.
Not his forte at all. He found out about their problems in a different way. He delved into their secrets
and didn't wait for them to reluctantly reveal them.

He didn't dissemble. "I agree. I'm more than interested in a quiet evening. And it smells wonderful already in here."

"Thank you. Have a seat." She pointed at a navy
chair that was modern and matched the vibe of the
place exactly. Maybe he should have her come redec-
orate his house. "By the way, you just missed Ellie
MacIntosh by about ten minutes."

He'd thought about the implications of maybe dating someone who saw several of his colleagues. Purely
by accident he knew Ellie saw Georgia, and not so
quite by accident he knew Jason Santiago went to her
too. He said succinctly, "Park Bench Killer case?"

She deftly poured wine into two glasses. "Let's say that it wasn't a private session, but if you want to know why she was here, just ask her. I take confidentiality seriously, so any secrets you reveal are safe with me." Georgia settled into an opposite chair after handing him his glass. "She sometimes just talks out loud to me. I think she believes she's getting advice. I think she's just working it through all on her own. I don't do much but listen."

Ellie was a good cop. He might go so far as to say she was a brilliant cop. He thought he fell into that same category. "Did you get the impression she was on the right track?"

"Maybe." Georgia considered him over the rim of her glass and hit a slam dunk. "You're interested in her case?"

"More than the one I'm assigned to right now." Why lie to a therapist? They probably took one look and knew all. At least the good ones did. "I have a frustrating murder that involves a lot of people who just don't want to tell the truth. In fact, they don't want to tell me anything. They don't want it solved. It's like banging your head against a wall. Besides the victim's mother, I am the only who cares, and half the time I think I care more than she does."

"Oh, you and I have a lot to talk about. People skirt around the real issues in their lives, and like you, I'm the detective, trying to figure it all out. I'd like to say on average I manage to see the light, but not always. A recent case for your department comes to mind."

He liked her. Especially he liked her sense of presence and her self-possession, because she didn't need him for anything except his company. He'd met way too many women who realized he drove an expensive car and lived in a neighborhood of old money and were suddenly warm and friendly. "That was an interesting one."

Dr. Lukens gave him a rueful smile. "I'll say. I missed the mark there."

"You hit the mark, actually." She had literally shot the murder suspect. "But you acted in a good cause when you shot your patient. Otherwise MacIntosh wouldn't be dropping by, because she wouldn't be around."

"Not an easy decision."

"I agree. I've had to make it myself once or twice."

"I know." She said it matter-of-factly, but obviously knew he'd been reprimanded once for a double shooting that he still maintained was self-defense. It haunted him he'd taken two lives, but he'd made the right choice. If he didn't believe that he wouldn't still be on the job.

He kept his tone neutral. "Just because it seems like the only course of action at the moment, it doesn't mean everyone agrees with us. I have the attitude that unless you are standing right there in our shoes, you can't judge what happened."

"That is very true. Change in subject? What a pleasant evening." She had nice long legs and crossed them, maybe just so he'd notice. He did, and was more than happy to abandon what they were currently discussing.

She asked him, "Do you like eggplant?"

That was an interesting question. He had no idea what she was making for dinner. He was a fairly direct person, so after a pause, he admitted, "Well, to be honest, not usually."

Her eyes glimmered. "We now have something in

common, Lieutenant. We both don't like eggplant. Do you like to snorkel?"

"I'm sorry, but no. I always seem to inhale half the ocean."

She said serenely, "We are on a roll then."

## Chapter 5

He had an idea.

Risky, but he was up for that.

This was catching fire.

He wasn't positive he was hiding it all that well either.

"Are you coming to bed?" Alissa's voice sounded off-key. She wore a fluffy robe that made her look even more overweight, which she complained about constantly, but he wasn't sure she did anything about. He was tired of her. When he'd met her she'd been slim and vibrant.

At one time he had maybe known this hunger was there, but he denied it.

They were really both at fault.

"I'm just fooling around on the computer," he said calmly. "I can't sleep, so might as well. There's a couple of projects at work that can use my attention."

"Your messed-up sleep patterns bother me."

"Don't worry about it."

*"I'm serious."*
*So was he. Dead serious. "I'm good."*


**"What are we** doing here?"

"I need some ketchup."

It was at least a testament to their association that Ellie completely disregarded his remark with a small snort. "For what? Frozen Tater Tots?"

"I swear I bake them first." Jason headed for the service desk. "Still frozen even I can't eat them. I tried it once and it was a less-than-satisfying experience."

The older woman at the supermarket counter took her time ignoring them until Santiago produced his badge. He said, "Excuse me. Milwaukee Homicide. Can we see whoever handles your flowers?"

Her rudeness didn't completely evaporate. She squinted at his badge. "What? Did someone beat someone to death with a bouquet or something?"

He didn't skip a beat either. "Florist crimes are really on the rise. Can we talk to her or him?"

"Her. Tammy. I'll call her up front here."

"That will be helpful." He flashed a boyish smile he must save for women over a certain age, because Ellie certainly didn't see it often.

She wished she could say she was one thousand times smarter than him, but Ellie wasn't positive that when it came to police work Santiago wasn't at least more on the game. They stood aside waiting for the floral clerk and she had to ask, "Why are we here again?"

"The tulips, if that is even a lead, were bought at a grocery store. I'm pretty ticked off, by the way. I didn't get any flowers. What am I? Not even worthy of a couple of dandelions or something? Jeez."

"How the hell do you know that? There must be hundreds of places that sell flowers in a city this size."

"I have super, secret special powers you don't even know about, but if you're willing to learn about them, I'm willing to share." He made his eyebrows go up and down in what she supposed he thought was his interpretation of a corny leer.

She sighed. "Just tell me and skip the world's worst sexual innuendos."

"There are times when you just have no sense of humor." He shook his head. "I thought that was pretty good."

"I might take out my service weapon and use it on you now. It has occurred to me before. Talk to me. How?"

"It isn't complicated. They smelled to me like grocery store flowers, and this place is near the park."

"They smelled like tulips." Ellie stepped aside for a woman who wanted to buy a magazine.

"You see, as someone who has always lived on a limited income provided by the taxpayers, I don't indulge in florists. If I buy a lady flowers, I do it at the grocery store, and if you've been in one, there's a grocery store smell. You happen to be in one now."

She was more than dubious. "That might be the most ridiculous thing I've ever heard."

"If you have a better lead, I'm standing right here wondering if they have toilet paper on sale, so go ahead and tell me and take my mind off of that. Maybe we should get a cart."

Ellie didn't hit him. Not with witnesses all around, but it was tempting.

And to make it worse than his irreverent sense of what he thought was humor, it turned out he was right.

Tammy, when she arrived, confirmed a little old lady had come in on the same day Ellie got the enormous vase of flowers and bought every single one.

Which made no sense.

Until the cashier remembered that the customer mentioned a man had paid her twenty bucks to buy them for him.

Okay, that was interesting.

Ellie wasn't positive it was a lead of any kind. But sometimes it worked that way, and it was some decent police work. "I don't suppose the little old lady paid with a credit card, right?"

"Nope." Tammy, young and with long dark hair, looked apologetic. "Cash he gave her. I kinda thought it was weird too."

They hashed it out driving back.

Ellie said, "So we have no idea who she is, and no idea who he is, and absolutely no idea if someone buying tulips and sending them to me has any significance to the two murders. Have I got that right?"

"You do, but there's a caveat here."

"Your ability to mangle the English language never fails to amaze me. What?"

"What the hell? I think I used that word correctly." Jason looked about as offended as he ever could look, and he was nearly impossible to offend. However, she suspected half of the time he used the wrong word just to annoy her.

"Please tell me why you think this is helpful information."

"The clerk said that lady shops there often enough

she recognized her. She didn't know her name, but she'd get it for us the next time she waited on her. I gave her my card and she promised she'd call. Maybe we can get a description."

Witnesses were so notoriously forgetful of details that it probably wouldn't help, but was worth a shot.

"Could be useful if A plus M plus W equals Z. In other words, a giant leap."

"If you can do better, you're holding back. Maybe this grandma can help us out. A stranger approached her to buy out a bunch of flowers and that's damn weird. Walk into the store and buy them yourself unless you are hedging your bets by not being caught on surveillance cameras. Notice he picked someone who wouldn't rip him off and run out the back door. I bet that sweet little oldster even gave him back his change."

She couldn't deny that was a good point. "I did notice that detail."

"So he calculates and weighs his options. What else?"

"Possible, but not probable, on the witness."

"Now we are cooking. I agree on that. Next move?" He braked for a light.

She'd been thinking about it. "I keep trying to decide if staying quiet is best, or if we should make the notes on the bodies public. It might be what he wants."

"Stay quiet." Santiago was emphatic. "I'm not playing with this asshole. Anyone who suffocates and strangles people is in the twilight zone. If he wants fame, I'm not in favor of giving it to him."

Ellie didn't disagree, but then again, cases were solved by outside tips often enough. "We should talk to Metzger and get his opinion."

"Better you than me. He hasn't forgiven me yet for being shot so many times in the line of duty. He acts like I was *trying* to get shot."

It was true. Santiago was a unique statistic, since most officers went their whole career without a shot fired in their direction. Ellie had been shot too, but he was the clear winner in the hit target division and she'd let him have and keep that title. "I'll ask him what he thinks about it all. In the end it's his call anyway."

"It just seems like we are on shaky ground. There's nothing but quicksand beneath us."

"I agree. How are we supposed to get what's coming next?"

"We aren't. Until we figure out his pattern, he has us by the—"

"Don't say it." Ellie had interrupted him so many times since she'd met him she'd lost count. She drummed her fingers on the dashboard. "I almost hate to admit this, but you're right. We have to shut him out to catch him."

"So we'll quietly ignore his ass and investigate, right?"

"He'll kill again."

"He's going to anyway."

It always scared her when she was in tune with Jason Santiago. "What I'm afraid of."

"I'm all for not giving him press. Cameras are at the park, so in case he comes back to fondly remember his favorite pastime we can get a shot at identifying him, and maybe the family of Calvin Hanes or a neighbor or someone will think of something."

It didn't help at all that Hanes was a bachelor and his elderly parents lived in Duluth. There had also been alcohol in his system, but not nearly as much as with the first victim.

"I think the perp is too smart for that."

Santiago rubbed his jaw in a characteristic mannerism. "Maybe his buddies at work could tell us what bar was his favorite. I drink alone, but I'm a sophisticated kind of man. Some people think social drinking is the only way to go. I solo most of the time."

If nothing else, her partner was good for a laugh now and then in a job that didn't provide a lot of levity. "Sophisticated? Yeah, that's you all right. Let's go see what we can find out."

**Jason wasn't optimistic** about the inquiries, which meant he wasn't disappointed either.

Calvin hadn't been much of a friend with anyone, so the lack of response wasn't surprising. He'd worked his shift and gotten off and then not shown up for work the next day. While he wasn't too connected to his coworkers, he was reliable. When his boss tried to call to find out what was up and got no answer, his supervisor was worried maybe he'd had a heart attack.

"No one answered the door and there was at least several days of mail in the box." The harried man shook his head, holding a clipboard and multitasking by talking to them and waving in a truck to the dock. "I know you aren't supposed to mess with anyone's mail, but I'm not a detective. I didn't know how else to see if he'd been around lately. I swear I didn't touch anything. I just looked. I tried knocking like fifteen times and found delivered newspapers still on the front porch. That's when I called the police."

In this case, Jason was a much better choice to do the questioning. "We aren't worried about his mail, and now neither is he. We'd just like to find who killed him. He a drinker?"

"I think he had a few beers now and then, but nothing over the top. Trust me, I know the signs, and I've fired a few guys for coming in hungover on a regular basis. Calvin wasn't perfect, but hey, who is. He was a good worker and he'd never missed before without calling in. I can't believe anyone would want to kill him. He went to work, and then I suspect he went home and just sat there and watched television. No girls, no gambling that I ever heard of, for sure no drugs because we test at random since a lot of our employees are drivers, so it's a company-wide policy."

"When you called you really helped us identify him. What else can you tell us about him?"

The man shrugged. "He was just an average guy. A loner, but not so much he wouldn't tell a joke now and then or even offer to pick up an extra shift if someone had a family emergency. I have a feeling he might have been gay, but if I had to call it, he just suppressed that. For my part, all I really care about is that they show up for work. Kind of sad if the only one who misses you is your boss."

They were standing in a loading dock and the big truck was backing in, beeping, and they moved out of the way. Jason said, "Thanks for the information."

MacIntosh asked as they walked back to the parking lot, "Why? Why him? It sounds like he wasn't bothering anyone, so he wasn't a natural target for murder unless maybe he was up to something illegal no one knows anything about."

"Why the pretty young woman if sexual assault

wasn't the intent? Has to be the same killer. The signature is a fairly conclusive bit of evidence there."

"Good question," Ellie agreed as they got to his truck. "Just being able to kill?"

"Maybe. Self-defense or revenge are the only two reasons I understand. The rest of it is just incomprehensible bullshit." He pushed the button on his key chain to unlock the doors. "I was in the military and I had no desire to kill anyone, but if they come after you, that's self-defense."

If someone harmed her, he might consider revenge. Those flowers really bothered him.

Of course she had moved fast to open her own door. They had some sort of contest going on over that act of courtesy and he wasn't aware of why. She quickly climbed in and commented, "I don't disagree."

They hadn't talked yet about his emotional and frank admission, and she deflected it if he even tried. Just the simple opening of a door was now a source of tension.

He was obviously an idiot for having told her. However, it was nice to get it off his chest, and he didn't think for a minute she'd been surprised. If he hadn't tacked on the part of what they were going to do about it, he might have been okay. He wanted to talk about it, but then again he didn't in case she took any possibility of a private relationship off the table. He got in and started the truck. "I have no desire to go to Duluth, and I doubt his parents can help us. Let's go back to my original thought and sift through his financial stuff and see if he frequented a specific bar. Right now we're fishing without a worm on the end of our hook."

"That usually doesn't produce stellar results, I agree."

"You fish?" He wasn't even quite sure why he asked.

"I'm from northern Wisconsin. Of course I do."

"I've never done it."

Ellie turned to stare at him. Her expression was incredulous. "What?"

He had to shrug. "My old man wasn't into anything like that. He watched television and drank himself to death. Those were his two hobbies. I started mowing the lawn when I was about six years old, because even at that age, I realized it was embarrassing to have the worst yard on the block. I'm lucky I didn't cut off a foot or something, but a nice neighbor showed me how to work the thing, probably because he wanted our yard to look better and not live next to a dump. My old man did me a favor there, since I eventually made some cash in the summers doing it for other people too."

"You've really never been fishing? You live by some of the largest inland lakes in the world, Santiago."

He wished, really wished, she'd just call him by his given name all the time. He used hers. "Just not part of my life experiences. However, if you need your grass cut, I'm your guy."

"I'll take you fishing. You haven't lived until you've fished up near Hayward."

He came close to blowing the whole thing by asking if they'd share a hotel room, but caught himself at just the last moment. "Sounds interesting. I've always wondered why people liked it so much."

"Trees crowding the bank, cool, deep water, and always intrigued by what you just hooked . . . it's addicting. It's also relaxing. No television, no e-mails, no ringing phone unless you're an idiot and bring one and leave it on."

"Teach me." He tried, but he didn't do casual well. There was a reason Metzger told him to just shut up on a regular basis when they were having a special chat; one of those he'd had often enough he'd just soon skip any more. "I could use another addiction. I'd thought about taking up smoking, but fishing sounds better."

"Um, yes, probably. Look at the upside for me: There's always the chance a giant muskie might drag you over the side of the boat into the watery depths."

"Don't sound so hopeful."

"A girl can dream. Did we gain anything from this interview?"

"He was quiet, middle-aged and withdrawn, and she was young and social. Those two were very different victims."

"Back at square one. There's a thread; we just haven't found it. Since we just mentioned it, he's like a fishing spider. He grabs whatever he can get and then crawls away. Nothing good happens after that for the victim."

"A what?" He really was mystified.

"Fishing spider."

"Never heard of such a thing."

"They literally jump into the water for prey. No webs; they are huge hunting spiders."

"You're making that up."

"No, I'm not. I saw one down in Indiana once. They are quite the predator. So is our guy."

Jason didn't disagree with that, but the idea of fishing had lost its gloss. A muskie he could handle, but a giant spider creeped him out. So did their perp. "I'm now considering bowling instead of fishing because of the spider thing, but wearing those shoes kind of turns me off. What do you want to do next?"

He wasn't just talking about the case and she knew it.

"I'll reach out to his parents in Duluth again. I want them to understand we're trying."

"Ellie, we *are* trying. What else? I'm wide open to all ideas."

"I wish I had some."

He couldn't argue that one. "This isn't our easiest walk in the park, and that wasn't intended as a bad pun by the way. Have we ever had an easy case?"

"Not really," she agreed, briefly closing her eyes. "At times I wonder why I do this, and then come right back to wondering what else I'd do."

He'd been through the same introspection. "I've considered being a greeter at a retail store, but I swear I wouldn't pass the interview. If they asked me if I would never tell anyone to go fuck off because they didn't answer my sunny smile, with all due honesty I'd have to tell the truth that the likelihood was pretty high I would."

Her mouth twitched. "Not the answer they'd be looking for if I had to venture a guess."

"I have no idea how they profile potential employees, but I'd guess you're right. So you see, I'm also stuck being a cop."

## Chapter 6

*It was a dual performance.*

*He was settling some old scores. Two down.*

*There were some inevitable casualties on the way, of course. It couldn't be helped. No one understood how the universe operated exactly. Countries went to war, people got sick and died, and now and then a blown tire made you veer into the wrong lane.*

*He was definitely the lane you wanted to avoid.*

*No one was home so he didn't even need to be quiet. He drilled the hole and took out the equipment, installed it, and it was as easy as promised.*

*After today she'd have no secrets.*

**Grasso was at** odds with himself for the first time. He'd always known where he was headed in his life. Solitude was his friend, but maybe the road less traveled was in the cards.

Georgia's e-mail had been simple. "Had a nice time. Repeat performance?"

He was all for it. "Tonight? My house this time with the warning included that I'll just pick up the food and not cook it as a favor to you. Do you like Italian?"

She typed back. "Absolutely. I have a late-afternoon patient. Will seven o'clock work for you?"

"Sounds perfect. See you then."

He almost wiped the smile off his face before Fergusson reached his desk, but not quite. "Oh, you're kidding me, Grasso." The chief detective was thickset and had the sense of humor of a colony of fire ants. "Did you just ask someone to prom and she said yes? I recognize that glassy-eyed look in a man's eyes."

Maybe the man was a detective for a reason.

"I'm unwilling to answer that question."

"Fair enough. Anyway, no progress on the gang-related murder, I take it."

"Did you expect any?"

"I was hoping someone would roll over. Nothing, huh?"

"They are a closemouthed group. Who can blame them? Roll over and you might be dead. It is the life they chose, and while I suspect most of them regret it sooner or later, it's like a tattoo. You can't just wash it off."

"Well, do your best and then we can cold file it if we have to eventually go that direction. It isn't like the kid's family didn't know he had gang ties."

"It doesn't make it any easier for them." Carl was someone who understood catastrophic loss.

Fergusson wasn't a bad person, he was just a man with a hard job. "I get it, but then again, you could also be helping someone else if it is going nowhere instead of spinning your wheels. I wish I didn't have to, but I'm assigning you another case. An older woman on the south side that it looks like might have died under suspicious circumstances. There's no crime scene and I'm going to warn you, the evidence is very muddy. This might not be a homicide, but her family thinks it is. Want to know why it's bugging me?"

Carl hated questions like those. He lived his life in an ordered way and made decisions based on facts and logic. "Go ahead."

"She lived very close to where the murders Mac-Intosh and Santiago are investigating occurred. I wouldn't have made my rank in the department if I didn't have some intuitive sense for a case, and I'm not saying I think there's a connection, I'm just wondering. Maybe she was a witness. They can't seem to find one so far."

"Near the park?"

"Very close. Too close. I don't like it, and when I don't like something, it makes me grouchy."

Grasso refrained from mentioning Fergusson was grouchy all the time. "Why does her family think she was murdered?"

"It's your job to figure that out, Grasso. They do. That's all I know. The regular officers that responded didn't see any evidence of it, but they aren't you."

He walked away and Carl thoughtfully watched him go before he picked up the file. Fergusson could be unrelenting, but he wasn't dumb by any means. Mrs. Armistad had died right outside her front door from trauma to the head. Her body had been found when her daughter had dropped by with a cake pan she'd borrowed. The daughter—an emergency nurse—had been alarmed that her mother had a very large bruise on her forehead that didn't look normal from a fall. No blood and no broken skin, but blunt force maybe from the position of the body. No natural apparent cause of death.

Carl didn't like it either, and neither did the assistant medical examiner who reviewed the case. He read the report and it said the manner of death was inconclusive based on the presented evidence. It was possible only if she fell and was still able to move, but he doubted if it was a fall hard enough to cause a hemorrhage to the brain that would knock her unconscious. But stranger things had happened in his expert opinion.

Inconclusive. What every detective wanted to hear.

Not exactly.

It gave you latitude when you started the investigation, but it also presented a complication that you maybe were looking for something that just wasn't there. The germ of doubt that might compromise any officer's resolve to ferret out the truth of any puzzle didn't really help the situation.

He left the office, ordered mozzarella chicken, a salad, and garlic bread from his phone with a set pickup time, and pulled out of the parking lot, still thinking about this new case.

For one thing, Mrs. Armistad hadn't been robbed. The first two victims had been stripped of any personal possessions that might identify them. She'd been killed right in front of her home, so that wasn't necessary.

If she'd been killed at all.

Old lady collapses and hits her head. End of story, but still better than butting up against stubborn teens with attitude that you know have the answers to your questions but just aren't all about talking to the police.

He had an hour or so and decided to cruise by the park. It was low key and pretty, as the sun had decided to make a fairly dramatic descent with streaks of crimson and dark blue, but there were some serious storms in the forecast. He'd been asked more than once why he didn't just sell that big house and move somewhere more hospitable. The truth was, he liked Milwaukee. It was in many ways a beautiful city in a beautiful state. The weather wasn't perfect—at all—but he didn't have to worry about hurricanes or earthquakes, and at least people knew how to drive in the snow in Wisconsin. There were worse places to live.

If he understood anything about himself, it was that he'd be bored in about five seconds on a sandy beach somewhere. The death of his parents had given him an urgency to stay busy to maybe just avoid thinking about it even all these years later, but he was settled into the pattern and it felt right. He was capable of making decisions that bordered on reckless, but he really had no regrets.

Mrs. Armistad's house was a regular suburban ranch style, probably built in the fifties or even earlier, and she had pots of flowers out front already, the blinds firmly closed.

He parked his car and got out, walking up the steps. There were bushes on either side, lilacs starting to leaf out, and they were mature, thick branched and offered some cover this time of year. Someone could certainly use them to hide.

He found a clear footprint of a man's shoe behind one bush, but it could easily have been of one of the cops, poking around just like he was right now. Still, he took a picture of it with his phone. It wouldn't hurt to have it. Since there was no clear evidence of a homicide, Metzger seemed to just want him to look into it. He had to admit he didn't like that the victim's house—if she was one—was so close to the park where two people had been evidently murdered and dumped.

It wasn't at all the same method, but it was quite a few bodies in a small area that was relatively quiet and crime-free. Between that and how adamant her family was that something had happened to her that didn't involve a simple fall, he was interested in the investigation, but not sure it was related to anything else. Until he drove halfway across town to talk to her daughter.

Mrs. Weston informed him that she was talking to her mother on her cell phone when her mother spotted a young man standing with a flower on her front porch.

Middle-aged and teary-eyed, Terry Weston swiped at her eyes with a much-used tissue. "I thought nothing of it. She didn't seem afraid. She said that to me. She said, 'How sweet. I know what this is about. How did he find out where I live?'"

A flower?

The flowers on MacIntosh's desk.

Carl suddenly didn't like it at all. "You have no idea who he could be?"

"None." The woman was decisive, but her eyes were still a mirror of misery. "She was suddenly dead on her front porch and there was a flower found next to her. My husband is an attorney who deals with your office often. They ruled it a probable accident on the report, but that man standing there . . . it is bothering me. My husband suggested we call Chief Metzger. My mother was the kindest woman in the world. I can't even fathom someone killed her, but I can't put it out of my mind either that it's a possibility."

Neither could he.

He drove home slowly.

Forty-five more minutes would give him time to at least check the bathroom on the main floor. It probably had cobwebs in it since he didn't use it often or even ever. He knew he had his ghosts. He still remembered when his mother had picked out the wallpaper because she'd dragged him along to the store.

Maybe Georgia Lukens could explain to him why he still climbed the stairs to use the bathroom off the bedroom he'd occupied as a child. But that conversation was for another time, and right now he needed to go set the table.

After he swept out the cobwebs.


**Santiago was always** an adventure.

Georgia considered him an interesting patient on any number of levels. He was honest. Most of them weren't. He wasn't really into dodging around touchy subjects, so she could ask him direct questions and get direct answers, and that was why he was there.

Good. They understood each other.

He paced instead of sitting in a chair, which was how he dealt with tension. She'd known him for a while now and he was wound up.

"I told her I loved her."

"Ellie?" Georgia took the low road and pretended surprise. "Do you?"

He rounded on her. "Why would I ever say so if I didn't? That's kind of a stupid question."

She had to stifle a laugh. "It's been obvious for quite a while how you feel about her. Accept the joke."

"Oh." He clearly wasn't himself. "Oh, right, funny, I'm laughing—not. Ellie now doesn't want to talk about it."

"Is there any part of you that hoped she would?"

"What? Yes." He paused. "Well, maybe no. I have no idea. I've never done it before."

"Done what exactly? Told a woman you love her?"

He said flatly, "Told anyone I love them. Maybe when I was a kid I said it to my mother, but quite frankly, if it happened, I don't remember it."

That wouldn't surprise her at all. "That would be very natural. She betrayed you in your mind, so you don't care to cherish memories of her. Detective Santiago, let's face it that you want Ellie to introduce the subject back to you and she hasn't cooperated. What's plan B?"

"Okay, I need one, and don't have it. I feel better just for saying it out loud to her."

"So, you accomplished what you needed and then it is out of your hands."

"Not exactly." He clearly wasn't happy. "If someone says, 'I'm in with love you,' I don't think the weather forecast should be your next topic of conversation."

"Have you considered it might have been as much of a major event in her life to hear it as it was in yours for you to say it?"

"Dr. Lukens, I'm just worried about myself at the moment. I'm not whining about it, but I have discovered the hard way that if you don't handle something on your own, there's a chance no one else will pick up the slack."

He had a point. A very good one. She'd been there.

"Okay, let's look at that angle. I have a question I think you should consider carefully. Which do you think you'd prefer, for her to say she also loves you, or for her to pretend you never said it? I think the answer either way scares you. I believe you chose Kate because you knew it wouldn't last from what you've said to me. When she left you, it didn't seem like you were devastated. For the first time in your life, you're worried about being truly hurt if this goes the wrong way, and you aren't sure what way that is."

He did sardonic very well. "First time in my life? Like when my mother walked out and left me with a man that wasn't actually my father when I was just a little kid? We've sort of made our peace over it, but forgive isn't forget, and I'm not going to be able to forget. I kept finding fault with myself, wondering why my dad didn't like me. Well, duh, I wasn't his child but he was stuck with me. She had her reasons, but I wasn't aware of anything except she'd just left me."

True, true, and true. Georgia could do a lot of things, but change the past wasn't one of them. Part of her actually admired his stepfather for maybe not doing the best job in the world, but not tossing Jason to the curb. He was abusive and alcoholic, but not all bad. He could have handed him over to the system as revenge against his missing wife. Maybe that would have been better, but maybe not. That would have involved Jason losing both of his parents and his home too.

"You had no control over that. This is different. You have choices now and you made one. Why did you tell Ellie how you feel? What did you hope to accomplish?"

Her patient sank into the chair in front her desk and exhaled. "Jesus, I don't know. Being in a relationship is like taking a run on Hell's Highway. This way and you hit fire and brimstone, and the other way you might find deep blue seas but they're full of man-eating sharks. Have a bunch of fun, jump right in, compadre."

That was pretty poetic for Santiago. Georgia stifled a smile. "If it makes you feel any better, everyone experiences anxiety when their life might take a drastic turn. You wouldn't be a normal human being if you didn't. If you want my insight, and I assume you do because you pay me for it, I'd say it might not hurt for you to sit down and think hard about what you hope happens next. Then you can decide what you're going to do if it doesn't happen. This isn't betraying patient confidentiality, but speaking as someone who knows Ellie as a friend, she'll talk about it when she's ready but not a minute before. I bet that isn't new information to you."

"I'm bugged about those flowers Ellie got."

He was bugged about a lot of things, but maybe this was the meat of their conversation. Georgia carefully considered her next words. He wasn't the hardest person to read because he didn't bother to hide anything, but he was also very smart. "Tell me why."

"It's the kind of shit you do to get attention."

"She told me about them and I put it out there that maybe someone just sent her flowers. We both know *you* think she's attractive, so let's just assume others do as well. Maybe you have some competition."

"I don't like the other player. Some stranger paid a woman to go into a grocery store and buy those flowers. Now it looks like it's possible she's been killed. It could have been an accidental fall, but there was a flower next to her body."

Georgia wasn't enthused about that information at all. "Ellie told me about the tulips. How did you find that out?"

For the first time in their session, Santiago laughed, but it was mirthless. "Detectives are supposed to be able to gather information. That's what we do. I'd like to think I'm decent at it. I've been practicing for a while. Grasso has been assigned her case as a possible homicide. It *could* have been an accident. If it wasn't, this is a very dangerous individual. He isn't convinced it is tied to our case, but it happened right in the area, and we know a man gave the little old lady money to buy flowers just like the ones on Ellie's desk. That lady is now dead."

"So she could identify him and he killed her? You're more than decent at being a detective, by the way. That's been proven. Now I'm worried about Ellie too."

"Because of me or him?"

That was an astute question. Santiago had his demons, no doubt about that. But for someone abandoned as a child to the not-so-tender mercies of a man who had never wanted him, he'd been a resilient spirit. Some children learn to repeat the behaviors that shape their upbringing, and some shun them. In his case, he shunned them, and that was a positive.

"Him." Georgia was firm. "You'll treat her well if she chooses that direction. I can't promise you she will, but I trust her instincts."

"My instincts are that the tulips connected to the dead woman bother me more than the bodies in the park. We took a picture back to the store to the clerk that waited on her. It was Mrs. Armistad."

"Okay, why did you go to all that trouble?" She truly was curious.

"He doesn't care about the bodies. The tulips are personal. I really wish he hadn't done that."

"We all wish he hadn't done any of it."

"You know what I meant. It really bothers me if he's paying special attention to Ellie."

She could see it did.

"You love her, so of course."

"Before now, if you'd have asked me if love came up and bit my ass, I would have said I might not recognize it. Just because I said it doesn't mean I know it. I thought I had strep throat once. It turns out I was wrong and I was just allergic to some disgusting drink made with peppermint vodka that Kate thought was trendy. I won't miss the sore throat or the drink either. For that matter, after she left me, you're right, I figured out I didn't really miss Kate. I'm still trying to figure out if this is real or not."

"But you would miss Ellie?"

"Hell yes." He ran his fingers through his hair. "Jesus, don't say things like that to me. My job is dealing with people who are missed by other people, and not for a good reason."

Dryly, Georgia said, "I think you truly have been bitten on the ass then, as you so eloquently put it."

"It has been pointed out to me I have a way with words. This nut job has me on edge, and I'm not all that relaxed on a calm day. Anyone who asks a nice little old lady to buy flowers for them and then in turn goes and kills her has a calculating mind."

In her professional opinion Jason had about a dozen reasons to have chronic edginess that held all kinds of labels, but in truth, she thought he handled life better than he thought he did. His childhood might not have been riding his tricycle down a sunny sidewalk, but he'd developed some serious coping skills because of it. Like most things, she'd discovered in the course of her career, not all good, but not all bad either. In her estimation, her needier patients talked about problems that someone like Jason Santiago wouldn't even notice.

"I agree. So what are you going to do now?"

He didn't hesitate, which didn't surprise her. "Catch him."

## Chapter 7

It wasn't like he didn't understand the dynamics.

For some reason, he didn't feel bad. He should, but he didn't. He wondered why, but then again, maybe people were just who they were. Some women who were pretty knew it, and some were maybe aware but not all that into the attention.

Detective MacIntosh was probably in the latter category. Not standoffish, but not receptive either. She might solve crimes, but she wasn't exactly perceptive on a personal basis.

She had no idea who or what he was.

Soon she would take notice.

**Carl answered the** door to an elegant frothy skirt and a silky blouse. Very eye-catching. The dark-haired woman wearing them wasn't bad either.

Georgia looked around the foyer with interest, and he had the feeling that inviting her to his home was a test drive for both of them. It was definitely dated, and he knew it, not to mention the peek into his personal life, but he could maybe use some constructive criticism. He led her into the kitchen. "I opened us some wine. No, I haven't changed a thing in this house for years. I realize I should, but am just not motivated to do it since I'm the only who lives here and it is comfortable enough. White or red?"

"There's no need to be defensive, since I'm not here to analyze you. Red?"

"I hope you like merlot."

"I do." Georgia settled into a chair at the antique table and crossed those legs he admired so much.

He took out the really nice crystal glasses. The ones his mother had inherited. They were so old he couldn't remember the century. At this point he figured that if one got broken, who cared? The child of parents who died unexpectedly, he wasn't concerned with passing on possessions. Life was short. Make yourself comfortable and forget the rest.

Georgia didn't seem to agree. Her eyes widened as he poured and went over to hand the glass to her. "Can you give me something else to drink out of please? These must be worth a small fortune. They are gorgeous. Where did you get these?"

"I inherited them. I think my mother said she inherited from a relative who mentioned Saxony, which to my knowledge no longer exists under that name."

She looked doubly alarmed.

He said calmly, "They were made to be used. Hence the term 'wineglass.'"

"If I accidentally broke one—"

"I'd forgive you on the spot and get out another one."

She went ahead and took a sip and then studied the etched glass. "Do you ever sit and wonder who has touched these?"

"I try to not think about them, quite honestly."

"I don't understand people like you and Santiago."

He about choked on his first drink of wine. "Oh, I'm dying to hear in what way the two of us are alike. I'd have made book on the fact that the two of us are pretty different. And excuse me, but I thought your profession was to understand people."

That statement made her laugh before she corrected him. "That's not accurate. My profession is to help people understand themselves. I have patients who have no idea why they do some of the things they do. Why they are unfaithful yet in a happy marriage. Why they shoplift and have the money to buy the item. Why they hate talking to their mother on the phone but panic if she doesn't call every day. The list goes on."

"I can only imagine. At least my job is just to find out who did it. Motive is not as important as most people think it is in an investigation. Opportunity is first and foremost. Who could do it and get away with it. Why someone would want to do it is more your field."

"I'm actually learning a lot about your profession. What I meant is you and Santiago certainly come from different backgrounds, but you're both actually quite sensitive. Yet you chose a job that would normally be considered difficult to handle on an emotional level. But you manage it. Why this path?"

Carl couldn't help it, he leaned on the counter and lifted his brows. "You think *Santiago* is sensitive?"

She didn't flinch. "I really do. Don't worry, he wouldn't believe me either. But don't avoid my question. This isn't an interrogation, so if you say you have no idea, I will let it go. I'm just curious."

"I've never really thought about it."

"Now see, right there, you are like Jason Santiago. He doesn't like to think about it either."

"That isn't what I said."

"No, but let's be honest, maybe what you meant?"

He liked her straightforward approach right along with admiring the way her hair caught the light. "I'll concede that, I suppose. I do it because I dislike man's inhumanity to man. A person's life has value. If I look at it that way, I think I see the similarity to Santiago. My impression is that he grew up having to fight for a sense of self-worth because he was pretty much on his own. My situation is different in that suddenly my security was also wrenched from me. I was on my own too."

Georgia nodded. "Very insightful, Detective. What else?"

"We don't like bad guys."

"I get that. Succinct and to the point. I think neither of you do. Ellie MacIntosh can be thrown into that mix as well."

Two could play this game, of course. There was a reason that was a saying. "Tell me about Georgia Lukens. Why does she do what she does?"

She was used to asking questions and so was he, but apparently neither of them appreciated answering any of them. She looked out the big window over the sink and obviously thought it over. "I'm not sure. I'm curious, like you. I want to help people stay away from their problems."

"Impossible."

"Okay, that makes me more optimistic than you."

"Is this a contest? The people who need me are all dead. At least yours are alive. Of course you are more optimistic."

She wasn't able to come up with an easy response to that one, so there was a pause. "Good point."

"I'm not for understanding the enemy, just catching them."

"Fair enough."

The doorbell rang then and it was their food being delivered, so that ended the discussion. She ate with predictable decorum and at a leisurely pace, so he did too, but usually he didn't think about the enjoyment because it was just necessary fuel.

They did the dishes together, and when her elbow bumped his she said very matter-of-factly, "You want me to stay the night. I'm considering it."

"What makes you think that?"

"Body language, for one. You haven't done a lot of deep looking into my eyes. You want something but aren't sure how to ask."

She was completely right. He was always amazed how women could read men so much better than men could read women. He'd been looking definitely at other parts of her. "I haven't even kissed you yet."

"I don't think kissing is really what's on your mind."

She was spot on there too. "Well, it could be involved in the equation."

"You aren't my patient."

"I'm not. You aren't a suspect either."

"So we're free to do what we want."

"Stay then?" Since she'd been so forthright, maybe he should be too.

"I want to and I don't usually take chances like this."

If she thought he didn't know that about her, she wasn't paying attention. He tried to sound neutral. "If you choose to stay, that would be great. If you don't, then that's your decision. It's up to you. I haven't opened the pool quite yet since I'm a Memorial Day kind of man, but let's go sit out on the patio because this is really a nice night for this time of year."

"Good idea."

It was starry and tranquil, and he was definitely a creature of habit and had to consciously relax. It had been a problem his entire adult life.

Georgia was a decisive person; he knew that from working with her on a professional level. She sat down in a deck chair and once again crossed those long legs and looked at him very directly. "I vote stay."

"That's my vote too."

She tilted her head back to look at the sky. "It is a really beautiful night."

He couldn't agree more.


**Ellie got off** the phone and sighed in relief. She knew she was tense over about a dozen things, not the least of which was one Detective Jason Santiago. Good news was most welcome, she thought as she settled in her comfortable living room. The only things she'd brought from her house up north in Lincoln County were some framed photographs, a needlepoint pillow her grandmother had given her when she was twelve, and her clothes. The furnishings were all new, but neutral. Beige couch and a matching chair. Nice polished coffee table, but the only personality was the selection of books she'd stacked there. She refused to part with that northern house for reasons she was still trying to figure out. Maybe she clung to it so tenaciously because it reminded her of where she grew up, which was certainly not a city, but it could be because her father had written her a check for the down payment and informed her with that smile she missed every single day that she'd better not even think about paying it back. So instead she paid rent in Milwaukee and kept the house up north in the woods.

She drank her tea with true enjoyment. Remission was a wonderful word. Her mother had sounded great. Her CT scan had come back clean, and both Ellie and her sister, Jody, had been worried but not talked too much about it. Breast cancer was definitely a wake-up call.

So was her next call.

"Hi. Is this Cinderella?"

A pleasant voice, calm, definitely male, tenor not bass, and completely without inflection.

There was a split second of confusion before she realized it was *him*. She dealt with killers, but the personal call was jarring.

He went on, "I wanted to know if you liked the flowers."

She found her voice. "I don't recognize you or the number. Who is this?"

"I have your missing shoe." He hung up.

She stared at the display that said Unknown Number, wondering what she could have done differently, or said differently . . . but she'd been definitely taken off guard.

Missing shoe. From the first victim. Cinderella?

She immediately called Jason, her hand not quite

steady. The man didn't sleep anyway as far as she could tell. "I think he just called me."

"Who?" He did drink and sounded like he might have actually dozed off.

"Our good friend who likes parks. I'm going to guess you'll agree it was him."

He did come out of it fast. The volume of the television went down abruptly. "What?"

She wasn't happy either. "A man called me and asked how I liked the flowers. I asked who he was and then he pretty much hung up on me. He also mentioned the shoe. When I answered the call he asked if I was Cinderella."

"He *what*? I knew it. Shit, Ellie, he's really bad news. I'm on my way over."

"Not necessary, since I have a gun and am trained in how to use it. I just thought you'd like to know."

"I'm coming over. Don't shoot *me*, please."

"I would aim to maim out of our alliance to each other, to not kill, if that makes you feel any better." It was easier to joke about it all than to acknowledge she was rattled. This man had an agenda she didn't understand quite yet.

Santiago was abrupt. "Either way, please hold your fire. You can't stop me. I'll be there in a few minutes."

He truly arrived in record-breaking time and she heard the actual shriek of his tires as he pulled into her driveway. Her condo wasn't very far from his apartment building, but still he must have broken a few laws. He had on shorts, which was a little optimistic, because it was still cool at night, and a Packers T-shirt that looked like he'd pulled it out of a laundry bag. He did, however, when she opened the door to let him in, seem perfectly clear-eyed and sober.

"Tell me about it, word for word. Let me venture a guess, a blocked number."

He was right, of course.

"Yes. I was having a cup of tea. Would you like some?"

He looked at her like she was insane. "Tea? What is this? Buckingham Palace? Do I seem like a tea sort of guy? I need to grow a bushy beard or something if I'm giving off that vibe." He pointed at a backpack he'd brought inside with him and set on the floor. "I have beer. None of it is cold, but I'm not picky. Help yourself if you want some because it still has to be better than tea. I'm sleeping on your couch, by the way. Now tell me what he said exactly."

"I'm perfectly capable of taking care of myself." She wasn't as sure as she sounded.

He sat down on the couch. "My ass is planted here until we figure out this guy. His exact words were what?"

"'I wanted to know if you liked the flowers.'" She sat down and picked up her cup. "Nothing ominous, necessarily, but he hung up on me. It could be not connected at all to the murders, just some strange guy, if it wasn't for the shoe thing."

"It bothered you enough you called me."

That she couldn't deny. "What was the purpose of it?"

Santiago fished in the backpack and got a beer and popped it open. "To make sure he has your attention."

"He has it already if he's killed two people."

"You and I are thinking along the same lines. That's why I'm going to sleep on your couch. I prefer your bed, but hell, don't worry about it. I fall asleep on my couch most of the time anyway, so don't feel bad."

He probably did, but she wasn't quite convinced yet it was necessary to have a sleepover, and as usual, she wasn't going to respond. "You didn't need to rush over here, but since you are here, fine, let's consider the evidence. Wait, we don't have any."

"I do sarcasm a lot better than you. I would have said we don't have jack shit."

"Of course you would."

"I'm more of a realist."

"Than me? How so?"

"I have no shyness in how I express myself."

That was so true she practically fell on the floor laughing. "No, you don't. You are a free spirit. So what now?"

"We're in a good place. He wants to talk to you."

"Oh, lucky me."

Santiago looked serious. "I mean it. He's killed two people, or maybe three, and we're sitting around scratching our heads and suddenly he calls. I wasn't in doubt we'd ever catch him, but this is not going to be nearly as hard as I thought it would be."

That voice on the phone, so measured and self-assured . . . she wasn't as sure. "I don't think I agree. He's sure he's smarter than we are."

"Maybe." At least he was willing to see her perspective. "I don't think anyone is smarter than I am, so what about the notes on the bodies?"

Funny. "Like with the flowers. He was just showing off."

"Ellie, he's into you."

She was afraid he was right. "I recognized his voice from somewhere. Maybe I arrested him at one point."

"Oh seriously? He's not going to have revenge on his mind if that's true. I'm glad you have a comfortable couch, because I've found my home away from home right here until we put on the cuffs."

"I didn't invite you."

"I didn't ask."

She'd noticed that. He amended, "I'm truly not asking to sleep in your bed. I just want to be here in case something happens. It makes sense to me. I can sleep on my couch or sleep on yours. Why not here? Now you have backup, and I want you to have backup."

"I don't think I'm in danger of any kind, but go ahead and sleep on my couch."

"Detective MacIntosh, yes, you do want backup."

"He was creepy," she admitted. "I am not a woman who says that often, but he did it on purpose. It wasn't anything he said, but I could tell he was trying to intimidate me. He was also deliberately disguising his voice."

"So now I really do have a new home away from home."

It was comforting to see him sit back and sip from his beer can, and she could swear she was the last person who needed comfort of that kind. "Why is it I think you'll be snoring and *I'll* have to protect *you*? That's what's going to happen. I clearly remember having to haul you into a boat one time to keep you from drowning."

"That was a fluke." He lifted an index finger. "I have stood between you and a serial murderer and arsonist."

"And you got shot twice. Metzger was all over me for letting my partner be in harm's way. Don't make that a feather in your cap. I took off my shirt to staunch the bleeding."

"Oh, and I remember that moment. Do people even

really say that, and what the hell does it mean? A feather in your cap?" He negligently crossed his ankles. "I have no feathers and it doesn't bother me to be featherless. I don't even have a fucking cap. What kind of cap are they talking about? Please not one of those poofy things you see in old paintings. I would look so stupid in one of those. Everyone does."

"I wasn't aware you even looked at paintings."

"The dogs playing poker is my favorite."

"That doesn't surprise me, and you so think you're funny and you so aren't."

"And yet you're laughing."

"I was picturing you in the hat with the feather."

"Please tell me you have an extra pillow."

She wanted him there. It would be unfair not to admit it. Ellie nodded. "I do. Let me go get it. Feel free to turn on your baseball game. I didn't even know it was that season yet."

"I have it recorded. It's my go-to if there's nothing else on. I'll just stream it from my phone."

Ellie did have to turn, gazing at him from across the room. "Seriously? You'd watch a game when you already know how it ends?"

"Seriously. Ever watch a movie twice or read a book more than once?"

There were some arguments just not worth it. She was going to lose this one. As a teenager she'd read *Gone With the Wind* probably fourteen times. "Let me go get that pillow."

Chapter 8

She'd slept alone.

He wasn't positive before now, but it calmed him to know. He needed it. In college he'd gone through a phase and continually watched a girl he'd noticed in his English class, but that had finally faded because he lost interest.

This wasn't going to go away.

He disliked the term "obsession," but he'd looked it up anyway in the dictionary. The state of a person vexed or besieged.

He wondered if either description applied.

No, he decided, he was simply fascinated.

Obsession implied imbalance, and he was completely balanced and in charge.

**Jason did something** he almost never did. He voluntarily went to see Metzger.

The chief was on the phone and yet looked as astounded to see him as he was when he'd decided to do it in the first place. Metzger actually ended the call abruptly and asked, "What now?"

Jason decided in the chief's defense that he was used to people coming to him with problems, and he wasn't actually any different. In this case, though, it was warranted. "I think the killer in our current case is contacting MacIntosh."

"Fine, good, I'm sure you'll catch him faster."

His thoughts exactly, though "good" didn't describe it. "Not good. I think it's personal."

Metzger rubbed his temples. "Why do you always give me a headache?"

"Sir, all of us give you a headache."

"Truer words never spoken. If I made more money, I'd consider moving to Bali, where I hear all the women want to do is rub your back and bring you tropical drinks. Fine, go on and tell me why this impacts my day."

"Speaking on the subject, I want to take a week of my vacation. I'm worried about her."

"Vacation? For what? To follow MacIntosh around riding a white horse and in a suit of armor?"

It was close enough to the truth, Jason couldn't really deny it. He still gave it a try. "We often have different days off. I just—"

Metzger was who he was. He never gave a quarter. "You're her partner, but you also have a thing for her. I see it and pretty much so does everyone else. The answer is no. You're with her practically every minute of the day anyway. If she needs to buy a tomato at the grocery store, you don't need to be lurking in the produce aisle just in case our perp leaps out from a pile of lettuce." The chief sighed. "Look, if you didn't work so well together, I'd just assign you each different partners. Do what you do best and find him. Ellie carries a Glock, and it is common knowledge she can use that gun. She's all good. The sentiment is admirable, but unneeded. If you're aware, she's aware. Put in for vacation when you can go lie on a beach in Bali for that lotion and drink therapy and let me know if it is all it's cracked up to be. Right now the most effective thing you can do is solve the case."

"You were in the military. If there's one thing you learn it's that anyone can be caught off guard."

"MacIntosh would not appreciate we are even having this discussion, would she? Get the hell out of my office, please. If you think you have paperwork to catch up on, try being me."

Jason knew when to give up.

Well, that was a bust.

He wasn't adverse to arguing, but with Metzger it was dicey. He went back to his desk, and to his surprise he got a call from, of all people, his mother. They really only barely knew each other.

"How are you?" Her voice was as always calm but guarded. They'd made their peace of sorts, but since they hadn't seen each other for over a quarter of a century before coming face-to-face again, it wasn't a perfect situation. They spoke occasionally now.

"I'm fine. Working a case that isn't exactly pleasant, but then again, none of them are."

"I imagine not in homicide."

"How are you and your husband?"

"Jason, he's your father." Gentle admonishment was in her reply.

"It's kind of hard to think of him that way, but I'll

take your word for it the one that raised me was the lesser of two evils. What's on your mind?"

"We all choose our own path."

She was the queen of that statement, that was for sure. He decided to not point it out. In truth, she seemed like a nice enough woman, if misguided.

"I wonder if you'd do me a favor."

He tilted his chair back on two legs and blew out a breath. "Let me guess, he's back in jail and you want to see if I can pull some strings to help him out." His father's family's ties to organized crime was the main reason they didn't know each other. It wasn't going to happen.

She said, "Not at all. I want to invite you to dinner. It bothers him that he doesn't know you. That's the favor. Just come have a meal with us."

That was an unexpected twist to his day. He really was at a loss for words. He was fairly sure his mouth was hanging open, so he consciously shut it.

"You can bring a date if you'd like. It's a fairly long drive. You decide and I'll send a text to confirm and you can say if it will work for you. I was thinking Friday."

Processing this was harder than processing a gruesome crime scene.

"Jason?"

"I guess that would be okay." He said it in a feeble voice and cleared his throat. Had he really just agreed? This woman had turned her back on her child but explained why she'd left. She claimed it was to protect him from being dragged into a circle of unsavory friends and family to inherit a legacy of crime that was traditionally passed from father to son. He was unimpressed with the argument initially, but there was no doubt now that he'd heard the story his biological father had spent time in prison because those records were public. Maybe she'd been right to just leave her child where he was—it was damned hard to say. It seemed to him her choice in men was dicey at best, but a small sliver of him—paper thin but there—wanted to believe her motivation was his best interest.

Now all he had to do was get Ellie to agree to it, and he wasn't even sure what *his* motivation might be. Someone to hold his hand? He'd never had dinner with his parents at all, much less alone. What? If he would shoot an intruder to protect Ellie, she should surely be able to have a bite of steak or some lasagna to help him out. She'd at least keep the conversation going.

Sounded like a fair trade.

His mother said, "Wonderful. I'll make your grandmother's famous strawberry cake. Your father will be very happy."

He wasn't even aware his grandmother had a famous strawberry cake recipe. "I'll get back to you. Thanks for calling."

After that interesting exchange he walked over to Ellie's desk. Maybe he even stalked over. That was possible. He was abrupt, but Ellie usually handled it fairly well. "Don't even try to get out of this, but you're the one that found my parents. I didn't even particularly want any part of it, so you and I now have a date for strawberry cake."

"What are you talking about?"

"You did it and you now own it. We're invited for dinner. You're the one that pursued this I-should-find-my-parents idea, and I'm not going alone."

"To dinner with your *parents*?"

"Oh yeah. I think I'm now officially pissed at you. Mexican for dinner tonight at your place, okay? I'll pick it up. We can talk about it then before I sack out on your couch again."

Ellie said in typical Ellie fashion, "You are such an ass. Yes, to Mexican food, I want a beef burrito. Fine, I'll go along to this family dinner if this makes you so uncomfortable, but I was just trying to help when I found your mother."

"My father is a criminal and she abandoned me. Surely they should get a plaque for bad parenting."

Ellie crossed her arms. "Your father paid his debt to society and has stayed clean, and your mother is the one trying, not you. There's nothing for us to talk about, and if there is, tell Lukens. Only talk to me if someone kills someone."

"I heard that and guess what? I'm talking to you. You have another body." It was Fergusson striding by with his usual abrupt approach. "Broad daylight. Different park. The report phoned in tells me it all adds up. He wrote on the victim on the wrist. Two was bad enough. This makes three, or if Grasso is right, maybe four. Get in gear. Metzger doesn't want to talk on the news, and I don't blame him. I've done it, and I hate it."

"Where?"

"I sent a text."

MacIntosh grabbed her jacket while Jason checked his phone.

"Oh shit," he said vehemently, "that park is right by my apartment. Coincidence? I'm starting to doubt that right away."

*  *  *

**This was calculated** and cold.

It was a show of power. Ellie knew every single case had a feel to it, and this one pushed the edge.

Was there a connection between her letting Santiago stay the night at her condo and this new killing? She was starting to think so when she knelt beside the body and read the ink on the victim's arm.

*Think about me.*

The victim this time was a young man, probably in his early twenties, and asphyxiation once again the method even if in a different form. He'd been hung from a tree, part of the rope still dangling.

She was cold all over. None of it made any sense.

One of his shoes had fallen off, and Ellie didn't want to look at it there in the nicely clipped grass, an orphan of a horrific crime. The scene was still being processed, so no one had picked it up yet, and she wouldn't either—she had her job and the technicians had theirs—but she hated it just lying there.

*Cinderella . . .*

"We cut him down thinking it was a suicide, and then saw that." The young officer sounded pragmatic. "I thought for a second it was a tattoo, but then realized it was just regular ink and made the park connection since I read the paper every morning with my infamous doughnut and coffee. We didn't touch anything else after we called it in as a possible homicide."

"Let me guess, no ID."

"You'd be guessing exactly right, Detective."

What if a child had stumbled across the body? She knew that when she looked over at Santiago the reason his jaw was clenched so tight was because he was thinking the same thing. This time it was a young mother, Mrs. Harris, who had thought her son's favorite ball had been left behind and gone back to get it once her husband came home and could watch the child while she ran back. She was as pale as an arctic ice floe and gladly accepted the offer of an unopened bottle of water. Santiago was nice enough to take off the cap for her because she was shaking so much she couldn't do it on her own.

When he gave it back, he said with un-Santiago-like sensitivity, "Describe the ball and I'll find it. It isn't going to be evidence. Detective MacIntosh might have a few questions, though, for you. Talk to her and I'll go look for it."

"It's blue and this big." She gave the dimensions with her shaking hands. "My son is three. He sleeps with it. He has to have it. Oh God. He loves to play here, but I doubt I'll bring him again."

Ellie said, "Let's go sit in my car and you can take a deep breath while Detective Santiago looks for the ball. The crime scene is almost processed."

The woman was young and dark haired, maybe in her midtwenties. She nodded almost frantically and downed about half the bottle of water as they walked to the car. Ellie didn't blame her. "Did you see anyone?" She tried to be matter-of-fact, but it was really difficult. "I'm sure at the moment you realized there was someone hanging there you weren't thinking about anything else, because that's how we work as human beings, but did anyone walk by or catch your attention beforehand? Maybe they weren't acting strangely, but something didn't seem quite right? You know about ninety percent of police work is about science, and the important ten percent is about how we sense things. It could be as simple as a bad feeling."

She was calming down, considering it, staring at the bottle of water in her hand. "I did have a feeling I was being watched from that way." She pointed toward the north. "I don't know why I thought someone was there, but I did. That doesn't help you one bit."

Well, maybe yes and maybe no. "But you didn't see anyone."

Mrs. Harris tearfully wiped her eyes. "A young man stopped and asked if I needed help, but I'd already called emergency services."

Oh, *that* sounded unfortunately familiar. "Can you describe him? Take a minute."

"The man? I don't really know . . . tall. Young."

"The color of his hair or anything distinguishing?"

"I can't think of anything. Blond hair maybe . . . or light brown."

"Was he white? African American? Hispanic?"

"White."

Same guy as with the old couple, Ellie knew it. "Nothing else? Was he wearing an earring in one ear?"

The young woman shook her head. "I didn't notice one, but I was so shaken up and he was just being nice."

Oh yeah, he was positively a delightful human being all right, but even if there wasn't a pattern yet to how he chose his victims, they had several, albeit vague, descriptions. Second was the park thing, third was he didn't stab or shoot anyone, he liked them to die from lack of air.

Santiago was successful with the ball quest and

returned the coveted item, opening her door and helping Mrs. Harris nicely out of the car. "One of the officers will drive you home. A patrol car will follow and pick him up. Don't worry, none of your neighbors will see you arrive in a police vehicle."

"Thank you." She clutched the ball like she was the three-year-old and made a beeline for her car.

Santiago climbed into her spot in the passenger seat. Ellie commented, "Good idea about having someone drive her."

After they pulled away, Santiago said, "I think she was more composed than the janitor dude and a lot cuter. Still, that ball evidently needs to make it home in one piece. I'm really starting to hate this guy we're dealing with. Did she help us at all?"

"She did. Not that we're any closer to catching him, but it seems to me like he hangs around waiting for the body to be discovered. Young, seems nice, brown hair, stops to ask if he can help. She didn't remember an earring, but for all we know, he took it out."

"I never thought I'd say this in my life, but I'd love to be the one to discover the next body. If he stopped by to ask if I needed help, I'd just cuff him and haul him in."

Ellie sent him a sidelong look. "Probably not in a gentle manner, I take it. I think we need a profiler on this one. He's contacting us, he's obsessed with a certain cause of death, and he wants to be right there to see the reaction to his crime. That said, we don't have a suspect. Let's find out what we're looking for."

"I've got the answer and I don't work for the FBI. He's a maniac scumbag."

"In this world we live in, that doesn't narrow it down enough," she pointed out dryly.

He conceded that one. "Fine. So call Montoya. He's your go-to guy for this sort of thing. Since we have almost nothing, it will take about two minutes of his time."

"*'Think of me.'* He's getting bold very fast."

This perp was a derailed loaded locomotive. "Call the FBI."

**Montoya was out** on vacation, but he answered anyway. She wasn't surprised. None of them rested, they just pretended to relax. Ellie said, "I won't waste your precious time. I have next to nothing, but I really don't know how to find him. He's killed three people already and we're thinking four is more accurate. Tell me something about this killer that will help. People are dying."

"You seem certain he's the same one."

She outlined the notes written on the bodies. "I can't be sure about the older lady. I think she was a casualty of having met him directly face-to-face. Others might have also, but she was our only real link. If he was the one who paid her to buy me flowers, he's not playing around, but that's *if* he's the one who sent me flowers. Someone did. No note."

Agent Montoya immediately said, "If he did kill your older victim, she didn't meet some criteria in his mind. It was necessary but not satisfying."

"He also likes to cruise by for the discovery of the body. He chooses a public place like a park to put the victims. He kills a diverse group so far, but floats on by to see the reaction of the people who find them. I have an unusable description, but in their defense, they only hear him asking if he can help. It isn't like they are committing that to memory; they are so shocked by finding a body that it is the only thing they are thinking about."

"Common. But you have a description, right? Make it fast. I need another Bloody Mary. I'm in South Carolina and there's a golf course with my name on it."

"Young male, tall, athletically built, and might wear an earring. I've been called on the phone by the killer. It was a burner. We couldn't trace it."

There was a sudden silence. Then Agent Montoya said, "He did *what*? Describe that conversation to me."

"He called me Cinderella and asked if I liked the flowers. The first victim was missing a shoe when she was found. You don't have to be top of your class in detecting school to make that connection."

"That doesn't make me happy."

Oh, good to hear from a federal profiler. She was already jumpy. "Yeah, I know." She said it tightly. "This latest victim had one of his shoes off and lying on the ground. If I were you I wouldn't plan on sneaking up on me anytime soon because it is very possible I'll pull my weapon. I'm worried I'll shoot a little girl who is selling cookies at my door if she knocks too loudly. My partner is currently sleeping on my couch at night, and while I would normally argue over it, I'm not. This killer has an agenda we don't get. He seems to want to take me head-on. So tell me about him. What do I need to know?"

Montoya didn't answer immediately but thought it over. "Does he kill just women, or men too?"

"So far your gender is winning a contest in which no one wants to claim the gold medal. One woman and two males; unless he did kill the older lady. We don't even know the identity of the last victim, as he takes their ID. We have to wait for someone to report him missing."

"I see. I'm processing. I think my wife just glared at me, but I get bored on vacation anyway and she's better at golf than I am, which is emasculating. I'm glad you called. What else?"

"He doesn't do it the same way, but asphyxiation is his thing."

"Sounds like a great guy. I'm glad he doesn't live in my neighborhood. You need to be very careful, Detective. He's forming a bond with you. It happens. Just like children misbehave to get attention, disturbed adults will do the same thing."

"He's very random. We can't connect the victims. The only similarity is that they've all had alcohol in their system so far. We don't have a full tox back yet on the third victim, but they did do a blood alcohol level test right away. Twice the legal limit, which makes you too impaired to drive a vehicle, but not falling-down drunk necessarily."

"That's interesting."

"I think so too."

"E-mail me the specs of the cases, but watch your back. You've gotten press for apprehending more than one serial killer in your neck of the woods. It could be he just wants you to know what he's capable of."

"I've pointed this out to other people, but there was no way of predicting I'd be assigned to this case. I'm definitely not the only homicide detective in this city."

"But you'd hear about him, you'd notice him. That's what he wants. I'm going to say he was fixated on you before this all started, but when he realized you were assigned to this case, he was in seventh heaven. Either way, don't discount how dangerous he might be to you on a personal level."

Apparently Santiago was spot-on. She wasn't particularly happy when she ended the call.

She sat there, pulling up the files. It was one thing to be the hunter. It was never fun to be the hunted.

If she revealed this conversation, Santiago would probably own her couch. She had very mixed feelings about it. She was confident she could take care of herself, but no one can handle everything. She had to sleep now and then.

A hard thing to learn, but she'd been over it in her head before.

"Hammett asked me to give you this." It was Grasso, handing over an envelope. He leaned a hip on the edge of her desk. "Everything okay?"

"I think so."

"I usually hate that answer."

"I don't usually give it."

"True enough. How's Montoya?"

"Santiago has a big mouth."

Grasso just smiled negligibly. "Um, no, he doesn't. I'm the next Sherlock Holmes, remember? With a third body, if I were in your shoes, I'd call the FBI to talk to a profiler, and you've worked with him before. I deduced you'd called him."

Ellie took a second to go over her response. "Montoya is sitting in the sun on vacation, but he's going to go over my notes because drinking booze and golf has him bored. Is there something wrong with every single one of us in law enforcement? Following the activities of a criminal is better than golf and a Bloody Mary?"

Grasso said without a blink, "Nope, we're the normal ones. I'm sticking to that story. Any insights?"

"From Montoya? He's just going to look over the notes. The man *is* on vacation."

"Nothing else?"

"I should watch my back."

"You should."

"You are as bad as Santiago."

He rose, as well dressed as ever in tailored slacks, an expensive shirt, and a tie that probably cost two hundred dollars. "As Santiago? That's the second time lately I've been compared to him. I'm not liking the direction this all is going, so cut me some slack for caring."

"Okay, you aren't as bad as Santiago. He would have said 'for giving a shit.'" She didn't like this investigation either.

Grasso did take that pretty well. "Okay, you win that one. He would say that."

"My impression was Montoya was alarmed, but not too much. Obviously we're dealing with someone dangerous, but we usually are. Once he reads the notes we'll know more where to look."

"Who to look for, maybe, but where is being pretty optimistic."

He was right, of course. "We have enough you'd think we could make some progress, but this killer seems really talented at being unmemorable."

"I'm not a profiler, but I'd say he's more adept at seeming to be a pleasant person. We remember someone who alarms us. We don't remember someone who just offers his help."

Grasso had been working this job for much longer

than she had. "I agree. 'Nice' seems to be the word that keeps popping up."

"Yeah, well, he's not so nice."

She thought about the body hanging in the park with a sick twist in her stomach. "No, he's not nice."

# Chapter 9

He ran with a steadiness of long practice, stride even, breathing controlled, the spring air fresh in his lungs.

He'd headed to one of his favorite trails, a long winding wooded path where the trees were starting to hold a shimmer of green.

He hadn't grown up in Milwaukee, but was from a small town in Dane County, a hole-in-the-wall place surrounded by dairy farms, and he'd thought traveling to Madison with his parents was a sophisticated experience when he was a kid, even if his grandparents' house smelled vaguely like cat urine and pipe tobacco. For a special treat they would all go to a small Swiss restaurant run by a fat woman who made the most amazing dumplings that he devoured like it was manna falling from heaven.

On one of those trips he realized his parents despised each other. He'd known in a childlike way that they didn't talk much even at home, but it had been a pivotal moment when he was ten and came to the *conclusion they truly were not and never had been in accord.*

*They were both cheerful people when the other one wasn't around, but put them together and dinners were eaten in total silence at the square farm table in the kitchen and his father scraped his plate clean and left as soon as possible. His mother brightened the minute he left the room and would bring out the cookies that were their special secret, as she put it, but by then he knew she'd just not been willing to share them with his father out of spite.*

*Their dysfunctional relationship had taught him nothing really about love, but a lot about hate.*

*He always ate the cookies—why not, they were good—but had wondered even back then how easy it would be to conceal your true feelings just by a false smile in front of other people.*

*Lesson learned.*

**Santiago had tacos**, and either they were extra delicious or he was ravenous, because he devoured them in record time.

He was also hungry for information, but he wasn't ruining her dinner. Ellie ate her burrito at a much slower pace, and he finally had to ask with one word, "Montoya?"

She set aside her napkin. "Now you sound like Grasso. Montoya is on vacation. He's going to get back to me. He wasn't encouraged by either the flowers or the phone call, but let's keep in mind we really can't connect either of those two things to what we're doing with enough level of proof."

"Oh come on."

She gathered up the plates she'd insisted they use and he handed over his cloth napkin. She said, "We are committing the cardinal sin of our profession by drawing conclusions. I think they teach that on the first day of cop school."

"I was probably truant. Skipping class was always one of my hobbies."

"Why doesn't that surprise me?"

"Let me help with the dishes."

"You mean putting two plates in the dishwasher? You got the food, so I'll clean up. Go check your precious sports scores. But I warn you, do it now, because I want to watch a movie and I don't have a television in my bedroom on purpose. I sleep in there and that's it, so that television in the living room is the only option."

"I hope it isn't going to be some chick flick, but it's your house. This is easier on us both. Metzger was probably right and you could handle it, but it's always the monster under the bed that got you. Besides, I'm fairly sure neither one of us would have gotten any sleep. I would have been tempted to call every hour just to make sure I got a response."

It was a nice night with stars out and a crescent moon and he walked outside instead of turning on the television, hands in his pockets. No doubt he was checking the street.

Her phone rang, showing an unknown number.

She stared at the display and gritted her teeth and answered anyway. She was a police officer, but she was also a woman. The idea of being stalked made her feel vulnerable and she didn't like it at all. He had an agenda and somehow she'd become part of it. "MacIntosh."

"Cinderella."

"I don't really think I like the nickname. I know who you are."

"No, you don't. If you did, I'd be under arrest. Do you like roses?"

"I—"

He hung up. Again.

Not chancing a possible trace. Technology was fine, but some of it should be banned. The call was from somewhere nearby, of that she had no doubt, and they could pick up the location maybe, but if he was clever about it, the phone would be untraceable.

Jason came in. Ellie obviously had an expression on her face that told him in just those few moments something went way wrong. She was sitting on the couch, looking at the television, which was not turned on, and her eyes were unfocused. In his usual not-smooth way, he asked, "Okay, what the hell just happened? I was gone for maybe three minutes, tops."

"He just called me again."

Jason muttered something under his breath that she suspected was particularly foul, even for him. "Are you flippin' serious? What did he say?"

"He asked me if I liked roses. Pointed out we don't know who he is." There was that flash of fear again she hated. He was right. They knew *what* he was but not *who* he was.

"He's making us guess at what he's going to do next."

"You have to admit it's working."

He did. "It could be the bag boy at the supermarket where you shop. I don't think so, but I've made it clear I don't roll that direction. I think he's someone you know in some way, Ellie."

"You and Montoya both."

"It's fine that you *finally* brought up that conversation."

"I wasn't avoiding it, I was thinking it over."

"Keep going. I need some microwave popcorn for the movie. All that health in the takeout is going to wreak havoc with my system otherwise."

"You are welcome to make some at any time. Make yourself at home seems redundant because here you are, and to be truthful, I'm glad you have such high marks when it comes to the firing range. The popcorn is on the shelf above the microwave."

He gave her a very serious look for him. "With all this going on, I'm not going to leave you alone. You know that."

She gave in a little. "I appreciate the concern, but I'll be fine."

"And I'm here to make sure of it."

"You know, this macho thing doesn't really fly with me. I believe we just had this conversation recently. We're working this as a team. Sir Galahad can stable his white horse. I don't need you to rescue me, I need you to help me catch him."

"Here's an interesting bulletin. You aren't allowed to tell me how I feel about this particular case. My therapist tells me it isn't unmanly to admit I actually have feelings. Damn, there goes most of my life doing it all wrong once again. By the way, dinner is on Friday."

The dinner. With his parents. Like the famous song, raindrops did keep falling on her head. "Like *this* Friday?"

"Yeah." His enthusiasm was at about a two on a ten scale. "I wouldn't mind if you called me Jason in front of them. I'm passing you off as my girlfriend."

For once they really agreed on something. Her enthusiasm wasn't all that high either.

**Her expression didn't** change. He knew Grantham was still out there; they were apart, but it might not be over, and Jason was skidding on thin ice anyway because he was 100 percent sure she thought a relationship between them was the worst idea on this earth. Luckily she nodded after a second. "That's fine."

"*Do* you like roses?"

Her mouth formed a firm line. "That isn't even remotely funny."

"I wasn't trying for funny. I was actually just curious."

"They are beautiful and smell good. Of course I do. Don't ever waste your very hard-earned grocery money on them, though, because they wither and die and the recipient is stuck with making the decision of when to toss them in the trash."

"That is the least romantic thing I've ever heard."

"Look, Mr. Romance, I thought we were talking about a serial killer."

He tried to be neutral about it, but he didn't do neutral very well. "Given I've said flat out how I feel about you, I think that was a perfectly valid question about the roses. Lukens tells me you'll talk about it when you're ready."

"You *told* her?" Hazel eyes regarded him with true consternation.

"She's a therapist, for God's sake, Ellie. Someone in my condition of emotional impairment needs a lot of that. Now, what movie are we going to watch? Please tell me it's *Beerfest* or something like that. What about *Animal House*? Now that is a good movie."

"Look, you Philistine, I was thinking along the lines of something more cerebral like *Amadeus*. It's one of my go-to favorites."

He'd never seen it, so it wasn't fair to groan out loud. "A musical?"

"It's *about* people, Santiago. It's really about how genius comes in all shapes and sizes. Keep an open mind."

He got up off the couch. "I definitely am going to need that popcorn and a beer."

He was halfway to the kitchen when he heard the crash. It wasn't terribly loud, but definitely audible even inside the house, so right out front, and he whirled around as Ellie jumped to her feet. It took a sprint to catch her before she rushed out the front door. Grabbing her arm, he said firmly, "Don't. Let me go look."

"We'll both go."

He had no choice, since she wrenched free.

It was his truck. The back window was smashed in and he was thoroughly unhappy but more than anxious to see if anyone was hanging around to get a thrill from his reaction.

"He's here somewhere." His voice was tight.

Crickets chirping, the smell of spring in the air, and glass just about everywhere all over her driveway and his truck made for a nice spring night.

"I'm just going to guess you're right." Ellie looked about as unhappy as he was and she didn't have an expensive broken window to deal with. "Let's see if he follows his regular pattern and cruises on by."

A car did come down the street then, but when they ran out and blocked it, flashing their badges, it just turned out to be a bewildered older couple.

"Vandalism. This just happened." Jason pointed at his truck. "We were wondering if you folks saw anything."

"No . . . I'm sorry." The man driving stammered. "We live down the block. I think I'll put the car in the garage tonight. Damn kids."

"Good idea, sir." He didn't want to mention it might be a personal agenda, because for all he knew it *was* a bunch of kids just getting their kicks out of riding around causing property damage. It had been known to happen all too often.

But his cop sense was telling him something else. "He's out there."

"I think so too."

Ellie looked both slender and vulnerable standing next to him. He felt about two feet taller than her, even though he wasn't, and wanted to carry her inside, set her down, and tell her firmly to stay put.

It wouldn't work. She'd be so infuriated she'd probably punch him. For all he knew he'd deserve it, but at least his motives were decent.

"Why is it I doubt he'd come by to ask either of *us* if we needed help, but he's watching somehow. I know it. It probably happened when we ran out. I didn't notice a car speeding away, but all he had to do is stand in the bushes across the street to catch his thrill and then just fade away on foot."

"Oh, we seem to be on his radar, dammit. Is he going to be able to pull this off?"

At least the movie wasn't too bad. He'd learned a

lot about Mozart, who didn't seem to have had a really happy life, so maybe genius was overrated.

He learned nothing about the killer.

**Georgia adjusted her** blotter. She did it about fifteen times a day and knew it was habitually a sign she was thinking about something other than typing out her notes or half a dozen things she should be doing.

Her night with Carl Grasso had been interesting, to say the least. As a lover he was thoughtful and took his time. She didn't regret the decision to sleep with him, but had to wonder if it had been a mistake.

The man was not all that emotionally available, to her or anyone else, in her professional opinion. He was intelligent—almost frighteningly so—and definitely attractive in a physical way, but he absolutely never talked about his feelings. That big house was more like a museum than a home. When he said he hadn't gotten around to changing anything, she suspected he hadn't gotten around to dealing with the sudden death of both of his parents even with all the time that had passed. It wouldn't surprise her if their clothes were still hanging in the closets. Clearly the room she and he had slept in was his boyhood bedroom, not that it had been childish in any way, but in a house that size it certainly wasn't the master bedroom, and the bathroom had been across the hall. It was an interesting quandary to be in. It was ironic that as a therapist she'd love to have a complicated patient like him, but that was certainly now out of the question. It was bad enough she saw both Ellie MacIntosh and Jason Santiago when they worked so closely together and had a personal relationship of sorts, but absolutely unethical to sleep with a patient. Besides, she had the impression that if she even suggested Carl needed therapy, he would be surprised, but maybe she was selling him short.

The light on her desk went on, telling her the next patient was there. Cindy was a resentful teen her parents forced to come to her appointments, and it was probably a good strategy they never asked about the sessions. All they'd said was please talk to her.

She walked in wearing a completely inappropriate ensemble for her age in about the shortest skirt Georgia had ever seen, a skintight shirt without a bra, and thigh-high black shiny boots. Her makeup was over the top as well, with bright green eyeshadow and deep red lipstick.

"I hate this shit," she announced, taking the chair in front of the desk. "I'm sure my parents told you already, but I've gotten suspended again."

"Actually," Georgia said mildly, "your parents don't talk to me. *You* are supposed to talk to me. Suspended for what?"

"Cheating on a test. The principal just doesn't like me. I've been called into his office three times now for violating the 'dress code.' I thought this was America."

She was certainly violating the dress code of anywhere at the moment unless it was a street corner full of prostitutes. "You dress to draw attention, so is it fair of you to be angry if you do draw attention?"

"Not to draw attention from that perv."

"Has he ever said or done anything inappropriate to you?" Georgia went on full alert mode. "Think over the answer very carefully. It isn't easy to live with it if you unfairly ruin someone's life with a lie, and I am mandated to report it."

The girl slumped down. "Well"—it was grudging—"no. I guess not. But he looks. And he calls my dad."

Cindy was smart, she was just rebellious. There was potential in her case for therapy to really help.

Georgia relaxed. "That's his job. If he sees you might draw unwanted attention from the wrong people, he would be negligent not to point it out. You should consider listening to him. I'm not saying you have to tell him he's right, but maybe tone it down a little. Now, let's move on. Tell me about the cheating."

"It was kind of reverse cheating, you know."

"Reverse cheating? Define it for me."

"I'm good at math. Like really good. I don't even have to think about it. My friend Matt sucks at it, so I did my test in about five seconds and he passed me his and I did his too. The teacher saw us when I passed it back. Now Matt's suspended too. I feel really bad."

It went to high potential for therapy to help at that moment. Offering up how she felt about something that didn't include resentment was a first.

"You were trying to help a friend, so your intentions were good, but now that you've thought it over, do you believe you were really helping? I don't mean to sound like I'm preaching at you, but Matt won't get better at math if you do it for him."

"I know." Cindy at least tugged down her skirt. It needed to be at least three inches longer, if not more. Georgia knew what color of underwear she was wearing. "He's really nice and math is hard for him. His parents are way harsh, man. Like, he doesn't have his phone or Internet now because they took it away until he's back in school. He can't even watch TV."

"What did *your* parents do?"

"Nothing, really. Made me sit down so they could lecture me for about the most boring hour of my life. My father wants me to be an engineer like him. They just want me to graduate and get into a decent university."

"Did they take anything away from you?"

"Well . . . no."

"How does that make you feel about your parents?"

She shrugged. "They are cooler than Matt's parents, anyway."

"Does it make you feel they love you less than his parents love him?"

"I think mine love me more than his love him. At least they just had to talk about it until I wanted to pass out. His parents were assholes."

That was real progress right there. Cindy had arrived for her first session hostile and hating her parents, and not feeling very generous toward Georgia either. Even the slightest of concessions was better.

When their time was over, Georgia contemplated calling Carl but then decided against it.

As it happened, he called her. "I was thinking about tonight. Are you free?"

"I'm quite expensive."

"If you thought that was brilliant, Dr. Lukens, try again."

She had to smile. "I'm not busy this evening, if that's what you're asking."

"I have a yacht of sorts. Want to go for a sail?"

Of sorts? Either a person had a yacht or they didn't. "I will be the worst first mate ever as I've never done anything like that. I can row a boat, but I learned that at summer camp what seems like a million years ago. That's about it."

"Don't worry about it. I rent out the boat, so the usual captain will take us. It sounds quite upper crust, but don't count on me not spilling champagne on my pants. We'll eat dinner on the water. Someone caters the cruises."

"Champagne and dinner on a yacht? I do that every night. I'm bored already. Count me in."

"I'm trying to impress you."

"You already have. I think you did twice the other night."

He laughed in his understated way. "Are you phone-flirting with me, Dr. Lukens?"

"Just give me a time for tonight."

"I'll pick you up at six."

"I'm looking forward to it."

She really was. When she got home she chose light-colored capri pants and a pink blouse, stepped into her favorite flats, and grabbed a bottle of chardonnay. She only drank champagne when celebrating and she wasn't doing that quite yet.

Maybe she was hopeful in a cautious way. That was about as far as she could go. Everyone has issues—she should know—and commitment was one of hers, but unfortunately, that same demon apparently haunted Carl Grasso.

Part of her wondered if that wasn't why she was so fascinated.

**Carl checked his** phone and then pulled on a pair of genuine deck shoes he'd worn only one time before.

He felt ridiculous and took them off and chose something more his style.

He never used the yacht.

Like never.

His father had inherited it and he had memories of sailing on it as a child. Georgia would probably have a field day with all of that, but he wasn't about to discuss it. Not that she'd ever asked personal questions, but more that she hadn't. She was probably analyzing him on some level because that was what she was trained to do, and he knew from personal experience it was hard to shut off work.

He wasn't sure he wanted to know what she was thinking. Of course he had his faults, because everyone did. It was no secret he liked to dress well and drove an expensive car, but he could afford it, so why not. He had a housekeeper, and if he ate home-cooked food, it was because she'd made it and left it behind with specific instructions on how to heat it up. He enjoyed solitude probably a little too much, and expensive scotch was a good friend and helped him sleep. He voluntarily spent too much time at work, had no real hobbies, disliked the idea of having a pet, and all of his relationships with women had been of the temporary variety.

This one, though, had some potential.

One of his faults was that he didn't truly *like* many people. He liked Georgia Lukens because she had a serene beauty he admired, but more because she reminded him of MacIntosh in a way, in that she was tough as nails under that feminine exterior. He sensed that resilient inner strength, and it was part of why he was willing to put some effort into getting to know her even better. Dependent women weren't his thing at all. The minute they started to cling, he started to let go.

He pulled into her driveway right on time and Georgia came out the door carrying a bottle of wine and a light jacket. Her hair was loose and she had also dressed for an evening boat ride.

She slid into the car and set down the wine. "I'm looking forward to this. I always remind myself I live on a lake and very rarely enjoy it. By a yacht, do you mean . . . a yacht?"

"My grandfather made a lot of money in railroad stock." He backed out carefully. "It's a yacht all right. I wouldn't have the slightest clue how to sail it. So there I am still in college and suddenly own that enormous house and a big boat. I have to admit I didn't know what to do with either one."

Just when he was positive he didn't want to make revealing statements, he did.

That was about as open as he was ever going to get about his past. He changed the subject. "There's been another park murder."

"I know. What do you make of it?"

Of course she knew. Maybe both Santiago and Mac-Intosh had told her.

"Without the note on the body, I'd have just first thought suicide and walked away, but there was no way he could do it on his own without climbing the tree, and that seems improbable. Not impossible, but not likely. He was unconscious, and the person who killed him threw the rope over the branch and hoisted him up and then tied it off. The note on his body nails it. It's a homicide tied to the first two."

"Are they making progress?"

"You mean MacIntosh and Santiago? Aren't they talking to you?"

"Can't answer that one because I take confidentiality very seriously. Are they talking to you?"

He drove toward the lake. "Someone threw a brick through Santiago's truck's back window. There's no way to connect it. Thoughts? So far the killer has stopped by after the fact to offer assistance. Not this time. He stopped by with a brick."

Georgia frowned at the windshield. "Hmm, I don't know. Santiago might want to be careful. That's a definite message. With the murders it is to wave an arm and say look at me. The brick was more personal."

"Than a human life?" Carl was skeptical.

"You asked and I answered."

"The brick was more personal?"

"He took a jab at Santiago alone."

Carl made a lane change. "Your assessment?" He truly was curious.

"He's jealous. When a male has an interest in a female he can tell when there's competition. This isn't new science; this is like extremely old science. Remember Helen of Troy?"

"I'm old, but not that old. She and I never met."

"You aren't old." Georgia gave him a reproving look that held a glint of laughter even with the subject at hand. "A late bloomer at worst."

"Oh, now I feel good about myself."

"So Helen launched a thousand ships, but I'm guessing that wasn't her choice. That was all male. You compete, and you do it in a ruthless way. It's how you work."

"How some of us work. What makes you come to this conclusion, Dr. Lukens?"

"He's evolving. The park probably means something, but I'm not sure what it could be."

"Childhood?"

"I don't know. It represents something important to the killer. I wouldn't think that except two different parks have been used. It could be something as simple as an easy place to dump the bodies. I'm inclined that it gives him a venue where he can watch them being discovered. You could take them to a mall or retail parking lot—can you imagine trying to pull that off? But placing them there is a much greater risk. In a park you can linger and no one would notice. You are supposed to linger in parks. That's why they exist. To relieve us as a society of endless concrete and busy streets. They are a place of joy for children and wildlife."

Carl nodded. "You might make a very good detective, Dr. Lukens. I agree. There's a dark thrill factor going on somewhere."

"I don't think you should even try to connect the victims. I believe he's being very random on purpose. He's thumbing his nose and telling you he can kill people and you can't catch him just because of that."

"But he's sending flowers to MacIntosh and has called her twice now."

"You can't trace the phone?"

He took a left turn, heading for the pier. "No dice. We tried and we have some pretty efficient technicians that can handle almost everything. He blocks the number, but we speculate that he used a burner phone the first time and one of the victims' phones the second time. Different location, and now, since he takes their ID, he probably has a third phone, because he takes that too. He isn't making it easy on us." For some reason Carl found that violation of privacy to really pile insult on top of the ultimate injury. For someone to kill a person and then use their phone to taunt the police took wrong to a new level, and he'd seen it all. How this person unlocked it wasn't really a mystery, since so many people were free with their passwords if they trusted the person. Even if they needed a thumbprint, the tech team said that could have been done easily.

Georgia said, "He's a clever opponent."

"I'm willing to concede that, but still not a fan. We'll catch him."

"You sound confident."

"He's taking chances, and Santiago and MacIntosh are good at their jobs. The killer will make a mistake. We all do. He's targeting his partner and Santiago isn't going to let that go. He isn't easygoing."

"I think I've noticed that."

"I invited them to join us for this joy ride."

"What?" Georgia looked nonplussed.

He lifted his shoulders. "That way we can keep an eye on both of them."

They were the closest people to friends that Carl had. There was a brotherhood that came with police work that he believed in moments of contemplation operated a lot like organized crime in some ways. Acknowledging what you did was dangerous, having the backs of people who had chosen your same path, seeing them for who they are, recognizing where they were strong and where they were not . . . the list went on.

It was hard to describe. He cleared his throat. "I'm apprehensive. I don't like this. MacIntosh is capable, but she's a woman. That might sound sexist, but one undeniable fact of life is that males are bigger and stronger. Her Glock might level the playing field, but if she didn't see it coming, she'd probably lose."

"Caveman stuff." Georgia's mouth curved into a smile. "Both you and Santiago are like guard dogs circling the perimeter."

He looked out over the city lights and said it. "Be happy. I think we'd both do the same for you."

# Chapter 10

The brick might have been a real mistake if he'd gotten caught. The sound of splintering glass had brought them running, and he'd known it would, so escape involved split-second timing. Still, he'd gotten to see the look of dismay and fury on the face of Ellie MacIntosh's partner, and it made it worth the risk.

If that old couple in the car had seen him, he would have been in serious trouble.

Timing really was everything.

He didn't think of it as luck, he thought of it as . . . well planned.

**It really was** a yacht.

Sleek and long with aristocratic lines. Santiago said incredulously, "This can't be it. He said boat ride. I was going to help offer to row. This is the *Queen Mary*."

Ellie pointed at the name painted in elegant script on the back. "The *Caroline Anne*. I think this is it. Be careful getting on. The last time we did this, you nearly drowned."

"Luckily you saved my sorry ass while I was trying to help you catch the bad guy. I'm anticipating a much better trip this time. I can't believe Grasso owns this. He's never mentioned it. She's a beauty."

Standing on the dock, getting ready to board, Ellie sent him a derisive look. "Have you met him? Oh wait, I think you have, pretty much every day. He's not a forthcoming person. That just isn't his thing."

"How much effing money *does* he have? Do you have any idea how much this cost when it was built? It's a classic. You can tell from the lines. A lady all the way and she has been loved. It's immaculate. Good for him."

"I believe he works because it gives him something meaningful to do. If you were in his shoes, you'd be on a beach somewhere watching girls walk by in thong bikinis." She elbowed him in the ribs. The sunset was bright red over the water.

"Ouch." He theatrically rubbed his side. "And damn straight I would. Toes in the sand and drink in hand, I'd just be admiring the view."

She didn't believe it, and she knew he understood she didn't. No one did their particular job without true dedication. "No, you wouldn't."

"For about two days, maybe." He gestured at the gangplank. "After you. You look hot, by the way, just in case you were wondering."

He was the most impolite/polite man she knew.

"Thanks." If she could level him with the lethal death glare, he'd have been gone a long, long time ago, so she didn't bother. "I wasn't wondering." After a moment, she did say, "I do, however, appreciate the compliment."

"I like the skirt. It emphasizes certain of your attributes I admire. If you think I'm being nice letting you always walk in front of me, think again."

One of their ongoing problems was she never knew exactly how to handle him. He'd been especially flippant lately, and she was well aware that part of that was her fault. Georgia was absolutely correct, she wasn't ready to talk about his abrupt declaration and question. "I'll pretend you didn't say that. You look nice too."

He did. Not that he'd dressed up, but clean jeans and a decent shirt were about as far as he went anyway. "I'm dying to meet Grasso's 'date.' She's probably an heir to an old family fortune or something like that. I'd guess she flew from the Hamptons on a private jet and will be wearing a diamond necklace worth a million dollars."

Not so, they found when they walked onto the deck.

"Oh shit." Santiago was as expressive as ever as he spotted her sipping a glass of wine. "You aren't serious."

Ellie rarely agreed with him, but right now . . .

It was really Georgia Lukens sitting in a chair on the polished deck. She didn't look any more comfortable than they did, but at least they all knew each other. Maybe too well.

No secrets and no privacy, really.

It took Santiago to break the ice. His lack of tact came in handy now and then. "What the hell? *You're* dating Grasso?"

Maybe there was a reason Ellie liked Georgia so much. She could even make Santiago speechless. Almost. She responded, "We know each other thanks to the MPD. I think you were there when we met. Chardonnay? The crab puffs are delicious, by the way."

Grasso said in his usual dry tone, "Have a seat. Look at it this way, no introductions necessary. Santiago, I assume you'd like a beer. I bought the cheapest I could find just for you. It was a little embarrassing, but I wanted to be a good host."

"We might know each other a little too well. And yes, that would be great."

Ellie accepted a glass of wine. She probably needed it for this evening.

It was a beautiful view with the lights of the city reflecting across the lake. As they took their seats, Ellie noted that Grasso as usual was a contrast to Santiago's inelegant style. But those two men had a different background, to say the least.

Why she was drawn to the bad boy was beyond her.

Perhaps because he wasn't bad and she knew it.

The wine was cool and crisp. Ellie wondered whatever would they talk about, but luckily Grasso took care of it in his usual succinct way. The job was his thing, hands down.

"This case you're working. Another body? What does Hammett have to say?"

Santiago answered. "There was alcohol involved again."

"So he's targeting them at bars."

"Probably," Santiago agreed, relaxing now in his chair, his hair ruffled by the breeze. "God, this is a nice boat. Sell your house and just live on this, Grasso."

The water did ripple like liquid gold under the moonlight as they got under way.

"There's no place to park my car. Okay, so the only link between the victims is the alcohol?"

There were times when Ellie thought Grasso had no sensitivity. Not that he was just brusque, but he was . . . detached.

Maybe Georgia could help him there. Ellie said, "There's no link. Different age, different sexes, and certainly there are no ties to a specific job. No luck on the tulip lady?"

Grasso shook his head. "The ME can't determine if it was an accident or an intentional death enough to rule manner was homicide. I don't believe for a microsecond it isn't, but there's no proof it was a homicide."

"Except he asked about the flowers."

"We're stuck." Santiago shook his head. "We have three witnesses that saw the jogger, and if she could confirm he was the same one who paid her to buy the tulips, we could bring him in for questioning anyway."

Grasso said succinctly, "If we can find him. We don't have her, so it is a moot point."

It was a frustrating case and Ellie was afraid she had a deep vested personal interest in solving it. The sum of the parts was mounting.

"Your killer is elusive." Georgia looked reflective as she took a cheese puff from a tray. "He has a goal, we just don't know yet what it is."

"His goal is Ellie," Santiago said flatly.

Oh, that was cheerful. This was dinner conversation on a beautiful night on the water? She interjected, "Montoya sent me a profile. The man doesn't know how to relax any more than we all do. Care to take a guess at what he said, Doctor? I'd think profiling would be right up your alley."

"I've already picked her brain on this," Grasso said,

comfortable in a deck chair, scotch in hand. "She's good."

Ellie was sure she would be. She'd place a bet Santiago would vote that direction also.

Georgia didn't look daunted. "I'll take a stab, though maybe that isn't what you should say to three homicide detectives. Let's try this, weighing what I've heard: He's affluent in background, but not very successful. Definitely athletic, probably nice-looking, but not enough to turn heads, so he can blend in and not be too memorable. He's isn't necessarily heterosexual, and that bothers him. How am I doing?" Georgia raised her brows.

"Pretty good. Montoya wondered also if he wasn't more interested in Santiago than me."

It was worth the entire evening—not to mention the canapés *were* delicious—to see the look on her partner's face as he choked on his swallow of beer. "*What?*"

She shrugged. "He just mentioned that we might be looking at this the wrong way. Montoya thought we should consider that angle. He might be gay."

"He isn't calling me, he's calling *you,* Ellie."

"What better way to draw your notice than to pursue your partner?" Grasso gave his two cents. "I can buy into that. There's a list, unfortunately, of serial killers, and some of them have been homosexual."

"That's just—"

"Possible," Georgia said in her calm way. "He's killing people. He has your attention, right?"

The subject wasn't funny in the least, but Santiago at a loss for words twice in one night was at least a little amusing to Ellie. He finally sputtered, "What? Really? Are you serious? He threw a brick through my truck window, if it was even him. We don't *know* that it was him."

"But that definitely got your notice, right? If you were spending the night with Ellie, he could have been jealous either way."

"I slept on the damn couch!"

"How is he supposed to know that? He saw your truck in her driveway."

"Why this guy has to figure into my life either way is pissing me off."

Ellie really couldn't agree more. "He's pulling strings, trying to make us dance. Since I don't understand what he wants, I have no idea what to do."


**MacIntosh always had** a way of getting to the point.

The idea Jason could be the target wasn't his favorite, but he'd learned long ago he couldn't control the universe, and maybe he was happier with that than if *she* was the target. He was protective even if Ellie didn't need it.

"I don't really care who he's interested in, he's not exactly our best friend." The beer was cold, the scenery great, and he was serious; he'd just live on this boat. Forget having a house. Why the hell did anyone who had this amount of money work?

Answer to a question that had already been discussed.

In a day Jason would be bored, so would Grasso. For that matter, he doubted if Ellie won the lottery she'd quit her job either.

"Montoya thinks he isn't a plotter, but an opportunist. Pretty girl comes in, so just buy her a lot of drinks, and instant victim. Old guy, buy him some beers, and victim two. We don't know who victim three is, but maybe our guy crashed a frat party or something and just picked out the one weaving on his feet near the keg. The vague descriptions we have of the killer say he's young."

Ellie considered her glass. "What if he's a bartender?"

Grasso nodded right away. "If anyone can spot someone overindulging, it would be the person serving them. In this fine state, it doesn't narrow the field very much. There's a tavern on about every corner."

That was very true. "I'm pretty grateful for that," Jason pointed out. "Go Wisconsin. Not a bad theory. Unless he just hangs out in some place. If he's a regular, he might know just who sometimes goes overboard, offer a friendly ride home, and it turns out not to be friendly at all."

"If he hangs you in a park, I'd say not." Georgia Lukens adapted to the less-than-relaxing conversation well, but then again, she would. He heard some crazy stuff on a regular basis, but he could only imagine what she heard. If Grasso had chosen a different date, then maybe they wouldn't be able to talk about this kind of subject. Luckily Lukens was not put off by the chosen topic. He commented, "He's methodical anyway. Not a single fiber or fingerprint."

"He's proving a point." The breeze brushed back Ellie's fair hair. "No evidence and so no arrest. We could bring him in if we had the slightest clue as to who he is, but we don't, and he knows it."

The caterer came out then to ask if they wanted dinner inside the cabin or out on the deck. Quite frankly, it was out of his sphere, so Jason decided not to comment and let everyone else decide. He'd eaten dinner more times than he could count in a basement that smelled like mildew when growing up, and a stint in the military made his picky level not all that high. There were no yachts in the Santiago legacy. Not even a cheap plastic canoe.

It was interesting realizing that he didn't resent that at all. Grasso didn't seem any happier than he was— maybe even less. Money was definitely not everything. Maybe it was just plain ironic that his only real serious relationship had been with a psychology major.

Maybe more ironic that she really hadn't understood him at all.

The ladies opted for the deck. It really was a nice night.

White tablecloths came out, heavy silver, fine china; the works. If Grasso chose to spend his time chasing criminals instead of sailing off into the sunset, he was at least smart about how he handled this enterprise. Jason could see how little old ladies or starry-eyed newlyweds would eat this up and rent the boat.

Speaking of which, he was happy to see a juicy seared steak, twice-baked potatoes, and a salad that had some exotic ingredients he didn't recognize but tasted good.

The discussion of murder was at least suspended during their meal. Instead, much to his surprise, the subject of pets came up, and while he had no input whatsoever and Grasso wasn't much better, Ellie and Lukens seemed to have solid opinions.

"I want a rescue Lab mix someday," Ellie said, and sounded like she meant it. "They love water and they tend to be good with kids. They aren't perfect, since they can get protective and bite someone, but in general those are great dogs."

"Give me a collie," Lukens argued. "Smart dogs. Such fast learners and so pretty."

"But if purebred, they are high strung. Plus all that hair everywhere. My sister had one and said once she vacuumed five times in one day when it was shedding."

"True enough. Quite frankly, those little cairn terriers are great guard dogs, and though very nosy and bossy, really cute."

It was impossible to stay quiet. Jason said with a bit of what looked like dandelion leaves dangling from his fork, "A what?"

MacIntosh gave him a look that indicated she thought he was a simpleton, which could be warranted. "Ever seen *The Wizard of Oz*? Toto?"

"Maybe once, I think, when I was five. Those trees tossing apples back at Dorothy and the Scarecrow while talking gave me nightmares. But I do remember what they passed off as a dog. Anything you can pick up and tuck under your arm is not a real dog."

Lukens took more salad. "Maybe you and I need to explore those nightmares in our next session. I need the recipe for this leafy stuff, whatever it is."

"Oh, there's nothing like having dinner with your shrink."

"Those of us who have a PhD in psychology do not like the term 'shrink.' "

"Those of us in need of one don't like it either." His steak was perfect, medium rare and seared just right. He was doing his best not to eat too fast. The lake was pretty calm too for spring, so the deck had been a good call. The moon was obscured by clouds, but they moved past swiftly like silent, flitting ghosts.

Perhaps he was more poetic than he imagined.

Well, probably not. That was being optimistic. "The salad is really good," he conceded, "but what are those green things in it? I think they were plucked from someone's lawn."

"Don't ask," Grasso advised him. "I just eat it, and if it tastes fine, I'll eat it again. I try to live the simple life."

"Says the man with the yacht," Ellie observed dryly.

"I can't take credit for what my grandfather did." He took a bite of steak. "Or what my father did. You and I have the same job, remember? This has nothing to do with who I am."

Jason's phone vibrated then. Fergusson had sent him a text. He read it quickly, feeling vaguely rude, but they were in the middle of a murder investigation, so Ellie and Grasso would have done exactly the same thing.

"Sorry to ruin the mood," he said, looking up. "Looks like we might have a name for the third victim."

*He thought the rose was a nice touch.*

*He wanted her to know he was thinking about her. Symbolic yet simple.*

*The front porch was a breeze. He wasn't taking any chances there. A few steps, a quick deposit, and he was home free and on his way.*

*He would like to see how she liked the gift.*

**Ashlie Riverton lived** in a Greek house on campus. The housemother, who had a grandmotherly air, informed them as they went up a curved staircase to her room that the young woman wasn't taking it well at all. The woman also had thoroughly examined their credentials. Apparently she took her job seriously.

"She won't cry, her roommate told me." The woman shook her head with a look of wisdom on her face. "She *needs* to grieve."

Unfortunately Ellie had seen that shell-shocked

reaction a few too many times in her life. It came with the territory.

"The girls don't tell me everything, but they tell me more than I want to know sometimes." Mrs. Peters said it as they walked through a hallway lined with doors. "I believe Ashlie and Zeke had talked about getting married after graduation. I'm still in shock myself if you want the truth. Boys aren't allowed in their rooms, so I saw a lot of him down in the common area. What a nice young man. This is her room. Let me tell her why you're here and ask if she can handle a few questions. Give me just a moment, please."

"Of course," Ellie said in a subdued tone. "This is difficult for everyone, even us, but we really do need to talk to her."

They waited outside and Santiago remarked, "I've never been in a sorority house before. Nice."

"The reason for your first experience isn't exactly a great one."

"That's the damn truth," he agreed soberly.

Ashlie was a pretty redhead and maybe slightly overweight, but still striking. She shook her head as she sat on her bed, and maybe their visit was useful because she instantly burst into tears. The housemother sat down next to her and put a comforting arm around her shaking shoulders.

She sobbed as she said, "He wouldn't kill himself. He wouldn't do that."

"We know." Ellie waited for the storm to pass. There wasn't a place for them to sit so they both just stood there. When she felt Ashlie could talk again, she went on. "We aren't saying he did anything at all. We are homicide detectives and worried someone did something to him. Can you think back? Is there any-one new and unusual in his life? A friend?"

"No." She thought it over and sniffled. "No. Well, maybe Jack."

Ellie suddenly had a bad feeling about this Jack. It happened sometimes. It was like knowing you felt dif-ferent and finally figured out you had the flu. "What about him? We are going to talk to everyone we can."

"He hangs out with Jack a lot all of a sudden. They met somehow, I think at a bar close to campus. I don't even know his last name."

Santiago asked, "The name of the bar would maybe help us."

"We all hang out at a place called Huffman's Pub. But near campus there are all kinds of places. I just don't know." She got up, sniffling. "Sorry, I need a tissue. I had to talk to Zeke's parents this morning . . . I've got finals coming up and I can't deal with all this. I still don't really believe it. I feel like I'm sleep-walking."

When Ashlie went into the bathroom, Santiago said almost under his breath, "I wish I'd just stayed in the car. I've seen grown men cry and I shrug that off, but a when a woman gets going . . . well, I'd just rather be somewhere else. You should have brought Lukens with you instead. She's worried about finals? Really?"

Ellie had to say, "She's maybe twenty, suddenly her boyfriend is dead, and detectives are on her doorstep asking questions. I doubt that conversation with his parents was a treat either. She's not able to change what happened to him. Of course she should worry about her finals. That's why she's here."

He wasn't without empathy if pushed. He exhaled. "Okay, you've made your point. Let's just find out who Jack is and where can we find him. Maybe he can be helpful."

Ashlie came out the bathroom with a tissue clutched in her hand, her eyes red and watery. "I don't know Jack's last name, but I do know he lives in an apartment close by. Maybe he can help you."

"Have you met him?"

"Jack?" She shook her head, her nose red and the tissue pressed there. "Not in person, no. Zeke just talked about him now and then. They ran together."

Ran together? The killer was a jogger, or pretended to be one . . . the look on Santiago's face reflected the same connection. A bar and running? Suddenly Zeke was dead.

Ellie consciously inhaled slowly and measured her questions. "Did he ever describe him? Talk about his family? Where he was from?"

"No." Ashlie started to cry again. "This is so horrible."

No one was going to disagree with that.

"I hate to ask this, but can we have a picture of Zeke?" Ellie didn't add that since she was fairly sure crime scene photos wouldn't help them out, they really needed something that actually looked like him.

Ashlie nodded, but it was like turning the spigot back on. "I'll text one we took together last week."

They left with her still sobbing, but luckily Mrs. Peters was able to step into the breach. Walking out into another spring evening that resonated with what might be coming, with hints of early blooming flowers, Santiago muttered darkly, "That sucked. I think I prefer being shot at; that I can handle. Maybe she did need to cry, but I'd really prefer it wasn't in front of me."

"You've made that clear." Ellie felt it too. "We help.

It just isn't under pleasant circumstances. So at least we know more about him."

"Not enough more. God alone knows if his name is really Jack, or there could be a perfectly innocent guy out there jogging down some trail whose name really is Jack. But my gut tells me he decided to target his supposed friend."

"I'm thinking the same thing."

"Maybe we should take up running to break this case."

"Go ahead." Ellie tried to picture that and failed.

"I walk from the couch into the kitchen to get potato chips and then go back. It was just a thought."

She'd seen him with his shirt off. He obviously worked out, but was just being a smartass as usual. "He's going to move on us again to a different spot," she said as she got into the truck. "It doesn't matter. We won't be able to find him."

Her partner nodded. "I won't be surprised if he does move, but it would really bother me if we can't figure him out. We're better than this."

It wasn't that she didn't disagree, but this wasn't a usual case. "I think he's coming at us sideways. This time, according to Montoya, we might be the cause, not just sorting out the effect."

"That's so wrong."

She usually wanted to argue with him, but Ellie felt the same way. "Very wrong."

"So it's time to try something different even if it isn't jogging, which I really didn't want to do anyway. I've tried it. No thanks."

"I'm afraid we have to talk to this victim's family. I know you hate it, but you signed on and it is part of the bargain."

His blue eyes were reflective. "Bargain? Where the fuck is the bargain? I wonder if I'd be good at driving a garbage truck. That's honest work right there. I can pick up trash cans. It would tone my biceps."

"I agree. But unfortunately you happen to be good at this, which means I'm stuck with you, and that is unfortunate for *me*. You can use those driving skills to take us over to interview the victim's parents."

"After waiting to talk to Ashlie, it's getting kind of late for a drive there and back, Ellie."

She thought it over and reluctantly agreed. She just wanted it over with. "We'll go first thing tomorrow morning. If those poor people can get some exhausted sleep, then I want them to have it. I think right now we need to follow a thin lead and go to Huffman's."

Santiago was typical him. He said, "Good, I need a drink."

**Huffman's Pub turned** out to be an average college bar. On the dark side, the tables scratched, and the music loud enough you couldn't talk easily. It smelled like spilled beer and spiced peanuts, and was crowded for just before finals in Jason's opinion. They edged in and flashed the picture from Ellie's phone at a harried bartender, who did take the time to at least look at it, but shook his head. "I'm new. Ask Ava. She's been here since the dawn of time. She's right over there, waiting tables."

Ava, with streaked gray hair and a no-nonsense air, was just as busy and glanced at the picture Ellie showed her and nodded while holding a tray of full glasses. "Sure he's been in here. Did you say detectives? Why?"

"We are investigating his death."

"Well shit. Are you serious? Let me deliver this tray and I'll be right back."

She did come right back, ignoring a group of students trying to get her attention by waving wildly. She took the phone and studied it. "He was one of the nice ones. Always polite, and believe me, not all of them are. He's really dead?" She seemed shaken. "I hate that."

"Really," Santiago confirmed. "We hate it too. So when was he here last?"

Ava looked like she was thinking about it. "He's been here recently, but if you're asking for a specific night, good luck. I don't remember what I had for breakfast this morning. Sorry, honey. Ask the management for credit card records."

"Was he with anyone? A tall guy with brown hair?"

"I'm five foot one. They're all tall to me, and if you notice, the lighting in this place isn't that great. I'm looking at you right now and I think you're blond, but I can't be sure. I only recognize him because he never failed to tip and always called me by name. Most of these yahoos that come in, even on a regular basis, just say, 'Hey, waitress.' It's rude." She handed back the picture. "This wasn't a stellar night already, but now I'm really bummed out."

"Thanks for your help."

"I didn't think that would work anyway," Ellie said as they walked outside. "We gained exactly nothing."

"Long shot," he agreed. The parking lot smelled like urine and he had to wonder how many drunken male students chose to just relieve themselves on the asphalt before heading back to campus. "We knew it was."

The night didn't get any better.

There was a rose on Ellie's front porch when they pulled up.

Jason drew his weapon and looked around as she picked it up. She, of course, was pragmatic. "Pretty nice with the pink and white petals. He went to some trouble. I wonder if you can get prints off of something like this. I'll have to talk to forensics. I don't see how, but now they can lift them off of human skin, so maybe. Even a partial would help us."

"You aren't walking through that door in front of me." Jason meant it, surveying the quiet-as-usual street. "But you aren't staying out here either while I check it out."

"Well, it has to be one or the other since you can't be in two places at once." She looked calm, but he knew that rose shook her too. He saw it in her eyes. "I am a police officer. I also have a gun. Please remember, you could be the target. Montoya knows his stuff."

"I don't think that for a minute."

"No, you don't *want* to think that for a minute. Different."

She loosened her jacket and took out her gun. "Can we go inside now? The nice night has gotten chilly. If it makes you feel more masculine, here's my key. I've got your back. Feel free to go first."

All things considered, he wasn't sure if he was more worried about the street or the house, but she was right. As Metzger had pointed out, she knew how to handle a tricky situation. Her condo proved to be empty and silent. Windows were closed, there was no visible entry, and he even looked under her bed and in the closets.

"All clear. Any dust bunnies?"

"Don't try to tell me you've never looked under the bed, so don't laugh at me. We all have at one time or another. It seems to me we have just cause to be cautious." He got to his feet. Her bedroom was more feminine than he expected somehow. Not that she wasn't feminine, but there was a collection of what looked like antique perfume bottles on the dresser, and a four-poster bed with a lacy bedspread, not to mention what appeared to be from the cover a romance novel sitting on her nightstand. "But all clear right now and I didn't notice a dust bunny, but don't look under *my* bed. Can I sleep with you tonight?"

Ellie stared at him like he'd spoken Mandarin or something. "What?"

He was not a great communicator; that had been made clear to him a long time ago. Kate had probably done a dissertation on it for her PhD. He tried again. "Okay, I'll clarify. I'll sleep on the floor with my gun right next to me but in your bedroom. I don't like anything about this situation, and if he came in through a window I might be too far away on the couch. I'll just sleep, but I'll at least be with you. He's killed three people and I think he's obsessed with you."

"Or you."

"Then you can protect *me*. Aren't we the perfect couple."

"Very funny."

"I'm serious." He really was.

"If this is a ploy for sex, you win an award for most imaginative effort ever, but really—"

"I said floor. I'd love to get naked with you, but tonight I'd be wondering if he was looking in the window. That might set me off my A-game. Let's just get some sleep. If you're here and I'm here all in one space, I'd think he'd have a hard time sneaking up on us. Ellie, we both know he's out there. He's making a *point* of letting us know it."

She had that damned flower to prove it.

"All right, but keep in mind my loaded Glock will be right next to *me*. Please at least wear boxers."

"When actively pursuing serial killers who know exactly where I am and have a doubtful interest in my well-being, I usually don't sleep naked. You're safe there. I can chase down a perp, but not with things I value hanging in the breeze."

"Did you really just say that? If Metzger ever hears of this—"

"I'm not telling him, are you?"

"No. Of course not." Ellie's cool look might have frozen the average person on the spot, but he was used to it.

"So we're all good?"

"Santiago, I'm not positive we'll ever be all good."

"Humor me for a minute. And I thought I was Jason."

She got up. "Fine. I'm going to go brush my teeth and change into pajamas."

"If you need any help with that pajama thing, let me know. Negligee by any chance?"

"I think I can handle it, and no. Shorts and a camisole."

He gave a theatrical sigh. "I just can't catch a break."

## Chapter 12

He was so furious he was shaking.

*That damned truck wasn't going anywhere.*

*Lights out except one low lamp in the living room, the kitchen dark and deserted, and her bedroom light was off.*

*That bastard was spending the night.*

*Calm down, calm down.*

*It didn't mean they were sleeping together, it just meant that after she found the rose and understood he'd been there, maybe she'd thought it over and decided it was best not to be alone.*

*Wise girl.*

*For the first time in his life—all because of her—he felt like a force to be reckoned with. If he didn't really have fortune, he still had fame. It was interesting to watch the news and read the paper and know they were talking about him.*

*He was more in love with her than ever.*

*It was imperative he see her.*

\* \* \*

**He was uncomfortable** sleeping on the floor. Jason came to that conclusion fairly early on, but he'd slept in bunkers and on the hard seats of helicopters, on deserts in a less-than-happy atmosphere with people with guns running around, and it hadn't been pleasant then either. Still, he'd been a bit younger then. He rolled over for the tenth time at least.

"You're keeping me awake. Look, just get into the bed." Ellie said it with absolutely no equivocation in her voice. "Just stay on your side and go to sleep. It's a matter of a few feet. I'm nervous already. You aren't helping. Every time you move, and it's about a two-second interval, I hear it."

In a different time in his life maybe he would have argued the floor was fine, but he really would prefer to sleep in a bed. He would argue the thirties were not the new twenties, but then again, he had some mileage on him the average person might not have experienced.

Next to her wasn't as good as with her, but it was better than the floor. The sheets smelled great and he was tempted to mention it, but he could swear from the cadence of her breathing she'd fallen asleep the minute he'd joined her, which was not exactly flattering.

So he was in bed with Ellie MacIntosh, but . . . she'd instantly gone to sleep.

If he ever told the story, he might skip that part.

On the other hand, he was going to have one of those nights when his head was like Grand Central Station and his brain was just racing from thought to thought, like trains pulling in and trains pulling out.

He hadn't really talked about it with Lukens other than mentioning he had some problems with insomnia. She had said for ex-military that wasn't uncommon, for police officers almost par for the course, and for a homicide detective probably to be expected, so she wasn't at all surprised. She wasn't licensed to prescribe medication, but she could refer him to someone who could. He declined because he shied away from drugs of any kind. He didn't even take aspirin.

So . . . live with the trains.

It galled him that they had many clues and no real handle on the murderer. They actually knew quite a bit about him, but it was all quicksand. Nothing solid at all. They were up to their knees already and sinking fast.

His first clue something was wrong was that he smelled smoke.

Good thing he was still awake.

"Ellie." He touched her shoulder because it seemed the least invasive of her personal space. "Something is on fire."

She woke up amazingly fast and sat up, sweeping back her hair. "What is this, a plot to not let me get five minutes of sleep? Okay, I smell it too. Dammit. Everyone in the world is going to think I'm sleeping with you . . . jeans would be nice."

"You can deny it without lying. I never went to sleep." He put his pants on and then grabbed his badge.

There were already sirens when they hit the pavement outside.

Condo next door had pluming smoke from the back. Luckily the young family was already out of the house standing in the driveway as Jason rushed up at full speed. "No one else inside? Full head count?"

The father shook his head, holding a little girl in his arms. "We're all here. I have no idea how it started. I never even saw it. I just woke up to the smoke alarm going off. I'm glad I'm diligent about checking those batteries, but I have two important reasons to be."

A small boy clinging to his mother whimpered. "Blackie."

Well, *shit*. He didn't say it out loud to his credit because he sure felt like saying it. "There's a dog or cat still inside?"

"Cat." That was Ellie right behind him. "Just let me go. He comes for a visit every now and then to my front porch. He knows me."

The father, Mr. Nichols, in a robe—he'd never given her his first name—and obviously upset said, "I left the side door open so maybe he bolted. Cats don't come when you call. I tried. He's hiding in the laundry room behind the washer. I just wanted to get my family out as fast as possible."

He usually only heard about stuff like this on the news, but Jason was willing to at least give it a try. "I'm right behind you."

"Officer Santiago and I will try to look for him," Ellie said to the little boy. "Just give us a minute."

The house was filled with smoke, but there didn't seem to be actual flames inside. It was a mirror image of hers and she went right to the laundry room. A pair of green eyes stared back at them from behind the appliances. "He's still here. You move the washer, and I will make sure he gets out. He won't like having his cover compromised."

Jason wasn't all that happy with the acrid smoke either. He coughed twice as he tugged the machine out, and the cat didn't exactly run to Ellie, but at least darted out far enough that she could snare him.

The animal was off like a shot once they got to the front door. "How badly do you think you're bleeding?" Jason asked while wiping smoke-induced tears from his eyes, because no doubt about it, the unhappy cat had clawed her.

She bared her arm, and sure enough there were deep scratches. "There will probably be scars," she said with dry humor. "But that seems the least of my problems right now. He's usually such a sweet kitten, but who can blame him? Here comes the cavalry."

The fire trucks screamed up. Jason said grimly, "Let's grab whoever seems to be in charge and tell them to look for arson. Death by asphyxiation again. Dammit, there were kids in there. When we catch him, I might strangle him myself."

"I'll help you dispose of the body," Ellie responded in much the same tone, her face set.

The firefighter shouting orders took a look at their badges, Santiago's scars from being shot in the line of duty since he was still shirtless, and nodded, and then told them to get the hell out of the way. He said he'd circle back around once the fire was out.

They did, standing back with the gathering of neighbors who had heard the sirens and commotion, and Jason knew Ellie was doing exactly what he was doing and observing every spectator. Arsonists tended to come watch their fires burn, but this particular individual, if he was responsible—houses did catch on fire sometimes—probably didn't qualify as an arsonist, but just as a lunatic on a mission to send a message.

"Maybe you need to talk to Montoya again."

The revolving lights reflected off her face. "Before tonight I wouldn't dream of interrupting his vacation a second time, but this is moving fast."

"He's gaining momentum, yes." He had the same bad feeling standing there and watching the process of putting out the fire, the hoses and the trucks, the smoke drifting by.

"He's not here. I can't believe he wouldn't at least stroll by."

"I'm also not picking a tall man with brown hair out of the crowd," he said.

"I agree. He should be here somewhere, but I can't spot him."

"Too smart."

She didn't argue. "Clever I can deal with, but smart is a real problem. The clever ones use angles. The smart ones are methodical."

One of the firefighters checked her out as he walked by and there was no doubt about it, Jason was annoyed. "Let's just go to my apartment. Obviously he knows where you live."

"He doesn't know where *you* live?"

"Maybe he does, but my place doesn't smell like smoke. It isn't on the ground floor either, so the only way in is through the front door unless he's some kind of a circus acrobat."

Her nod acknowledged he had a point, even if it wasn't a happy one. "Fine."

**"Smoke bomb." Riley,** the firefighter in charge, took them around the garage and showed them the contraption set under the back bedroom window. There was black soot all up the wall and across the window. "This one is homemade. Never seen one quite like it before. So not technically arson, but whoever put it there wanted to make it seem like the place was on fire. The good news is these folks won't have water damage. They'll just have to live with the smell for a while." He was heavy shouldered and had a goatee speckled with gray. He shook his head. "Why inventive people don't spend their energy in positive ways is beyond me. Anyway, we're out of here. I don't know if this qualifies as a crime scene to you, but I don't need to call in the troops to analyze how it happened. Maybe it's just a prank."

"I wish." Ellie did qualify it as a crime in that it was meant to intimidate, but at least no one had been hurt. "The owner is a science teacher at a high school. I suppose that's possible."

"It was a decently sophisticated device, but there have been teen geniuses before."

She and Santiago walked back to her condo in contemplative silence. Both were too aware of every possible threat, because that could easily have been just to get them out of the building. Luckily, all was silent.

"Not a prank. It's just my opinion."

She agreed.

"Apparently we're roommates," she said acerbically, even though none of it was his fault. "Thanks to Montoya and Lukens I'm now worried about you, so we are living in the same world."

"I always wanted you to care. That's so encouraging." He was as flippant as ever.

"Yeah, right. I just don't want to adjust to a new partner."

"Hey, I meant that. Let me go put on my shirt."

She liked the view without the shirt, even though she was resistant to that realization. It was not a good idea to get involved on a serious basis with her partner. Bad for her career was the number-one point.

Though she *had* become involved with Bryce when he was still a suspect in a murder case, so she wasn't pure as white snow in that judgment category. Still, Jason had been pretty honest, so she at least owed him that too. "Can we just get through this case please? I always need to evaluate whether or not you're serious. Let's watch and see if a car follows us."

"Why don't you let me start your car? I have a painful prior experience that proved car bombs do exist. My truck is fine, but I still miss that sweet ride. If he can rig a smoke bomb, he probably can plant an explosive device."

"That's cheerful. I don't see why you should risk your life more than I should."

This time he *was* serious. "Because I would really miss you. Give me the keys. My personal belief is that smoke bomb was showing us what he could do if he wanted to, but if it was just to deflect us so he could do something else, let's not assume anything."

He had a point. She went and checked. "The garage door is still locked, dead bolt and all. We were right next door. I think we'd have seen someone walk up."

"So it should be fine." He held out his hand. "Keys?"

She handed them over. "Fine, just because I need to grab clothes for tomorrow and at least a toothbrush and my phone and laptop."

"Wash off those scratches. I don't want to catch this psycho and then have you die of cat scratch fever, whatever that is. I used to listen to a lot of Ted Nugent back in the day."

That didn't surprise her at all. It also wasn't bad advice. She sincerely hoped Blackie would come back home when all the commotion faded away. Her next door neighbors were nice polite people and she guessed had just suffered because of her. Why it should make her feel a twinge of guilt she wasn't sure as she examined her arm and the collateral damage of three bleeding spots, but maybe if they'd lived next to a minister or an insurance agent, it never would have happened.

There was no explosion, but when she walked out to get into the car, she made a point of bringing the remote for her security system. She told Santiago, "I'm still wearing pajamas in the faint hope of getting some sleep tonight, so drive safely please. Enough people have already seen me in my sleep attire that I'm starting not to care, but let's keep it to a minimum. I don't want to stand in a street talking to a patrol officer wearing this."

"I always drive carefully."

He was a cowboy behind the wheel; she'd experienced it firsthand. Not too flashy, but if he needed to do so, he could go over the top. They'd done one pursuit where she was fairly sure her life was about to end in a headline on the news, but he had pulled it off safely at the last minute. "No comment."

"You don't trust me?" He did back out carefully and she hit the garage door closer.

"In some ways yes and in some ways I know you are a risk taker, so no."

"Calculated risks are different."

"I'll grant you that, but I want to get some sleep. It's hard to sell yourself as a detective wearing cotton shorts with little hearts all over them."

"I think they're cute."

She let it pass, brooding at the lights glinting past. She had no illusions he wasn't just as concerned. "So tonight proves it is about how he's in control. How do we get it back? For all we know he's in my condo right now, lighting it on fire."

Santiago took a left and shook his head. "No, he's going to prolong this as long as possible. Historically a lot of serial killers have taken on the police, and some have gotten away with it, like Jack the Ripper." He braked for a light and looked over at her. "Oh shit, didn't think of that. Jack? Didn't he send notes to the police?"

It hadn't occurred to her either. "He did. Not at all the same method of death, though. The Ripper used a knife, and though this conversation is likely to give me nightmares, he disemboweled his victims."

"But the police never figured it out."

"Exactly."

Very slim theory, and it didn't help them at all.

"Both Montoya and Lukens might help with this. I'm hesitant to work with anything but solid facts. One name isn't enough and it doesn't lead us anywhere."

"It's a thought, though."

"This isn't a novel."

"I didn't think, by the way, homicide detectives are supposed to even have nightmares."

"I think we probably have more than the average person. Don't you?"

"Oh hell yes," he admitted ruefully. "It's usually worse for me when a case is over. My brain decides I should live it all over again just for fun. The Burner case was particularly bad. All I wanted was to dream about blue skies and maybe something like a picnic in a park. Bologna on white bread with mayo like when I was a kid. Now this bastard is going to ruin parks forever for me, so I'm going to have to pick a new theme."

"Try puppies frolicking or kittens and a ball of yarn," she suggested, but she knew what he was talking about all too well. Some images were too haunting to erase. "I think we need to check out this parking lot pretty carefully. For all we know, he anticipated us changing location."

## Chapter 13

He used a portable printer and a digital device to enhance the detail and alter the picture. It wasn't hard—they'd made it easy, actually, and almost ridiculously so.

It was hard not to laugh.

He wanted to bury them both to a certain extent, in different ways, but never dreamed it would be so simple.

Nothing he had to do but install the camera. They'd hung themselves and he didn't even have to supply the rope.

That could come later. Zeke had been satisfying, but just practice.

When they'd left, he could move around without worrying about them hearing him, and he took full advantage of it.

He loaded the footage up on his computer, watched it, and felt much better

Nothing had happened.

\* \* \*

**Carl heard about** the smoke bomb through the very tight precinct grapevine. This was heating up—with or without smoke—in his opinion, and he knew Santiago hated family interviews, so he stopped by his desk. "I'm free this morning. Want me to go with MacIntosh instead to interview the family of the latest victim?"

Santiago looked pretty tired, but still glanced up sharply from concentrating on his computer screen, his blue eyes slightly bloodshot. "Seriously? That would be fine with me. She usually handles the whole thing anyway. I barely survived the interview with his girlfriend. I'm starting to worry I'm a sensitive guy. It's not true, is it?"

"I think that worry is unfounded if it makes you feel any better. I'll go tell her it's me instead."

"I think you just made my day."

Ellie was putting on her jacket when he caught her, since the day was cool and rainy as per spring weather, and she lifted her brows. "What?"

"You're stuck with me. I'm along for the ride."

"That's fine," she said immediately. "That's good. Santiago hates it way too much. His discomfort makes it worse for everyone—including me—and it isn't pleasant in the first place. He's good at a lot of different aspects of this job, but not at what we're about to do. You ready then?"

"I'm all set." He wasn't happy about it either, but he hoped no one got used to it.

"Offered accepted. Let's go."

Gone was the pretty blonde in the long flowing skirt, the no-nonsense police officer taking her place. Hair in a ponytail, minimum makeup, blue shirt and black slacks. Professional as always when on the job and he respected that. "I'll drive."

"That's fine."

The Grays lived in a neighborhood that consisted of expensive houses that all looked the same with minor differences in decorative shutters and different colored mailboxes. It was moderate affluence at its finest with manicured lawns and sedans and SUVs in the driveways.

"If I lived here, I'd just jump off a cliff," he muttered as they pulled up. "After a glass of scotch I wouldn't be able to find my own house."

MacIntosh remarked as she parked, "We can't all sail away on our yacht. I have a condo that looks exactly like all of the rest of them on the street. You can't get more generic than that. I do miss my house up north. Let's go see if they can help us."

At first it seemed like no one was home, but finally a man answered the door, and when they produced their identification he turned away for a moment before he composed himself and let them in. He was dressed in pressed khakis and a golf shirt, but it looked like maybe he'd forgotten to shave. He was fairly young to have a college-aged son; late thirties at the most. Mr. Gray said hoarsely, "I haven't been looking forward to this, so please forgive me. I'm not going to lie, I'm not glad to see you."

"We understand." MacIntosh definitely took lead, and it made sense since it was her case. "No one is ever glad to see us. We're just here because we are investigating your son's death and it seems to tie to a series of other homicides. We want to help not just you but other families."

"Please feel free to sit down. My wife will not join us. Believe it or not, all these years of trying after Zeke, she's expecting another baby. I'm doing my best to make sure her inconsolable grief doesn't result in a miscarriage. She won't eat. Neither of us can even begin to figure out how to deal with it, but if she loses this baby . . . well, then whoever did this will have killed both my children."

At that point Carl was glad to have Ellie in charge. She said very calmly, "We can just talk to you and you can reassure her we are just trying to piece together what happened and make some sense of it all in a world that doesn't always make sense. I can't imagine your loss, but please understand that we don't want anyone else to feel like you do right now. Talk to us about Zeke's friends. Do you know someone named Jack?"

Given something to focus on besides the crime itself, Mr. Gray settled on the edge of a chair. "I don't think so. Jack? No, it isn't from high school. Did you ask Ashlie?"

"We did. She gave us the name." Ellie made a few notes on her phone. "Anyone else? Maybe someone he ran with now and then? We know he was a jogger."

His eyes were shiny with tears. "He mentioned he sometimes ran with someone he'd met. He was very health oriented when it came to fitness."

The autopsy revealed Zeke Gray had been hit with a blunt object and was probably unconscious before he was hung. His father was right, he was capable of defending himself, so obviously the attack had taken him by surprise. Carl was forming a deeper picture of the killer and he could see Ellie was doing the same thing.

"No name?" she asked.

Mr. Gray shook his head. "I don't remember. I wish, in retrospect, I'd not adopted the philosophy that he was now an adult and should be able to live his own life without constant probing questions. I'm angry, devastated, and quite frankly, I have lost belief in humanity. We are decent people who raised a good child despite being very young when he came along. He had a nice girlfriend we love and was doing well in college. This is unbelievable. I really still don't believe it. I don't know how you do your job, I really don't."

"If you think of anything, please let us know." She set her card on the coffee table. "We are very sorry for the reason we are here."

Carl finally put in a word as they rose. "We'll get him."

When they walked out, MacIntosh said with legitimate censure, "A nice promise I hope we can deliver on. This suspect is a ghost. A nasty, malignant ghost, but he's so elusive I have no idea where he is or who he is, and I was working it three bodies ago."

"If you don't doubt yourself now and then, you don't care enough. We'll get him." Carl got into the car. "I know it. Smoke bombs and flowers? He thinks he's ten feet tall. He's going to trip and we'll be there to catch him. He's too showy. The ones who bury the bodies and fade away are the kind that make you wonder if it will happen. He's not an easy meet and greet, but he's not trying to hide. He's daring us to catch him, and you know, anytime that happens, your shoelaces tangle together."

She backed out of the driveway, her expression absorbed as she mused out loud. "He's young, tall, athletic, and strong or he couldn't hang a grown man from a tree. He's a runner and he must be not just personable, but I'm thinking charismatic."

"Give me a lever and I can move the world," Carl

said, also contemplating the murder scenario. "With a rope over a branch and some leverage, it could be done, but you're right, it wasn't done by some portly guy who eats doughnuts in his cubicle."

"I agree he does think he's ten feet tall. He wouldn't do it now, but I believe he delivered those flowers himself right to my desk. I've viewed that video several times and he's wearing gloves as he walks up to the front door. He's been to my house. He's probably the one that vandalized Santiago's truck and left the smoke bomb." She slowed way down as a kid who seemed to be a novice at riding a bike wobbled too close to the edge of the sidewalk.

"Our real problem is some of those things just could be explained away. Santiago's truck . . . well, he's not the first to get a brick through a window. The smoke bomb at a teacher's house? That's maybe his problem because he gave someone a failing grade on a test. The flowers could be because you really do have a secret admirer out there with a crush on you. Maybe the gloves were just not to smudge the vase."

"And the bodies with the notes?" she asked as the child decided to get off his bike and wheel it instead back toward his house. "Can you explain those away?"

"Sure. There's a very disturbed individual out there who needs our attention."

She said quietly, "Oh, he's got it."


**Georgia wasn't sure** exactly how to handle this session. The dynamics of her relationship with Ellie Mac-Intosh and Jason Santiago were hardly textbook.

The latter came into her office and took a chair, but she knew he wouldn't stay in it for long. As usual, he was forthcoming. "You and Grasso? What's up with that?"

"We aren't here to talk about me. We're here to talk about you."

Those direct blue eyes were *very* direct. "Nothing is that simple. People are people, and while we are going to sit here and talk about what I'm feeling, I also study people, just in a different way. Grant me that. Grasso has a lot of flotsam floating out there. Is that it? What interests you?"

"Aren't I the therapist?"

"He's a good cop. I trust him. He isn't a perfect choice, but he'd always be there for you."

"Are you counseling me, or am I counseling you, Detective?"

He then did a Jason Santiago thing and simply put it out there. "I'm not sure which one of us needs it more. Let's just talk."

She still tried to sidestep. "How are things with Ellie?"

"I'm sleeping on the couch, remember? How are things with Grasso?"

"I'm not seeing you for therapy."

He burst out laughing. "Oh, God help you if you were. That would be perfect. Here's the sum total of my advice. If life kicks you, get over it."

She took something from that and rolled with it. "Is that what you did?"

To his credit, he did think about it. "As a kid? Sort of. I didn't have a mother, so soccer games were out of the question. My old man had neither time nor inclination to take me to practices. Not the cards dealt to my table. I accepted it."

"Did you *want* to play soccer?"

"No. I played football. I walked to practice until I got kicked off the team for getting caught breaking the rules by smoking a little weed. I think that was the day my old man decided as soon as he could do it, I was out the door. He'd been pretty decent when I was playing well. He wasn't ticked about the pot, he was just mad I got caught. I look back on it and regret being stupid, but we all are from time to time. He was going to show me the front door pretty soon anyway." He shrugged. "For all I know he did me a favor. I'd already learned a lot about self-reliance from him, so the military was a breeze for me compared to some of the other kids, and we really were still kids, but it was time to grow up fast. He wasn't a good example; he just didn't worry about my tender feelings. A drill sergeant was nothing. He was a kind and caring man compared to my father."

Georgia had to admit as a psychologist having someone like him as a patient was like wandering through a chocolate shop. He was smart but wary, he didn't deny his issues, but he didn't really acknowledge them either, though he clearly knew they existed. While a lot of patients became dependent and needy, trust was off his plate. Maybe he trusted Ellie, but if Georgia had to call it, that was on a professional basis, but emotionally, he was still skirting the edge. He was going to have a problem with total commitment.

However, he had mentioned the word "love" before.

Major breakthrough right there. Maybe they needed to address it.

"Do you want to talk about your personal life?"

"No man wants to talk about his personal life." He

stirred restlessly, but he did that frequently when they addressed issues that made him uncomfortable. "Thanks for asking. Couch, remember? I'm not sleeping with her."

"I wasn't asking about your sex life, I was talking personal life. You want to sleep with her, I understand that, because any man who is in love with a woman would naturally be interested in sexual intimacy. But have you really asked yourself yet what you *want*? Is it marriage?"

That was going out on a limb with someone like Santiago. He was never going to be an easy study. He looked irritated. "What kind of question is that?"

"A valid one. For instance, children. Small little beings running around with blond hair? Looking like you and Ellie?"

"Like she'd ever agree to that."

"You don't know she wouldn't."

"I don't have a high opinion of marriage."

Meat and bones right there. "Why?"

"My parents were married. Yeah, that worked out. My mother walked out the door."

"You can't predicate your life on the mistakes of two other people. Aren't your biological parents married again now?"

"Legally? I have no idea."

"So you just signed off on it?"

"Ellie could have probably married Grantham."

"But she didn't."

"No, but he's rich and good-looking."

"Does that threaten you?"

That stopped him, but it was just a bump in the road. He really would be hard to handle, so she didn't envy Ellie. "No. She isn't in love with him."

Insightful, and she agreed. "Is she in love with *you*?"

He was Jason Santiago. If this was the old West, he'd have walked down that street for a good old-fashioned gunfight. He shot from the hip always. "She sure doesn't want to be."

"But maybe she is?"

"How the hell do I know? Ask a question like that of a woman and you might not like the answer. You're the one that told me she'd talk about it when she was ready, and she isn't talking about it."

"Do you think the professional ramifications are being weighed against the emotional ones? She values you as a partner, and perhaps she doesn't want to compromise that relationship. For a dedicated police officer, that's an issue."

"I'd ask if she's said that, but you wouldn't tell me." He ran his fingers through his hair.

"No, I wouldn't. I'm asking you if that is what you think."

He admitted, "Metzger has made it pretty clear he wouldn't be happy about it if we had a more personal relationship. Not me and him, but me and Ellie. He does nothing for me, but don't hurt his feelings by letting him know."

Georgia did laugh. "Have you decided one way or the other about Jason Santiago's preferences, setting Metzger's aside?"

"I think you expect some answer that includes intro-spection, and I try hard as hell not to do that."

"Why is that?"

"I don't always follow positive thought patterns. Your guess is better than mine."

## Chapter 14

It had been a misty day with a brisk wind, so he didn't stand out wearing his hood up to cover his face.

At some point they'd add cameras to her security system, he knew it. In her shoes, he would.

So it was easy and he was good at this game, he was discovering. He really wasn't positive before now he was good at anything in his life. Average at best at wrestling when he'd given it a try, decent grades but no scholarships, and with long-distance running he'd at least found a small niche.

His parents would have preferred he was the quarterback on the football team, but he recognized that was not his avenue toward fame.

No question about it, he was much better at this.

So he dropped off his gift and thought about where he might go next.

**Black roses in** a vase.

This time he hadn't left the blooms, but just a

framed picture propped against her front door. Ellie stopped when she saw it, took in a deep breath, and then went around to the garage door. She unlocked it, went inside, and put on gloves to open the front door and pick up the picture, hoping she didn't smear a clear print, but she'd bet there wasn't one.

Smart. Smart. Smart.

A refrain going on there like a popular song. Just throw in a tune.

There wasn't a note, but the message didn't need one.

The communication was clear enough. *I'm here.*

Security cameras were being installed on her front porch. As luck—bad luck—would have it, there had been a delay, so it wasn't happening until tomorrow morning.

The picture went carefully into a plastic bag and she picked out clothes for the next day, texted Santiago she was on her way to the restaurant, and carefully locked the doors and activated the alarm from her phone. It was infuriating to think she felt relieved to safely leave her own house, but she did.

Her partner had suggested an English pub that was in a neighborhood full of shops and seemed so unlike him she was surprised, but also not in the mood to cook either. She managed to find a parking space, which wasn't easy and involved someone leaving at just the right moment in a BMW. She nabbed the spot and saw Jason's truck several spaces down.

At the moment she was pretty convinced they were on a date. It wasn't like they hadn't eaten out together dozens of times, gotten coffee, and had slept in relatively the same space, but he wouldn't have normally chosen this place with an elaborately trendy facade and a hostess dressed like an eighteenth-century bar-maid. In the background they were playing a ballad that involved a lute when she walked through the door.

Not at all his style, since he was more like rock bands with no stringed instruments except electric guitars in sight.

*Date.*

She told the hostess, "I'm meeting someone. Tall man with curly blond hair. I'm guessing jeans and a denim shirt."

The woman pointed. "Over there. Second booth."

"Thanks."

Santiago did the usual and stood when she ap-proached. She wanted to ask him to quit that, but everyone was the sum of their parts, and he might be profane in a million ways, but would always pull out her chair. He waited for her to sit down before he slid back into the booth and went straight to the point. "I ordered you some sort of white wine thing. How did the interview go?"

"About like anyone could expect. Please tell me it's chardonnay."

"I just said dry. The waitress asked what kind and I did my best. That's all I know. Nothing helpful from today?"

"No. Be happy you skipped it, though. The father is hovering on the edge and the mother is pregnant with a long-expected second child but just lost her first one. Not my favorite day ever. I never even spoke with her. It wasn't great." It had been heart-wrenching.

"I was happy to skip it before you ever walked out the door."

"Let's just talk about it later."

Their drinks arrived, a lager for him, and what seemed to be her first lucky break all day was that her wine *was* chardonnay.

She waited to tell him about the picture. A nice dinner without discussing it would give them both a respite. She'd tell him later, of course, and get his take on it, but for now she'd listen to the lute music and sip a glass of wine and pretend a killer wasn't stalking her.

"How's your sister and the new baby? It was her third, right?" He asked it very casually, as if that was normal conversation for them.

It wasn't.

Definitely a date.

"She has her hands full, that's for sure. I believe she said flat out that she wouldn't mind going back to work soon so she didn't see visions of cartoons in her dreams. Apparently she can sing all the songs from *The Little Mermaid* by heart, and can give lessons on how discreet breastfeeding in public is possible."

"Those are some marketable skills right there. I've been to her house because of the thing with your grandfather, but really didn't meet her. What's she do?"

He had been with her when they stopped by Jody's one time after a skeleton had been found on her grandfather's property.

"Marketing. Do you have a fever or something?" Ellie couldn't help it. "You haven't said one swear word yet. Stop freaking me out."

"I'm trying to be polite and make small talk. That's what it's called, right?"

It was time to skip back to common ground. "Our killer, if it is him, left me another present. A picture of black roses propped against my door. Maybe forensics can lift a print. He must have downloaded it, so that might be a lead. Black roses can't be all that popular. If he paid for it online we could track him down."

"You have to be fucking kidding me."

She took another sip of wine. "Now I feel better and like I'm talking to the real Jason Santiago. No, not kidding. He was at my house again."

He absently took a piece of bread and ate it, obviously thinking it over. "I don't normally plan to shoot people, but he's number one on my shortlist. There wasn't a note?"

"No."

"What did Grasso say?"

"He wasn't there."

"You were with him. You didn't say anything about going to your house alone."

"I happen to be a grown woman."

"I've noticed. Don't do that again until we fix this. He could have been lurking in the shrubbery . . . oh hell, do people even say shrubbery? He could have been anywhere. Jesus, Ellie. A grown idiot."

"As far as I can tell, he was long gone."

She wasn't as calm as she sounded. It was one thing to track down killers, but another to have them tracking you down. Her intent was to keep them from killing more people by arresting them and their intent was to make sure that arrest never happened.

This was different.

"Ellie, he's in your face."

"We've had this conversation." She opened her menu. "I'm thinking of being boring and having fish-and-chips."

"Shepherd's pie for me and don't deflect." His eyes held a stubborn glint of reproof.

She looked at him directly right back. "Am I bothered? Yes. Let's let it go for a few minutes. I really think this person wants my attention and I don't want to give it to him one hundred percent of the time. That's a transfer of power. I want to eat dinner and not think about him."

He didn't concede easily, but agreed. "Fair enough."

"You are too high strung. I bet if Georgia were here she'd say you want him to try something so you'd have an excuse to just wipe him out."

"High strung makes me sound like a lady who would faint in one of those novels you read. I want to stop him, and if that means dead in his tracks, well, let's face it, he's asked for it."

**He really *did*** want to just wipe him out.

Gone. Refuse off the face of the earth. He wasn't a stranger to vigilante justice.

The food was really good and the place wasn't his usual, but Jason had to admit his taste tended toward a burger at some bar. However, he'd allow her a quiet dinner, even if it was an effort to rein it in. At least the food was delicious.

"I'm thinking of moving to England and taking up sheep farming," he said after the last bite. "Maybe you could come along and be my serving wench."

Ellie had gradually relaxed during the meal, and she laughed. "You wish. I'd just pour the ale over your head. Besides, I don't think you farm sheep. You raise them. It really was good. Not a bad diversion from our current problem."

"Also no grocery store and no stove involved. Ellie, I know you don't want it, but I think we made a good call asking to put a security camera on your front porch. He's paid a couple of visits now."

So much for leaving the job out of it.

"He'll expect it."

She could be right. He still argued. "It might discourage unwanted deliveries and we could get a visual."

"He'll just change tactics. I think he'll choose another park too."

The music switched to bagpipes right about the time the check arrived and he quickly handed over his credit card. He could handle most music, but not bagpipes or opera. Every man had his limits. "I wish I didn't agree with you, but I do. He's going to hit again."

"I just wish we knew his direction. He's a wild card."

Luckily the waitress returned with his receipt quickly. This discussion was ruining the ambience of the evening pretty fast. He scribbled in the tip and then suggested, "We can head for my place. If you insist on going home I'll have to bring my sleeping bag and crash on your porch."

"Your place is a good plan." Her brows lifted as she got out of her seat. "*You* have a sleeping bag?"

"No, I was showing off. Camping isn't my thing."

"That makes more sense to me. I'm not much into camping either, but I do like the serenity of the woods. A hot cup of coffee sitting on the dock listening to the loons on the lake with the mist drifting over the water . . . there's nothing better."

He could picture her there sipping from a mug on a cool day, feet up. "I'm going to have to take your

word on that one. I like a window with a view and
*SportsCenter* playing in the background on the TV
while I drink beer on the couch. Shall we go?"

She didn't argue, which was unusual in their relationship. This was getting to her and he understood,
since it was getting to him too. He wasn't used to a
killer tracking a police officer. Usually it was the other
way around.

She nodded. "Thanks for dinner. It was . . . nice."

Nice. Well, he supposed she was right. It had been
nice, but he wasn't positive nice had been his goal. He
wasn't even sure he'd had a goal other than food.

Not true. He just plain had a bad premonition
about how this was going to play out and he wasn't
going along with it. Ellie wasn't safe by herself. He'd
known some fallen officers. Every single one of them
was competent and capable. No one could handle
every contingency.

He held the door for her and kept it open for two
middle-aged ladies with shopping bags who thanked
him with bright smiles. "I want to see this picture," he
declared darkly as they walked across the parking lot.
"I bet he didn't sign it just because it would directly
tie him to the murders."

"I expect you're right there. At the moment we still
can't link the phone calls and flowers to the murders."

"We both know it's him, Ellie. I'm more bugged
than ever. If you'd argued over our destination I'd
have had to go all caveman or something and cuff you
and sling you over my shoulder."

The breeze had picked up and there was a hint of
rain in the scent of the air. "Kidnapping is a federal
offense, may I remind you, Officer Santiago." She
pushed a button on her key chain to unlock her car.

"But I'm still craving that good night's sleep, and the idea of someone crouching in my—what is it, shrubbery?—watching me turn off the lights doesn't help that. So fine, it's your place again."

"Well, shit, I was looking forward to cuffing you and you just ruined it. Give me a break, everyone has fantasies."

"Just don't share yours, please. I doubt at even my advanced age I'm old enough to hear about them. I'll meet you there."

He was smiling when he got into the truck because he'd just won what he'd worried might be a serious argument. Independent was an understatement when it came to Ellie. That smile faded when he thought about that picture. Metzger was wrong. Yes, she could take care of herself, but this was some scary shit.

The cameras might help, or maybe it would just make the guy adjust his strategy.

This deviant was sending her flowers and leaving them on her doorstep. Black roses weren't exactly a positive message.

She just wasn't going to be out of his sight at this point and they were going to fight about it. Ellie might cooperate now, but she wasn't going to stay that way. He didn't blame her. Life needed to return to normal so she could go back to the regular pattern.

Without anyone else being part of the problem.

His apartment was quiet and dark, which he fixed quickly by turning on all the lights. Ellie followed him in, and by the way she glanced around he could tell she wasn't quite settled. This was an unusual case and he got it. "He isn't here, and if he was, I'd know it, but let me look around," he said, and meant it.

It was hardly a palace, so it didn't take long. "We're good."

He bolted the door, and as a precaution, even checked the balcony. Nothing but the cheap beach chair he'd bought to sit in on warm summer nights and his small folding table. He went back inside. "I think there's still some of that wine you brought over in the fridge. I know I haven't touched it. Now that I don't have to drive anywhere, I'm going to have another beer. I can scrounge up a clean glass."

"No need. I think I'm going to call my mother, just to check in on her, and then I'm going to sleep."

At that moment her phone rang. She took it out of her purse and swore softly. "Blocked number. I think I know who this is. Our good friend."

Jason wished they really knew who it was because that would make the case a lot simpler. "Answer it. Or let me."

"I'll do it. Detective MacIntosh." Ellie was brusque and professional.

It was frustrating to not be able to hear anything but one side of the conversation.

"Yes, I did receive your gift."

He was on his phone in a second. "I need a trace right now to this number." He reeled off Ellie's cell as fast as possible.

No dice. His partner said in resignation, "Good try. He hung up."

He still had forensics on the other line. "Is there a way we can trace all calls to that number? I don't need a report on every single one, but can we nail the ones that count by location, and that means Milwaukee? This is part of a homicide investigation. I'll get you the server and account information."

Ellie glared at him. "Hey. My phone."

He pressed a button and was unrepentant. "Good idea?"

"Oh. I love the idea of someone monitoring my calls."

"Incoming calls. Did you enjoy this last one?" he asked pointedly.

The answer was no. He could tell. She was definitely at least a little pale.

"So let's find where he's coming from. We can't get a straight trace, since he's not using his phone anyway, but we can maybe get a general idea of what part of the city he haunts."

She pointed out, "This is a big city. All he has to do is call from somewhere and drive away. I just don't see how it will help us or I would have suggested it the minute he called me Cinderella because of the missing shoe."

Jason shrugged. "Look, the more information we have, at least in my opinion, the better."

"I've dealt with a lot of criminals and he's . . . different."

Jason was cautious usually about touching her for several reasons, one of which was he'd told her straight up how he felt about her, another that he was aware they had a professional relationship and there were boundaries, but he did reach out and take her hand to tug her toward the couch. "Call your mother. I'm going to get my beer. Sure about that glass of wine?"

# Chapter 15

He was running late. It was annoying because he'd hear about it, but he'd make up something about a flat tire or small fender bender. No one at work would, or even could, check that out.

Maybe that he was behind schedule would be noted, but not in connection to the real reason.

What a good morning.

It hadn't been as easy as the others. She'd been a smart cookie, as his grandmother would say, and knew full well he didn't like her and never had. There was no friendly drink, there was no pleasant conversation, and there certainly was no joy in her expression when she'd glanced up and seen him standing by her car.

It had been very satisfying to see the one person who had always seen right through him panic and try to run. She couldn't, though, the old bitch; she was too heavy. He caught her in about three strides and then it was over. Not done, though; he'd worked pretty hard

*to haul her into her car and fumble through her purse*
*for her keys.*

*He was happy to see she was still breathing.*

*Not for long.*


**Ellie woke up,** took a shower—his shower was clean
for a bachelor—and prepared for her day. As far as
she could tell, Santiago didn't sleep much at all, so she
could already smell coffee as she dried off, did the
minimum for her day by just pulling her hair back
and touching up with some foundation. She felt out
of place, but maybe not as much as she would have
expected.

He was out on the balcony even though it was still
very cool in the mornings. There was a clean yellow
mug set out with the logo Go Hawks. It was a small,
thoughtful gesture compared to how he'd insisted on
sleeping on the couch, which was therefore between
her and the door, which was a big, thoughtful gesture.
Iowa Hawkeyes were apparently a college team he
favored. Ellie filled her cup, sniffed it, and felt like
that was enough caffeine to fuel her for the day.


**This morning she** was grateful he was sitting there with
his long legs propped on a little table, drinking his
coffee. She'd always operated on the premise she
could deal with almost anything with level calcula-
tion, and maybe that was true.

The man was undeniably considerate at times and
rude at other unforgettable moments. It was hard to
know how to take him, and she was undecided on
how to handle it all.

Much like the killer.

At least she'd slept knowing Jason was there.

She slid open the sliding door to the balcony. "Hi, well, I'm headed to work."

He said contemplatively, not even looking over but at the railing, "I think we're going to have another murder. He talks to you and then kills someone."

That did stop her cold. She looked at him reclining in his chair, holding his mug of what seemed to be very strong black coffee. "What makes you think that?"

"Ellie, he called you last night, and now he's going to kill someone. There's a pattern developing."

All of this was so appalling she wanted to go hide in a closet somewhere. But she couldn't discount it either. He knew his job. "All right, talk to me."

"This psycho nut job is killing people *for* you, not just because of you. I still think it is an obsession, but I'm starting to readjust my thinking. He wants to hand you crimes to solve."

"Look . . ." She struggled for words. "I have plenty of work. Don't we both? Why?"

"Montoya is wrong. I bet he hates me more than anyone on this earth." Santiago drank some more toxic coffee, his legs relaxed but the rest of his body tense. "I spend all day with you. I get he wants to shoot back at me. I feel it."

"Or he hates *me*?" She wasn't sure.

"Wrong." He finally glanced over. "Don't even think of leaving without me. Give me five minutes. We'll go to work together."

Like he got to give that decree. Except maybe she liked the idea of not walking out the door alone. She had to admit it, she was wary.

Santiago was definitely a John Wayne and would

leap out in front of her, guns blazing. It wasn't that she couldn't defend herself, but it was a good idea to have backup. That's why police officers had partners in the first place.

She gave in. "Five minutes. I'd have some coffee but it smells like you could pour it into your gas tank and it would work just fine."

He got to his feet. "I like it strong. You aren't going to catch me having vanilla latte or some wimpy shit like that."

Ellie couldn't help it. She raised a brow. "You're just worried Montoya is right, aren't you? Are we going to stop off at the gym so you can lift weights or at an outdoorsy store so you can buy camo gear?"

"I actually don't care how anyone lives their life, unless they are killing people, and then I take a serious interest. I'm going to take a quick shower and then we're out of here."

She had to give him that one. She pretty much felt the same way. She actually thought about the coffee again, but was hesitant to go there, so she instead checked e-mails from her phone, and it was then she noticed a car cruising through the parking lot for the second time.

Slow circle. Possibly someone picking up a kid for school and they just weren't down there yet? Santiago's building's parking lot had more minivans than a car dealership, but this was a sporty car. From this distance it was impossible to get a license plate, but she took a picture of it with her phone anyway.

Third circle. Then it sped away. Not picking up a kid.

She was, after all, a police officer. It didn't feel quite right.

Santiago came out, his hair damp and probably only finger combed, which she suspected was how he operated. "Maybe we had a visitor."

"Like what?"

She showed him the picture. "Recognize this car?"

He studied it. "No, but we need to keep in mind random things happen all the time. Different people move in and move out."

He was right, of course. She said, "I just can't imagine why anyone would drive through three times and take off."

"We have suspicious minds. Good call on the photo. Let's go."

She drove, since they might as well carpool, and just to irk him, she stopped and got a vanilla latte to brighten her morning. Santiago drawled sarcastically in his signature way as they pulled out of the drive-through, "If I'd said I wouldn't eat worms, would we be stopping off at a bait shop or something?"

"Maybe."

The coffee was delicious, but the rest of their morning was not.

The first person she saw as she walked through the door was Metzger hovering by her desk. Not in a good mood. He was not a man who hid his feelings well. He demanded, "Do you mind telling me why we have another body with writing on it and no suspect at all?"

"What? Where?"

"A different park. The mayor is getting involved because it really is such a bad reflection on the safety of our city. The two of you can get your asses over to this address and *you* tell *me* what happened. Last I checked, that was your job." He jabbed a finger at a report and a flicker of dismay went through her entire body. "Just so you know, I told them if they don't get in those cameras today someone will be terminated."

Santiago took her keys from her hand. "I'll drive and you read. Tell me this happy story on our way. I'm kinda doubtful there's a satisfying ride into the sunset at the end."

He didn't get off scot-free either. Metzger said, "Get a haircut, Santiago. How often do we have to have this conversation?" Then he stalked away.

Santiago muttered, "Whenever he's pissed, he mentions my hair. What does that have to do with anything? By the way, I told you so."

Ellie was processing the report even as they walked out the door and was not at all happy. "This guy is so erratic. This time it's a drowning. "

"He's sticking to suffocation. Nice. People don't swim quite yet in this balmy climate in the spring and scribbling on yourself is old school. Just get a tattoo. Not an accident. I believe I mentioned I thought this would happen. I take it no ID?"

"No. Of course not, because that would make it easy on us, and he isn't interested in that at all."

"I think the real question is just what *does* he want?"

She wanted to know as well.

Maybe.


**There was nothing** like a facedown body to ruin your morning.

The woman was wearing a skirt, jacket, and had gray hair. The team had dragged her from the water and Fergusson had sent in crime scene techs, so they were all over the place, working their magic.

Jason looked around at unfurling leaves and daffodils and asked the pertinent question. "Who found the body?"

"Some old guy walking his dog." A young patrol officer handed over a slip of paper. "I wrote down his information from his driver's license. He seemed just to be in the wrong place at the wrong time. I saw no real reason to hold him, but told him you'd probably pay a visit. He had a dog on a leash, waited for us to respond, and was eighty if he was a day and maybe a hundred pounds. He was wearing a sweater vest. I didn't think anyone even made those anymore."

"Hey, I have about six of those in my closet." Jason couldn't resist. "They're comfortable. I wish he'd stuck around so we could ask him a few questions."

The officer said dryly, "Detective, you don't somehow seem to me to a sweater vest sort of guy. Anyway, I don't think he killed anyone, because he couldn't physically manage it. I let him go because he said it was time for the dog's medication. I swear I think that dog was older than he was. It peed on my foot. Maybe I looked like a tree or something. Geez, this day had better improve."

Jason couldn't agree more. When the officer left, Ellie said tightly, "Hang on to that note because I want to know if a jogger happened to stop by."

He was interested in the same damn thing and just as sure that it probably wouldn't help them at all if someone had, because unless they were wearing a name tag, it wasn't going to give needed information.

A deputy medical examiner named Halden came over and gave them a solemn nod. "Detectives. It seems all wrong to say good morning, so I won't. Until we get her on the table I can't say for sure, but it seems to me she was probably dumped here after a struggle. There are some bruises on her neck. If there is water in her lungs she was still alive when she went into the pond, and if there isn't she was dead first. I'll let you know, but you might want to look at this."

He lifted the victim's hand. Inside of her right wrist in indelible ink: *Not all roses are red.*

Ellie shut her eyes for a moment, but she snapped out of it. "He's really making a statement. Time of death? Can we get an estimate?"

"Water temperatures change things, but I'd say it happened just a few hours ago. Rigor really hasn't set in and that water is pretty cold."

Interesting. The killer had certainly been busy last night and this morning.

The DME said, "I have no idea what that writing means, but that is more your job than mine, and from the look on your faces, it struck a chord. Now if you don't mind, we're going to put the body in the van. I'll send the report as soon as possible. We're all aware this is an ongoing case."

Jason stood there with the breeze ruffling his apparently once again overlong hair as they loaded the victim. He needed to take time to look in the mirror more often. "You do realize he just gave us the link we needed. Not all roses are red, and he gave you that picture of black roses. It's not DNA or anything, but circumstantial is better than nothing."

"Trust me, as someone who is not enjoying his special attention, I've already thought of that. Without sexual assault, DNA is a lot harder to pin down. I don't have to remind you of that."

"No, you don't. Maybe she fought and scratched him."

Ellie stood, looking out over the small pond. "I think he puts something over their heads. Like a pillowcase. A long one that goes down their arms. They don't know what's happening and are disoriented because they can't see anything. It was morning, so I doubt she was drinking. She's older than the other victims and less likely to put up a fight she could win."

"Maybe, but we can't go to every retailer that sells textiles and ask if their pillowcase sales have gone up. You do realize I'm now following you into the women's bathroom, even at the police station. I'm sure no one will mind."

"I can think of three female officers who might enjoy it, but some who would arrest you on the spot. I'd be inclined to just arrest you myself."

"Three, huh? Can I have names and numbers?"

"Thelma is one of them. She keeps telling me to give you a chance. Maybe you should ask her out."

Thelma was a dispatcher who far outweighed him, was twenty years older, and regularly showed everyone she could trap pictures of her grandchildren. He said, "Now you can tell her you've slept with me."

"I thought you said you didn't sleep."

"I didn't, but you did. There you have it, it's official. You've slept. With me."

She ignored that comment. MacIntosh had a sense of humor, it just didn't always match his. "Some of the older ladies think you're cute. I've never understood it."

He could ignore her too and pointed at the departing van with the body headed toward the morgue. "He's not fooling around."

"No," she agreed, hands in the pockets of her fluffy pink sweater. "I really am going to go ahead and call Montoya again. I'm sliding down a slope and don't have a sense of where our target is going. This is number four."

"That we know of."

"He seems to have a focus and be good at this. I'm still wondering if it's a cop."

"And he's a young jogger. Let's not forget into flowers, but without a lot of imagination unless he's killing someone."

"Oh, listen to you. If you sent me flowers, what would you send?"

"Roses." He had to admit it. "Woman equals flowers, and the more expensive the stronger the message. Roses imply strong and sincere admiration. Our killer has sincere admiration."

"You don't lack imagination. I would never have tracked down the tip about the older lady through the cashier where she bought the supermarket flowers just by their smell. I wonder if he realizes that's the murder that will probably hang him on all the other ones."

They were walking back to the car and he said, "Ellie, call Montoya and we'll talk afterward. I never flip out, but I'm heading that direction. You don't want to hear about my fantasies, fine, but I bet you really don't want to know about his."

"Thanks for that observation. You aren't always the most cheerful of companions."

He shrugged. "I'm not in a cheerful mood. Maybe it was the corpse."

## Chapter 16

*Another ticket cashed.*

*He sat on his back porch and thought it all over. She'd deserved it. Didn't she know that?*

*That was the frustrating part.*

*She hadn't recognized him.*

*It might have changed everything if she had, but he doubted it. He was careening down a treacherous path.*

*That harsh, vindictive harridan hadn't even recognized him.*

*Her death had been a pleasure.*

**"My informant rolled,** but the word of one man who has a rap sheet a mile long isn't going to impress a judge." Carl didn't offer it as a disclaimer, but it was the cold, hard truth. "I know who did it now, but haven't one shred of evidence except the word of a convicted drug dealer. If the shooter was smart he traded guns with one of his buddies, so the murder weapon is now in the hands of someone with a solid alibi. I hate these gang-related cases, but Metzger keeps giving them to me."

Georgia just smiled, elegant in a black suit. She could really pull that off. "I suspect you're very good at solving them, or at least better than anyone else in the department. I think he's a smart man. You represent authority more than someone, for instance, like Santiago. They would never talk to Ellie either. She's a woman. My impression is it's a very misogynist culture, and Santiago looks like he left his surfboard somewhere. They wouldn't take him seriously either. You *look* like a detective. You look like authority."

"I like the free counseling." Carl actually did like talking to her, so he wasn't entirely joking. "And the other perks, of course." He'd rarely spoken about his job with any other women he'd dated. "Last night was . . . memorable."

Her place this time. Drinks and dinner and a good aftermath in the bedroom, and now they were having lunch.

She was amused too. "I'm good with memorable." Then she stopped smiling. "I understand there was another murder."

"There's always another murder. I assume you mean the Park Bench Killer. We have no idea who the victim is, as usual."

"Another note?"

"We've been trying to keep that out of the press, but yes."

"He seems very motivated. I wish I had a better word. Let's say intent. I know Ellie."

He had polished off his meal and felt better because he frequently didn't eat enough. Georgia was not only interesting as a woman, but maybe good for him. "I'd agree with intent."

She'd ordered biscotti for dessert and took a lady-like bite. "There hasn't been a breakthrough?"

"I don't think so. I'm helping, but not a lead investigator."

"Ellie is lead and not Santiago?"

He considered it. "They are a unique team. She's got insight and a way with a witness, and he's a tough street-smart kid that became a cop. I don't think the chief says one or the other and they decide. I think he just assigns the case and lets it fly. Good call. Let them handle it together."


**It wasn't as** if Georgia liked her job all of the time. Counseling certain patients took extraordinary patience and left her wondering if she'd actually helped. Ninety percent of the time she was sure she'd done more good than harm, but 100 percent was her goal. She'd say that after her lovely night and pleasant lunch she was maybe 70 percent helpful this afternoon, which ruined the nice afterglow. Her patient, who was a victim of domestic abuse in a previous marriage, had met a nice man and he'd proposed, she'd accepted, and now she had nightmares and actually had taken her engagement ring and dropped it in the toilet and sat sobbing in the bathroom for hours before she decided not to flush it. Then there was the man who was so sure all meats and vegetables were bad for you he only ate bread and took supplements, and his primary care physician had referred him because of his deteriorating health. Georgia had tried, but if she had to predict it from their first session, he would end up in an institution at least until they could sort out some meds that might help.

But things were looking up.

Her rebellious teenage patient Cindy said, "I'm thinking about trying to take some early college classes. I'm pretty sure I could get in. What do you think?"

*What do you think?*

That was a first. "In math? You are good at it."

"Oh, hell no. I can do math already."

Georgia considered her response carefully. Cindy was wearing a shirt that could pass for reasonable and some low-cut but barely respectable jeans. Definite improvement. "Is that what you are interested in doing?"

"I'm not interested in engineering. I kinda have a few other ideas like maybe graphic arts . . . I love comic books and movies using pixel animation."

"Have you discussed this with your parents?"

Cindy looked away for a second. "They think it's stupid and a waste of money."

"They said that, or is it what you took away from the conversation?"

"We didn't have a conversation."

"Then how do you know it is what they think?"

"I've only lived with them my whole life, Dr. Lukens."

Well, maybe she deserved that rebuke, or maybe she didn't. "I'd like to point out that you can't find out what people think without asking them. I do grant you that you might ask and they have the option not to tell you the truth, but I have learned from working with a lot of police detectives that there's a reason they are supposed to not draw conclusions."

"Do you really?"

"Do I really work with police officers? Yes, I do. They are pretty clear that hard, cold evidence is all that flies."

Cindy bit her painted black nails. "You really know cops? I've thought about that too."

That came out of the blue. Maybe Georgia wasn't as insightful as she thought. Cindy was opposed to authority as far as she could tell. Better reassess that. "It certainly is a tough job, but a very worthy one in my opinion."

Homicide detectives, not beat cops. Georgia had to admit she paused. But she had a policy of being honest with her patients, at least as much as possible. "Most of the ones I know work murder cases. It isn't where you start. I see them if they've been injured in the line of duty or have had to injure someone else. What makes you so interested, Cindy?"

"I've just always thought that might be pretty cool."

Since Cindy didn't think anything was cool, that was certainly a positive sign. "If you'd like, and your parents either call me or send written permission, I can probably arrange for you to talk to one or two of them and ask questions about what they do."

Carl might be too well dressed and well mannered for a teenage girl like Cindy, but Ellie and Santiago might be perfect, since Ellie was female and Santiago was light-years away from formal. He might appeal to someone her age.

Georgia went on, "That means, of course, you'd have to actually tell your parents you are considering other options for your future besides engineering."

"I don't want to," the girl confessed, slumping in her chair. "My dad will freak."

"It seems to me that your dad cares enough about

how you feel that he arranged for you to come see me and pays for our time together. I certainly can't promise he won't be disappointed, because those are his feelings and not mine, but you might be surprised. Avoiding the problem will not make it go away."

"Yeah, yeah, I know." Cindy didn't look happy, but at least she wasn't so sullen. "You should try living through dinner at my house. I have to effing stay at the table until he finishes his coffee and 'talk about my day.' It's stupid."

"Or else maybe he's interested in your life and well-being and wants to be a part of it. Have you considered that? I know someone who was raised by an alcoholic stepfather that kicked him out of the house before he was even out of high school." She would never mention Santiago's name, of course, but that information wasn't a breach of ethics, since he was upfront about it and plenty of other people knew so it wasn't a secret. "I believe he would have preferred to have someone care about his day."

"And there are children starving in Africa, I know. I've heard that about three million times from my parents, right after they take my cell phone away for some lame reason."

Well, Rome was definitely not built in a day, Georgia thought, but in her notes she was going for tentative progress. "Do you really think their reasons are lame or are they trying to help you learn to cope with consequences if you make a mistake so you are more prepared for life on your own? It sounds to me like you don't want to live at home forever, and most people don't, but it is their job, don't you think? They want to teach you how to do it."

"Whatever. If you can really do that cop thing I

might go ahead and tell them. I think our time is done, right?"

She was no stranger to having patients—when it was getting into difficult territory—to decide to abruptly leave.

"As soon as I hear from your parents, I will see what I can do."

Cindy left right as Georgia's cell phone vibrated. It was an old friend from college who breezed into town now and then and wanted to get together. It was telling that she hesitated to accept the dinner invitation because she hadn't heard yet from Carl. Maybe her session with Cindy made her revert to her own high school days. But they'd just had lunch, so . . .

"That sounds lovely."

Laurie said, "Fantastic. We need to catch up. Pick the restaurant and we'll meet you there. Reservations for three please. There's someone I want you to meet. I'm not traveling alone this time. Bring someone too."

She was the one to call Lieutenant Grasso. "I have an old friend in town and I think I need a date for dinner. Interested?"

It turned out to be reservations for four.

## Chapter 17

*Storms rolling in.*

*As a kid he remembered deer hunting up north with his dad when a freak winter thunderstorm broke loose and there was absolutely no place to go for shelter. The trees were clawing at the sky, the wind moaning through the branches, and the few remaining leaves were scattering and swirling around them when a big buck came bounding through the patch of woods where they were trapped and getting drenched.*

*He shot it. Clean too, just one bullet, and it went down like another burst of thunder. Ten points, a big boy, and his father wiped at the rain running down his face with a gloved hand as he went to kneel by the animal. Then he looked up and said, "Good kill, son."*

*High praise from a man he could never seem to please in any other way.*

*She was home.*

*He'd followed her from the station, keeping well back, taking a different street now and then once he knew the direction she was headed. It was too diffi-*

*cult to do any surveillance in Detective Santiago's apartment complex, since all those vigilant mamas and fathers distrusted a man sitting in his car alone, so he'd tried it once and driven away.*

*This quiet street was different.*

**She was being** watched.

There was no conclusive evidence except that she sensed it, but Ellie walked swiftly toward her front door, and at the last second turned around, her hand in her jacket, gripping her weapon.

No one she could see.

It didn't help that the sky had turned a lurid green and they were under a tornado watch. Ellie didn't hear sirens yet, but the air was heavy and anything was possible this time of year. Thunderheads had built in the sky like monoliths all afternoon and there were rumbles in the distance. The wind had also been picking up, never a good sign.

It was spring after all. She let herself inside quietly, checked around, then relaxed, opened her mail—she knew now how the caller had gotten her cell number because her last cell bill had never arrived. Since it was paid automatically she hadn't registered it was missing right away. Taking someone's mail was a serious offense, of course, but murder was even more serious, so she doubted the killer was losing sleep over taking something out of her postal box.

Still, it was a violation of her privacy and she deeply resented it. Santiago would be all over her for going home alone again, but what was she supposed to do? They worked together as a team but not always the exact same hours, and he also mentioned an errand after he got off work. She'd decided to run by the condo and check on things.

A crack of lightning lit up the window to the south as the front gathered momentum. The thunder that immediately answered said it was close and Ellie heard a plaintive meow from her front porch, more like a feline wail. She ran to the door and was very relieved to see it was Blackie, seeking asylum under the overhang. She'd wondered if in all the confusion of fire trucks and smoke if the cat had ever gone home.

"Oh, thank God." The next door neighbor dashed up and scooped up the cat. "She loves your front porch. I was hoping she was here. I want to thank you again for going in after her when we thought the house was on fire. My son is very attached to this animal. I saw you pull in but we haven't seen you for a while. I hope everything is okay."

So she technically *had* been watched, but it wasn't as sinister as she'd thought. They knew what she did for a living, so she just said, "Working long hours on a case."

"We're going to lose power. Our lights have flickered already."

Blackie liked being held in a thunderstorm about as much as she'd liked being held in a smoke-filled house. Ellie told him, "I think you'd better run for it."

"Good idea." Nichols took off in a sprint, the cat squirming in his arms, and barely made it before the deluge started in earnest. The rain didn't arrive gently; it came in with a vengeance in sideways sheets that lashed at the windows and seemed to shake the walls.

As predicted, everything went dead and dark.

It was actually soothing, because surely only a complete maniac would be out in this weather, so she could relax for a few minutes. Not that she didn't consider the killer a maniac, so maybe she wasn't safe after all.

Of course her phone rang.

"Nice weather out there." It was Grasso with his cool voice. "I think it might be spring in Wisconsin."

"Let's name this Hurricane Walleye. It is pretty wicked out there."

"You're telling me. I'm going down KK at about two miles an hour. I wanted to tell you my case has shifted. The older lady really was probably murdered. The family paid for a very expensive forensics specialist to fly in from California and go over the scene and the body. Hammett's conclusions were verified and our guys are good, but this guy did some sort of fancy mathematical probability curve on it being an accident based on his findings and those from our department, and it came out as improbable. Metzger is now glad he gave the case to a homicide detective right away instead of dismissing it as a slip and fall, because he saved face. I'm going to drag Santiago to the supermarket with me to see if he can find the clerk that told him about the lady buying the tulips so we can show her a picture. If she can be directly tied to the flowers sent to you, when we get him, there's another charge of murder."

The worst part was Ellie definitely felt responsible somehow. It wasn't rational, she knew it, but anyone would regret the death of someone who had helped out another human being and it ended up in their death.

Grasso went on. "I'll send the report, but what the autopsy suggests is dual blows to the head, which means someone hit her and she went down. It is possible she tripped and was stunned, staggered up, and fell the other way, but the expert thinks it is improbable. It looks like she was slammed on the side of the head and it dropped her. She also fractured her arm, but it was from the fall."

"One big bogeyman or multiple ones?"

Grasso didn't mince words. It wasn't his way. "One. He was put on this earth to simply ruin my life and yours, but we have it better than the others where he took away their lives. Damn, did you hear that crack of thunder?"

"Hard to miss it. I'm fairly sure my ears will stop ringing soon. Our guy killed her, I'm sure of it."

"Someone did. Enter suspect who is our already suspect."

"We need a name." Ellie stood there in the dark except for the vivid lightning flashes and was amazed she still had cell reception.

"Let's get him." He paused, and then said quietly, "I'm concerned about you, but I am way more concerned about Santiago. What better way to get your undivided attention than by killing your partner? I don't like crawling around in the heads of people who consider murder a sport, but if I were him, he'd be who I'd go for."

That wasn't comforting. Grasso knew what he was doing. She asked, "Speaking of Santiago, was he still at his desk?"

"No. I assumed he was with you."

He so wasn't.

"No."

"Maybe give him a call? I need him anyway and he isn't answering me."

"I will. Unless we lose signal in this mess, I'll call you back."

She tried, and nothing.

She tried again and no answer until the fourth ring, but Santiago picked up. She inhaled in relief. "Where are you?"

"Riding the storm out by leaving a place that still has electricity, aka the Underworld. We keep our dead nice and cold. I can hear the generator running. That's a good thing. If it went dark when I was down here I would flip shit. I had a question for Hammett. Where are you?"

She didn't want to actually say. "Grasso needs to talk to you."

"Fine. I'll call him. Where are you?"

"My condo."

"Jesus, Ellie." He was emphatic. "Don't go there without me. Are you nuts? He targets you there."

"Of course I'm nuts. I like you as a partner, so I must be. This weather is awful." She could barely hear him over the roar of the storm.

"I must be nuts too. Don't set a foot outside until I get there."

"Like I would. Rain is coming down in buckets. I'm safe enough."

"I'll be there soon. I'm headed upstairs."

"Don't drive in this."

"Try and stop me."

**True to his** word he arrived in a deluge and sprinted to the door at record speed, shaking off like a wet dog once he got in the front door. Ellie looked at him accusingly. "You're an idiot."

Maybe she was right, but it was a relief to see her safe. The pitch-dark street had not been a comfort.

"I'm not the one that left without backup. Dammit, Ellie, don't do that again."

He needed a beer and some dry clothes, but either was highly unlikely. He couldn't really sit down. She had nice furniture and he was soaked. Her place was dark without power, but she'd lit some candles. "If I could have a towel that would be great, or I'll just have to sit on the floor."

"I have an extra robe, but it's pink. Or this over-sized white shirt that has lace ruffles down the front." She actually smiled. Since this all started those had been few and far between. "That I'd like to see. Let me take a picture of you wearing it."

"Very funny, but I think a towel will work out fine."

It literally had been a cold front, so he was shivering, but no regrets. He'd heard the ping of sleet on his windshield even through the slashing rain. Spring seemed to have taken that part of *out like a lamb* as just a suggestion. She disappeared down the hall and brought the towel. She also brought him a beer. It was higher end than what he usually drank, but he wasn't picky at the moment. He twisted off the cap as she asked, "Did you call Grasso?"

"In this shit? No dice on questioning anyone on anything. Thousands of people are without power. I got his message, though. I'm lucky I didn't get pulled over coming here because I was going too fast for conditions. Patrol officers aren't anxious to stand there in this weather and issue tickets. What's up?"

She told him about the older lady who was now not ruled an accidental death as he toweled off his damp hair.

"Okay. That's interesting and makes me feel bad. Why didn't Hammett say anything to me?"

"It's his case. You know her. She follows the rules meticulously."

That was true enough, but might have been good information in a face-to-face conversation. "She and I have some trouble with communication now and then." His voice altered but it couldn't be helped. "My mother called to reschedule due to the weather. I have to admit I'm not looking forward to it so I said fine."

"I know you aren't, but maybe an open mind would be the better way to go?" Ellie looked comfortable on the couch in the flickering light, drinking a glass of wine.

"You have to admit my situation is quite different from yours."

She was close with her mother and sister. He didn't really even know his family.

"I admit if I was you I'd be more curious."

He loved the shape of her eyes. He got lost in that for a moment before he responded. "I think our life experiences are so different that maybe it is impossible for us to judge each other."

"I'm not judging you. I'm just weighing in."

He considered his response. "Curiosity, in my case, could be the worst idea ever. Those are skeletons I don't want grinning at me from the closet."

"Well, now that's a pleasant picture."

"My point."

"At least you aren't shivering any longer."

"It's damn cold out there. That's why I'm here."

No, it wasn't. He just couldn't ever live without her.


**It was time** to make the decision.

She'd felt it over and over again, maybe like the

rumbling in the distance that made the earth move just a little before an earthquake. Thunder and lightning wasn't just reserved for the outdoors.

Ellie stood in the flickering light and took off her shirt right in front of him.

Decision made, apparently. She just stripped it off her head and tossed it. Unfastened her bra and also dropped it onto the floor.

What the hell was she doing?

Maybe it was the chaotic weather and high-powered wind, maybe the way he'd come dashing to the rescue she hadn't needed, but he'd worried she did—maybe it was a growing realization that there was going to be a swing one way or the other and he was leaving the decision up to her.

He was Jason Santiago, so his position was clear—he didn't have much of a problem with that—but in his favor he hadn't pressured her to go to bed with him.

At all.

If he had, no way she would ever do this.

He understood completely.

To say he was astounded was an understatement. He was beyond blindsided, she could tell it and sympathize. She was blindsided herself.

Maybe it was all the sexual tension between them that needed to be resolved.

He didn't speak or move, just stared at the curves of her breasts in the flickering light. When he could finally speak, he said hoarsely, "Don't do this to me unless you mean it."

She wouldn't. "I don't do anything unless I mean it. I thought you knew that." She was admittedly self-conscious, uncertain about her decision, aware he could possibly be the worst choice of her life.

And she could be the worst decision of his life.

There were no promises. She wasn't even sure she wanted promises. She just knew this had been in the back of her mind for a long time and he'd been more straightforward than she had been about it.

Responsibility on both sides.

This was about as direct as it got.

"Ellie, I don't really walk around with protection. Do you—"

"Don't worry about it."

He accepted that without argument, and also accepted the invitation by getting to his feet and coming toward her with his unmistakable intensity. "I'm probably dreaming, right?"

"You said you were in love with me and asked what we were going to do about it. I guess this is what we're going to do about it."

"Finally make love? Good call."

She didn't respond, since he pulled her up against him and kissed her. Hard. That didn't really surprise her; he wasn't someone who wrote poems and sang under balconies. She was fine with action, since she really didn't expect—or want—chocolates and flowery notes.

But he did say "make love"?

"Bedroom." It wasn't a question, since he just backed her into the hallway that direction.

He didn't ask if she was in love with him, and she was grateful for that as he stripped off his clothes and pulled her close again on the bed.

She was afraid the answer would be yes.

He whispered in the dark, "Oh God, Ellie."

That was it. He didn't talk and she was perfectly fine with that, because if anyone could say the wrong thing it would be him, but while passionate wasn't a word she usually used, maybe it applied. It had never been in question that in general he was a physical person.

Definitely the case in bed. He was focused and intent but not selfish, and since she didn't know just what to expect, it was very enlightening. They connected in more ways than just like-minded thinking when it came to solving crimes. He wanted what he wanted, but he also wanted her to have what she wanted.

It was interesting that she thought maybe that would be the case all along.

Jason drifted to sleep afterward, maybe more relaxed than she'd ever seen him, one arm carelessly over his head, but the other one protectively over her.

They'd just crossed a bridge, and it had fallen into the river behind them. No going back. She finally drifted off as well.

## Chapter 18

The storms had rolled through.

He'd watched the lightning, mesmerized by the spectacle. The sky sizzled and cracked.

He'd also wanted to watch something else. The cameras were battery operated, but as far as he could tell, the whole city had been affected.

The bedroom was too dark. He enhanced the images but it didn't really help.

He leaned back and regrouped.

Some things were out of his control.

He couldn't see, but he could hear. He'd whispered to her and she'd made occasional telling sounds, and then it was all quiet.

Then they were asleep.

Pacing, he tried to decide what to do.

He'd changed the lock to the back door. She'd figure it out fast enough, but it wasn't like she unlocked it often from the outside. She went in through the garage or the front door.

*He could maybe take care of it all tonight, but then decided that was just too soon.*

*Santiago had crossed a serious boundary.*

**Ellie rolled over** and registered the tall male body next to her and had a serious moment. She was sure she'd made worse decisions in her life, but this could be up there. Jason had lived up to what she'd imagined; intense but not forceful, ardent but not aggressive, and to make it more romantic, they'd both kept their weapons within easy reach while a storm raged outside.

Interesting.

He was just so *him*. Of course he was instantly awake. He murmured, "I'm pretty sure I wouldn't mind doing last night again. And again. Keep the refrain going."

There were worse compliments she supposed. Ellie responded, "At least we survived the night. I thought the wind was going to blow us off the planet."

Talk about morning-after panic.

He sensed it too. His arm tightened around her, those blue eyes vivid as he lifted up on one elbow. "Ellie, we're fine. From a personal standpoint, I'm way better than fine."

"We slept together . . . what the hell is wrong with us? We just shouldn't have done that."

"What? Be human beings?"

Okay, he was being logical and she wasn't. "I know."

"Nothing I could name is wrong with us." He leaned over and kissed her neck. "I'm a fan of Ellie MacIntosh. And in case you were wondering, that isn't exactly what a guy wants to hear the morning after."

He had a good point there. It *had* been her suggestion.

Maybe it had been the storm, or his obvious sense of protectiveness, or even this unusual case that had her so off-balance she would even consider something like waking up naked in bed with Jason. The sexual tension between them had been growing for a long time, so the circumstances of being together even more than usual hadn't helped matters one bit.

"Bear with me." She actually moved closer. "I live in a male-dominated world. Now the next time Metzger looks at me directly and asks if we're sleeping together, I can't look right back and say no."

"Relax. I doubt he'll ask again."

"Why?"

"I know him." Santiago rolled to his back, taking her with him, and his tone was matter-of-fact. "He doesn't want the answer, Ellie. It doesn't really change anything. He's told me face-to-face he knows how I feel about you. I doubt he'd be happy it happened, but I also highly doubt he'd be surprised. I was the one who was surprised. In a really, really good way. You?"

He could be right. There was a direct way Jason approached things, and that was one of them. It wasn't she was really sorry about what had happened and it had been her decision, but it wasn't what you were supposed to do and they were cops. Rule one was no romantic involvement with your partner.

Major violation.

Not to mention the man had more issues than a third world country.

She needed to talk to Georgia Lukens, but maybe Georgia needed to talk to her since she was involved with Grasso. That was one complicated man who also had issues.

It was odd, but she felt comfortable, and Santiago was not a person to inspire comfort. Quite the opposite. "On a personal basis, I'm okay. On a professional one, not so sure."

"Repeat performance?" He touched her lightly. There was a side of him that didn't leap toward trust. There was no way, she reminded herself fiercely, she could possibly get truly involved with this man on an emotional level.

Sex. Sex was fine.

Love was something else.

Too late?

"I mean, there's still no power, so I can't watch television. What else is there to do?"

"Oh, there's a line no woman could resist." She jabbed him in the shoulder.

He grinned, unrepentant. "I take charming to a whole new level, I know."

"I'm not sure that's a level anyone should aspire to achieve, just for your information."

"Hmm." He tickled her bare shoulder. "About that repeat performance offer?"

She shouldn't. She just plain shouldn't for several reasons. Up and down she would have sworn Jason wasn't her type; far too intense, sophistication was just not in his vocabulary, his idea of an outdoor sport seemed to be drinking beer in a lawn chair, and . . . the list went on.

But she didn't refuse, which said a lot.

"I vote yes."

\*    \*    \*

**Jason and Grasso** did not strike gold at the supermarket. There was no power restored in a lot of parts of the city and gutters weren't handling the overflow.

The checker wasn't there either.

"She only works a few days a week." The service desk lady was trying to be helpful, but really wasn't. "She takes classes at a community college. Her shifts change depending on whether she has a test coming up. She's very serious about getting her degree. I don't think I've seen her all week."

The store manager was a little better in that he saw their badges and gave up Tammy's address with alacrity. "She's a good girl," he told them earnestly. "If she can help you, she will."

"Glad I'm wearing boots and not those thousand-dollar loafers you have on," Jason remarked as they had to wade through a small lake to get back to the truck.

Grasso shot him a suspicious look. "Thanks. You are in a cheerful mood today, at least for you. Just grateful you lived through the storm? I know I am. Any leaves from last fall sitting in someone's unraked yard ended up in my pool. I ate cereal for dinner and took a cold shower this morning, and I'm investigating the murder of a little old lady who did a favor for a stranger who probably turns out is a serial killer. I don't even want to talk about my wet shoes. I'm *not* cheerful. Why are you?"

No way Jason was going to say anything about his night with Ellie even to Grasso, so he merely remarked, "Considering the weather, I knew MacIntosh was safe enough and I got some sleep. Now and then I do crash. Last night I zoned. I learned in the military to sleep with one eye open, and trust me, that isn't real sleep. That's pretend sleep. Let's hope this Tammy is actually the one I talked to and is at home. At the time I asked about the flowers, I was just sniffing around, but not positive it was a murder investigation yet."

Her building ended up being a square modest collection of prefab apartments designed for people with modest income at best, and maybe government subsidized. Tammy answered the door in pajama bottoms and a sweatshirt and Jason wanted to tell her to never do that to a random knock when you are a young woman who lives alone and not expecting someone, but maybe he was just a jaded soul. He produced his badge. "I don't know if you remember me, but—"

"I remember." She nodded, eyes wide. "My boss called me because he started to worry maybe he shouldn't have given you my address without a court order or something. It's okay. I want to help. Come on in, but I warn you, it's a mess. Finals are coming up soon. I haven't done laundry in, like, two weeks."

So at least she was expecting them. That made him feel better. Her small apartment *was* a disaster and there were books open all over a generic desk, the coffee table, and empty scattered cans of diet soda pretty much everywhere. Grasso produced the picture. "Is this the woman who bought all of those tulips?"

Tammy studied the photograph and then nodded decisively. "That's her."

Pot of gold, right there. Jason asked, "You're sure?"

Tammy pointed at the picture. "She always wore pearls. She had that antique brooch thing on her jacket every single time she came in. I think I recognize that more than I recognize her. I made a comment on it once and she told me it belonged to her grand-mother."

It was absolutely the small kind of detail that made a difference in court. Jason could tell Grasso also felt the same flicker of not exactly what a person would call triumph, but confirmation anyway.

"That really does help us," Jason assured her truth-fully. "It's what we were looking for. If you remember anything else, please call."

"I will."

They squished back to the truck, Jason ruminating. "So he killed her to make sure she couldn't identify him and we've got that nailed."

"I think that's true."

"What an asshole . . . I'm always blown away by how a human being can be . . . well, less than human. Get into it with your neighbor over the fence line, or get pissed at the people who talk during the movie at the theater, but don't kill a little old lady that was nice to you. No neighbors saw anything?"

Grasso didn't seem any happier about his shoes, but they were his problem. "No one *I* talked to saw anything, and I talked to anyone in her neighborhood who would answer their door. Now that we tied it all together with a neat little bow, you guys better get on it. I have one imprint of an athletic shoe, but that's it as far as evidence goes."

"I love how everything seems to be my problem."

"That's just your perception, Santiago. Stop grum-bling. It's your problem by proxy. Your killer killed my little old lady and all because of his interest in your partner." Grasso's tone was somber when he added, "I'd really watch my back if I were you, because I bet there's a bull's-eye on it. I've said it to MacIntosh already."

Jason started the truck. "Yeah, well, I'm not as easy to kill as a young drunk girl or a pudgy middle-aged dock worker. Speaking of Ellie, she better have stayed put at her desk."

"I think maybe you should get over thinking you can tell her what to do."

"Oh, I can tell her, it just doesn't mean she'll listen to me." He glanced over after swerving around what appeared to be a clogged sewer drain because someone could swim in the pool around it. "You and Lukens. How's that going? I admit I was kind of surprised, but maybe she is your type."

"Meaning what?"

"I don't know. Just seems like it. Maybe it's the polished exterior but tough underneath. We've all shot people, so quite the gathering the other night. Lots in common. Great for conversation. That breaks the ice every time."

That comment wrung out a laugh. Grasso said, "I'm not sure I want to have that come up at a dinner party, but then again, I usually decline dinner parties anyway."

"I usually don't get invited, so I'm safe there."

"You had dinner with the governor, Santiago."

That was true. "Well, okay, can't deny that, but even though the food was good, the entire time I wished I was eating a burger and drinking lukewarm beer while sitting on my couch watching a Packers game. I'm going to order a personalized license plate next time that has Philistine on it."

"I'm astounded you know what a Philistine is,"

Grasso observed dryly as they parked and then walked to the building.

"Thanks for the vote of confidence. By the way, my feet are perfectly dry. I'm astounded you wore those shoes. I might *be* smarter."

"All right, you win that one."

He didn't win all the way.

It turned out Ellie absolutely hadn't listened to him. She wasn't at her desk, there was no note, just her empty chair and a closed computer. Jason said tightly to Grasso, "No need to worry about the killer getting to MacIntosh, I'm going to strangle her myself."

**"So . . . I don't** even know how to put this except bluntly, and I wouldn't share this information with anyone else, but I slept with him."

"Jason? I'm not surprised," Georgia poured from a pitcher into two glasses filled with ice. "But I am curious why you are."

Ellie dropped into her usual chair. She was curious too.

"He isn't exactly every girl's dream guy. His past alone would make anyone consider they'd made a very questionable decision. It's stupid." She picked up her iced tea. "I've risked my job on a man who is so frigging out there . . . oh lord, you see? I just said frigging. He's *not* a good influence."

"I happen to know him and he would stand between you and a speeding bullet. I think he's already done that. He has challenges, but we all do. If you are looking for the perfect man, Grantham would have been a good choice. Quiet, considerate, absolutely independent both financially and emotionally. Consider that last part. Take the physical out of it."

"I have. For one thing, he's in New York. Physical is impossible."

"Ellie, if you wanted to do so, you could go there."

It was true and she'd thought about it, but then decided against it. "It would probably make things worse for both of us."

"Because you feel you'd be pursuing a relationship that isn't going anywhere?"

That was a truth she'd come to acknowledge months ago. "I don't feel rejected . . . I just think in the end we weren't right for each other. We wanted to be and I can say I know we both tried, but you are making a big mistake if you try to force something too much."

"I don't disagree, but my opinion isn't gold. I think the issue we need to address is Jason Santiago really is going through a transitional time right now. It is a leap for him to care for someone else. You are getting my perception only."

That perception was the reason she was there. "Bryce had been burned before so he was also transitional before he got the break he wanted and headed off to New York. Is this *my* problem?"

Georgia said, "If you are asking me if I think you are drawn to damaged men, no I don't. I wouldn't describe either of them as damaged. Wary would be a better word, and who could blame them? They've both been burned in the past, Bryce Grantham by his ex-wife and Jason Santiago by his mother walking out the door in his childhood. You are on the wary side yourself. I think you are confident and attractive and the same type of men are drawn to you. That isn't comforting when it comes to this killer."

"Keep talking." Ellie said it grimly.

"I think you probably would intimidate a lot of men just because of your profession alone. You don't have that problem with Jason because it is common ground. My impression is that Bryce might have thought about committing again but the hesitation was on your part, he sensed it, and then fate intervened. He had to choose, but the book deal was a certainty and you weren't. So he chose."

Ellie said ironically, "Just in case it didn't work out."

"What would you have done in his place? From what you told me, he can still work his other job from there too, so the logical choice would be to go."

She was done discussing her personal life, because while it had been rocky before last night, it was a true mess now and all of it her fault. Santiago had called twice and left messages, and finally she'd texted him back and simply said: *I'm fine, I'm with Lukens.*

*I'll pick you up. Her place or the office?*

*I'll drive myself and meet you later at your apartment.*

*No way. Give me a time. We'll get your car tomorrow.*

*Office.*

Ellie gave a heartfelt sigh of frustration and looked at Georgia. "Sorry about that. I hate people constantly on their cell phones. Jason needs to get over this sudden quest to keep track of me every minute. I appreciate the concern and I'm not going to claim I'm not frightened, because we have no idea who this killer is or what he might do next, but I'm a police officer not a rock star who needs a bodyguard. Trust me, I'm paying attention."

Dr. Lukens merely lifted her brows. "He's got a lot

invested in your welfare. You are his partner and apparently now his lover, and if I may remind you, someone out there is killing people just to impress you. Besides, I don't think it is all that sudden when it comes to his interest."

"I talked to the FBI profiler again. Montoya says he dislikes the fast pace. Most serial killers operate over time and are methodical. The impulsive ones get caught fairly quickly, but some never get caught at all. Santiago thinks he's calling himself Jack for a reason if our jogger is a true suspect. That name is well known to represent someone who got away with it if you consider London in the late 1800s. From a psychological viewpoint, what do you think?"

Lukens obviously considered the question seriously. "I don't do your job, but maybe that theory has some validity. Association exists. If indeed, though, he's a part of the equation. He could just be someone who came along, met your victim and they decided to go running together, and his name really is Jack."

It was possible. "My take on it too. He also could be someone who should be locked up in a prison somewhere with the key to his cell buried in a padlocked box."

"Maybe."

"That isn't a 'maybe' right there if he's the one. Or an asylum. As odd as this sounds, I understand somebody killing a person because of a sex crime so they don't want to get caught, but this one is all over the place. He has no personal interest, or at least that we can see."

"Except in you and Santiago."

"Santiago is worried it's me and I'm worried it's him."

"It might be both of you." Georgia definitely looked reflective. "Don't sell my theory short here. He's intrigued by you, but also trying to tick off Santiago. You are operating under the assumption that people think the same as we do. I can tell you, they don't. He knows you in some way. It could be someone you work with."

It took a minute, but Ellie admitted haltingly, "That's certainly has occurred to us. I've thought cop. I've even said it out loud. We've also thought military or ex-military. This person knows too much about how to move around and not be seen. He's visited my condo on numerous occasions now and no one I've asked has seen a thing. I think the people he murdered trusted him in some way. Ask yourself why they'd put themselves in that position."

"A police officer is possible, or a doctor, dentist, or lawyer? Someone that you should be able to trust with your well-being? He could present himself in many different ways."

Ellie mused, "All along we've been puzzled about how random the victims are. I'm starting to think once again there's a tie of some kind. I never thought of health professional. I'll check and see if maybe they all visited the same office. We were originally thinking it was the same bar, but the older victims I can't see in a college scene, so I think that's a dead end. They also were definitely not runners."

"I will say it is puzzling to me. Carl is pretty convinced the cases are tied to his now."

Ellie considered her friend/therapist with equanimity. "You know, we have the most bizarre friendship ever, right? I meet you because I'm investigating a double murder and now you are pretty involved with the MPD homicide division, including dating one of them, apparently. How is that going?"

"Carl Grasso is an interesting man."

"I grant you that."

"I like interesting." Georgia's smile was reserved.

"He qualifies."

"He does. I'm undecided on how it will turn out, but I guess if you take no chances in this life you will get nowhere. I think you and I are in the same boat right now. Grantham was pretty grounded. Santiago is not."

"And Grasso?"

"Professional opinion? Not grounded either."

Someone knocked on the office door without pushing the button on the light. Georgia said lightly, "I think your ride might be here."

**Chapter 19**

He visited the grave.

There had been flowers there but the storm had decimated them, scattering forlorn petals everywhere. He wasn't at all worried about being seen, he had a good reason to be there. There was an explanation anyone would accept.

Not that at this time of the morning he expected to see anyone. The mist drifted by in thin veils and the air smelled like turned soil and green grass.

There was no sense of melancholy, no remorse, no feeling at all as far as he could tell. He stood there and listened to the singing birds trill in the background, his hands in his pockets.

That first obsession had been like a slow-spreading disease. It wasn't like he didn't recognize it wasn't entirely normal at the time, but then again, define normal.

It was probably a solid truth that the line between normal and abnormal was very blurry.

*He studied the gravestone with complete detachment.*

*Just . . . nothing.*


**Metzger slapped down** the roster. "I don't think he's a cop, but here's the list and the access code. You two can run it, but I think I only hire the best, so feel free to check. We screen carefully. I'm surprised either of you two goofballs made it."

As they walked back toward their desks, Jason said under his breath, "Goofballs? Where the hell did that come from? I thought we were angels with magic air under our wings and he just said goofballs. I'm in shock."

He was joking. Metzger was tough, but he was protective of the department's reputation as good clean cops who worked hard to keep the city safe.

"That's because you would have said something much worse." MacIntosh was studying the list already. "It was a term of endearment. He was being nice for him. All I think we need to do is a profile of physical characteristics and see if any of the witnesses can identify an officer."

"They'd better not." Jason meant it. "I take my job seriously. I don't want it to be one of us or anyone remotely associated with this or any other department. In a closet somewhere I have a white hat. I can't find it most of the time, but I have it."

"I'd love to see that hat." Ellie, looking young in a light green sweater that set off her hazel eyes, punched up her computer. "Let's narrow it down. Height, age, and coloring as components. That should make the search easier."

It did. Only seven of them were young, fit, and had brown hair.

"What about Wright?" She squinted at the screen. "He matches the profile."

"He might," he agreed, leaning over her shoulder, enjoying the fresh scent of her hair. But then shook his head. He was doing his best to not touch her when other people could see them, but hell, he really wanted to even if it was just resting his hand on her arm. "I know him and I can't see it. I realize people have been fooled before, but not him. I don't feel it."

To her credit, she moved on, accepting his intuitive verdict. "Moreland?"

"He isn't smart enough."

"Oh, that's nice to know about a fellow police officer. Khara?"

"Let me put this nicely, he wouldn't send *you* flowers. Maybe he'd send them to me, but not you. He's really a nice guy, but you aren't his preferred gender."

She caught on. "Oh, I didn't realize. Fine, okay, but maybe he just considers me competition?"

"He's not in the closet, but he doesn't advertise it. He's a nice guy, but I don't think I'm his type, and you sure aren't either. I'm looking it over and it isn't anyone on that list, Ellie. We aren't searching in the right place."

"Great. That just leaves the whole world, but in a way that's a relief. I swear Metzger would be furious with us if it started an IA investigation, even if we were right."

"He'd go along with it, though. But we'd have to be really convinced and I'm not. This morning I made calls and no dice on the dentist or doctor connection either. None of the victims saw the same medical professional. Not even a match on any of them."

"That's disappointing. I thought Lukens had an angle."

"No clue on the identity of the last victim. I'm worried she was a lady living alone and no one will miss her for a while."

"We aren't exactly batting a thousand, are we? No wonder Metzger is on edge." Ellie sat back. "I'm on edge myself. Okay, new game plan. What is it? Enlighten me. I'm not coming up with a thing."

"I don't know," Jason admitted. "I wish I did. Grasso's case is essentially our case at this point. His murder is tied to us, but won't give us any insight. She's a casualty only."

"That's once again not a cheerful thought."

"But I'm thinkin' pretty accurate. Someone somewhere has to know one meager fact we can investigate."

"If they do, they are keeping it to themselves."

"I realize that." Jason rubbed his forehead. "Okay, let's go over the chalkboard again. We have four very different people murdered and left in various parks."

"I'm aware."

"No clues that lead anywhere."

"We are still casting out those hooks without bait."

"I don't disagree."

"I told her about last night."

"Her?"

"Lukens."

It took him a moment.

*Well, shit.* His private life wasn't very private. "Not a moment-by-moment description, I hope."

"Those kinds of comments are what have me questioning my sanity."

He, of course, made it worse. "I was kind of hoping on a scale of one to ten I was an eleven, but—"

Ellie gave him a disgusted look. "I swear I'm poisoning your food tonight. They will never find your body."

He truly did try to look contrite. "I'm sorry. What did Lukens have to say about *that*?"

"I'm under the impression she thinks it isn't the smartest thing I've ever done, but maybe not the dumbest. I *was* of the same mind. If you'd stop hovering over me and move about three feet away to the chair by my desk, I would be a lot more comfortable. I think everyone is watching us."

He did it, but thought she was being too sensitive. "I just don't believe our relationship is that interesting to anyone but us. We work together, so we are together a lot. That's the story."

"There's together and *together*."

That was a point he couldn't argue. He stopped himself from pointing out he didn't care what they thought. He did what she asked and crossed his forearms on her desk. "Could you relax?"

"Maybe if we had a solid lead."

"Back to the case? I meant about us."

"No, I can't." Ellie looked away. "I don't sleep with anyone casually, which indicates it meant something and I have no idea what it meant. That is throwing me off. Give me space."

Fair enough. "I don't sleep with anyone casually either, so the word doesn't apply to either one of us. Let's solve this damn thing so we can move on to whatever is going to happen next."

"Not to mention make people stop dying."

"That's why we're here."

"He might know them another way."

"You are thinking . . . what? The gym or something? Sorry, I can't see the older victims doing that any more than I can see them out for a morning run."

"Maybe at church? It seems all wrong to meet a murderer at church, but the world is a very interesting place and stranger things have happened."

"That serial killer in Kansas that got away with it for thirty years was an elder in his church. Maybe we should check that out." It wasn't a bad idea. "All kinds of people can attend. They don't ask questions, you just show up."

"I'll call the families and see if we can make a connection."

"I'll check missing person reports. Maybe someone is worried about the drowning victim." He stood. "My place tonight? What kind of food would you like to poison? Think it over."

**It was a** bust all around.

No clear church ties, no missing person report that matched the last homicide, and Ellie was feeling frustrated and ineffective, not to mention confused on a personal level.

So what she needed to do was head north and think.

Not an option.

Maybe when this was all over.

The question was whether to just invite Jason to go with her, or if she wanted the argument if she didn't.

There would be one. She opted out, stopping by his desk. "I'm tired and hungry."

"Invitation or ultimatum?"

"Just telling you my plans."

He shut off his computer. "I'm inviting myself as your resident bodyguard."

"We won't have the most pleasant dinner conversation," she warned.

"I consider that par for the course."

He would. In other ways, a little distance might not hurt. Unlike Bryce, who had told her outright he felt he was crowding her, Jason Santiago was never going to offer any such apology. His straightforward approach never left you in doubt of where he stood.

"Fine. I'll meet you at your apartment."

He didn't agree. "I'll walk you to your car. We'll go together."

"I don't need—"

"We have hours to argue," he interrupted. "Let's not spoil that pleasure by doing it now. If we're going, let's just get out of here for a while."

She couldn't disagree with that. "I want to walk back through the parks where the bodies were found."

"Sounds like a cheerful date. Be right there."

True to his word it took him only a couple of minutes and then they headed toward her condo so she could pick up her mail and clean clothes. The hobo existence was getting old.

Blackie the cat was on her front porch again, right beside another long-stemmed rose. This one was a deep pink and it really spoiled her day, which hadn't been that great. Jason was already swearing before he even got out of the car and snatched it up.

"You're fucking kidding me? It looks like you've had a visitor again, and this is exactly why I was so ticked you came home alone yesterday. Ellie, you need to face it that you're being stalked. Not just a little but a lot." He got out his phone and took a picture of the rose. "When we catch him, do me a favor and don't leave me alone in an interrogation room with him. I don't need to be slapped with police brutality charges."

It didn't thrill her either, but she had to say, "Giving up your white hat would be a bad thing. Not that I'm positive you really have one."

"I did make that up."

At least he still had a sense of humor. Hers was starting to go south. "Give me a few minutes. All I need."

"After I check inside."

"I'm perfectly capable of doing that."

"I know you are, but I'm not capable of sitting in a car while you go in there alone. Think of me."

He wasn't capable of it, so she'd go ahead and concede that. The sum of his parts did not include letting a female go into a potentially dangerous situation alone.

She liked that about him.

So she let him go first yet again. While he roamed around, she took out a shirt, two sweaters and a pair of jeans, and anything else essential, and dropped it all into a tote bag and headed for the door. It was almost as record time as Jason's packing.

When she went out the door, he was talking to her neighbor, who was once again retrieving his errant cat. If she wanted to be popular it was much better having a cat around than drawing the attention of a serial killer. She liked Blackie a lot more than the killer. The feline was more than welcome.

"I asked Nichols to please watch out for anyone near your house." Jason fastened his seat belt as they both got into the vehicle. "Any car, *anything.* He seems to get it. He said he'd asked his wife to be really careful and they'd talked with the kids already about 'bad' strangers after the smoke bomb thing. I wonder how many parents had that conversation with their kids after my car exploded in a parking lot that is a school bus destination. Now I feel like crap. Maybe I should move. We could both move. I hear Siberia is nice."

Ellie understood. "*You* didn't blow up your car. I hear Siberia is darned chilly. Don't say I didn't warn you. I think Siberia must have some good points, but isn't it just too cold to go around killing people? We'd be unemployed."

"Ah shit, nothing ever works out. There goes my little slice of paradise."

She carefully backed out of the drive. "How do you think I feel that thanks to me my neighbors have to talk to their children about bad strangers?"

"They should do that anyway," Santiago pointed out pragmatically. "Maybe having you next door is doing them a favor and making their kids more aware this world can be an unfriendly place sometimes. Everyone needs to learn that eventually. It's better early than too late."

Considering his childhood, he was telling the plain truth from a point of view that had some heft behind it. "True enough. There's that place on Appleton that serves Scandinavian food. I need some comfort in Swedish meatballs and mashed potatoes. I vote we stop there for dinner."

"Fine with me. By the time we get there I'd eat a piece of shredded tire from the side of the road. Thanks to your propensity for Scandinavian cuisine, the sum total of things in my refrigerator right now are outdated milk, beer if I remembered to put it in there, and a jar of pickled herring. I need to ask Lukens to evaluate why I like that stuff. It's all wrong. I don't really eat much fish, I'm not Swedish or Norwegian, and yet I like it. The next thing I know is I'll be opening a can of sardines." He sounded peeved.

Ellie laughed, and that felt good because that rose was an unwelcome grim addition to her day. "I apologize for expanding your cultural horizons. Maybe we can go fishing sometime soon and you can try freshly caught pan-fried walleye. The bigger lakes don't still have ice. The Wisconsin River is clear and beautiful to paddle. I have a canoe."

"I know a woman who owns a canoe and a man who owns a yacht? Seriously?" Santiago shook his head. "I never cease to be amazed at life. That sounds like a date. What *did* Grasso have to say?"

She sped up to keep with the flow of traffic. "He'd be there if anything happened, but he'd really appreciate it if we could crack this case."

**Chapter 20**

They weren't there.

He'd watched them come and go. It was a mission to make sure Detective MacIntosh understood he was in charge. He'd taken the time to dismantle the security sensor for the back door when he changed the lock, which had actually been a piece of cake because he'd had a technician show him exactly how to do it.

People felt safe but they really weren't from a determined, skillful predator.

Detective Santiago thought he was tough. He had a street kid edge to him that was familiar because he'd seen it many times. He'd have to be taken swiftly and by surprise and absolutely not given a single chance to defend himself. Planning it was taking some time, but the purest pleasures always did.

Her kitchen was cleaner than his by far, no dishes in the sink, the counters shining, towel neatly folded over the handle of the oven. He checked the cupboards until he found a vase, filled it with water, and put a rose in it.

He left it on the nightstand by her bed.

*  *  *

**She was right** about the meatballs. Jason ate his and the rest of Ellie's once she was finished.

Maybe he needed a vacation.

"I need a glass of wine." She toed out of her shoes. "And my warm pajamas and fuzzy robe. I told you it would be cold tonight."

"I used to ride my bike to school in blizzard conditions. Don't get all cocky and think Milwaukee boys can't handle this stuff. My old man forgot to pay the heating bill often enough that I slept with about four extra blankets."

"Was it that bad?" Her voice was soft.

It was the first time she'd ever asked him directly. Jason wasn't exactly sure how to respond. Kate had grilled him on his childhood, Lukens had asked some probing questions, but no one had asked so simply. He shook his head. "It depends on your definition of bad, I guess. He never really intended harm, but did his best as he knew it. I'm going to have a beer. I'll open the wine."

"I'll be right back."

Subject closed. Good. He found the glasses, thanked the stars above for his cleaning lady, and opened the wine Ellie had brought. When she emerged wearing patterned pajama pants and the famed pink robe, he handed her a full glass. "Don't worry about a coaster. I never do. I define this place as urban lived in."

She settled into a chair. "I chose the condo because I can't seem to commit yet to living in a city. I'm pretty used to woods and water. And a fireplace. I admit I love a wood fire."

"Aren't there bears? I can picture a hungry one by the woodpile just waiting for me."

"You always overestimate how attractive you are. Who says you are invited?"

"A personal fault, but if I can be excused from the bear camp, I think that shows intelligence instead of conceit."

"You can think that."

The banter might have gone on except her phone rang. She glanced at it. "Unknown number."

"Let me answer it." He didn't wait but just took the phone from her hand. "This is Detective Santiago. MacIntosh isn't available."

The bastard hung up. It was her phone, so instead of chucking it against the wall, Jason handed it back. "He didn't like me on the other end at all. It was him. Just an educated guess."

"I'm furious he has my number."

"I just hope he isn't going to kill anyone else as per his usual pattern."

"Don't even say that."

"We're both thinking it now." He tipped back his beer. It wasn't that he didn't care, it was just the waiting. Until a crime was committed—another one—they could hardly anticipate what the killer would do. He wouldn't sleep tonight.

"I have a chair like your couch up north." Ellie observed it quietly. "It used to belong to my father. Not really ugly but broken in. The good news for you is he spilled beer on it all the time, so don't feel nervous. He fell asleep watching television, can in hand, because he thought it was so comfortable. My mother wanted to get rid of it because of the memories, so I took it."

It was nice to picture that trip, and even better she pictured him going along.

"I'd settle right in. He sounds like a man after my own heart. If dozing off holding a beer can was an art form I'd be Picasso or da Vinci. I've never asked, but what happened to him?"

"My father?"

"I'm pretty sure I know what happened to the other two I just mentioned. History was never my strong point, but I paid some attention. Yes, your father."

It took a second and another sip of wine. "Heart attack. He was pretty fit too because he loved to play tennis and golf. It came out of nowhere." Her expression changed just enough Jason could tell the memory was still painful.

Sentimentality was not high on his skill set list, but he at least understood it to the extent that if he'd had a loving father he expected he would miss him also. "I wish I'd have felt something when I learned the man who raised me passed on to wherever he went. I didn't care, one way or the other. I thought I should . . . but I just didn't, and I finally decided that it didn't really say anything about me, but sure said a lot about him. We were like wolves, living in the same den. He should have had a plaque that said Stay Out of My Face."

Ellie sat up. "Speaking of such things, aren't we supposed to go to dinner at your mother's house tomorrow?"

"Yeah." He tried to sound casual, but then gave up. He was very bad at casual. "Look, I'm not sure I want to know my real father. The man has done prison time. And I'm still pissed at my mother. She's made some pretty questionable decisions in her life if you ask me. I'm not sure I want to sit all warm and cozy over a hunk of meat loaf with either one of them."

"I like meat loaf well enough. Did you ask her what we could bring?"

"I have no clue what we're having. I made that up. Ellie, really? I don't even know these people. I'll bring beer and you can bring wine. I suspect we'll both need it."

"That's your call, of course. What does Lukens have to say about it?" Her tone held only neutral inquiry. "Tell me or don't, that's also your call. But we are talking about it, so if you want to comment, go ahead."

The cozy familiar atmosphere, comfortable couch, the quiet outside was calm and serene and he had a cold drink and a beautiful woman looking at him . . . if there wasn't a murderer out there, life would be good, but this wasn't bad.

He said, "She doesn't give opinions too often since she wants you to come up with your own answers. I used to think therapy was pure bunk and maybe it is, but it does make you think out loud."

"She's asks the right questions."

"I agree. Ellie, I'm not good at talking about stuff like this. "

She looked away, accepting the change in subject. "Sorry. I just wanted a break. The average case where they do terrible things and we go find them is bad enough. This is getting to me. He's . . . sinister."

"Hopefully that last call was traced."

"I don't think it was long enough."

"I don't either."

He was so much more comfortable with the case than with talking about his dysfunctional family. He wasn't even sure he considered them family. "I'm thinking this over and I agree one connection is going to make the dominos fall. This might sound funny, but I honestly think I have a suspect in mind, I just don't know who it is yet."

"That isn't funny, it's ridiculous."

"Um, can I remind you I don't have small bleating sheep all over my pajamas? Now *that's* ridiculous."

"You don't have on pajamas."

"I'm kind of counting on that staying the case and persuading you to take yours off."

She didn't say no or yes, but just took another sip of wine.

Then Ellie took off her pajamas.


**Decisions to be** made and she'd already made some of them. Ellie made coffee that would probably not be strong enough for Jason and took it to the chair by the window. The floor was still cold, but the apartment was warm. Sunrise was just glimmering over the tops of the trees and houses.

Was this just really great sex and for once not being the good girl?

No, she had to grudgingly admit. How could she *like* Jason Santiago?

She did, though. He had an unswerving purpose she related to, and while his methods weren't always by the book, they were definitely in place for the people he protected.

She curled her legs under her and looked out at the view, just sipping and thinking about how much the series of murders in Lincoln County had changed her life. If it hadn't been for the Northwoods Killer case she wouldn't have been offered the opportunity in Milwaukee or met Bryce Grantham. Quite frankly, if it wasn't for her, more girls would have tragically disappeared. She'd diligently worked that case from the minute a young Realtor had been reported missing at the time and she realized there had been other missing person reports that could be tied together. It had taught her a lot about investigating homicides. She'd been the one to pick up on the pattern, and she'd been the one to hunt down the killer. The case had caught national attention as had several of the cases she'd worked since taking the job in Milwaukee. She'd been contacted by several police departments as a result, but had no desire to leave Wisconsin. If she had, she would have more seriously considered moving to New York with Bryce.

Maybe. It would have been a bad call in retrospect.

Bryce was really no longer in the picture, but she'd learned a lot from that experience as well. They'd both picked their jobs above each other, and she still loved him, but apparently not enough. They were definitely still friends and he e-mailed regularly, just to check in and to update her on his life. There was a part of her that wondered if he'd ever fully put his bitter divorce behind him.

Get over thinking about the past, she told herself sternly. She should probably sell her rustic house up north, but by renting the condo, she could keep it as a getaway when she just needed quiet woods and an escape from the city. Luckily, there were enough management companies for vacation properties. She had hired one to check in on the place on a regular basis and it wasn't too expensive.

Playing Russian roulette with her life was how she viewed her current situation, but she was doing it anyway, juggling homicide detectives and killers and worrying over her mother's battle with breast cancer. She was relieved the latter seemed to be going well, but only cautiously. Hope could be a deceitful friend.

"Do I smell coffee?" Jason came out of the bedroom barefoot in faded jeans and a white T-shirt, hair rumpled. His weapon was holstered, but he even slept with it in reach.

She said dryly, "It won't put hair on your chest like yours, but I set out a mug anyway. I'm comfortable, so you'll have to help yourself."

"A chest like mine?" He looked down, being his irreverent usual self. "What's wrong with it?"

"Like your coffee would, smartass. Just get your own."

"Bachelor cops are fairly self-sufficient." He poured himself a cup and wandered straight to his beloved couch. "Damn, I actually slept. It didn't hurt being right next to you. Have I mentioned your hair smells really good?"

"Yes." She wasn't even close to being ready to talk to him about that. "Speaking of bachelor cops, nothing about another murder," she told him. "I checked my messages. Maybe he's being kind and letting us take a weekend off."

That familiar moody look on his face took over. "You're an optimist. I don't suffer from that problem."

No, he didn't. His dark side bothered her, but everyone had issues.

Ellie said, "Let's plan our first fishing trip so I can forget about roses and parks while we drink our coffee anyway. Sometimes a little distance helps. No news is good news. Let's leave it there for ten minutes."

"I don't know about fishing. That spider thing—"

"I've never seen one up here, so relax. Didn't I say Indiana? For heaven's sake, I've seen you pull a gun and shoot without blinking. Even if there was one lurking in wait behind the door, I think you could handle the spider situation."

"Don't underestimate my cowardice. Man, I hate spiders and bowling shoes. I hope this fishing thing works out or I'll have to climb Everest or something. No, strike that. I hate being cold."

"I've noticed. You gripe about it all the time, but yet live in Wisconsin."

He shrugged. "I was born here. I'm capable of un-reasonable loyalty."

"Unreasonable loyalty? Never heard that one."

He patted the couch. "Like I feel toward this piece of furniture. It doesn't match anything else, but unrea-sonable loyalty makes me want to keep it. I stay in Wisconsin because I love this state. It isn't all I know, since I was in the military—hell, I was stationed in Hawaii for a while—but it's home. I suppose I could do Minnesota in a pinch. Michigan would work if it was the Upper Peninsula, but I'd rather be right frick-ing here."

She was going to fall out of *her* chair laughing. "I haven't had enough coffee for this intellectual dis-cussion."

"This isn't coffee." He peered into his cup. "This is brown water."

She'd already known he'd make a comment. "When we trapped the killer in our last big investigation, you were the bait; maybe I should go there this time."

"Be the bait? No." The refusal was emphatic. "I thought we were going to take ten minutes not to talk about it. Subject closed."

"You don't get to make that decision all by your-self. This is *our* investigation."

"I'm sticking by it. Yes, I do. Subject is closed. Do you want more brown water? I'm getting up for an-other cup."

"Feel free to make a pot of the sludge you like."

"Sludge? I just want it to get my attention."

"Please tell me you own a flannel shirt."

He looked at her like she'd just lost her mind. "That's an interesting switch of the conversation. I don't know if I own one. I'm kind of doubting it. Why?"

"Men who fish have to have flannel shirts."

"Hard-and-fast rule?"

"Hard and fast."

"Come to think of it, when I accidentally stumble across a fishing show, they all are wearing flannel shirts. I think I have a denim one, will that do? There is a hole in one sleeve."

Ellie laughed at his mock hopeful expression. "Okay, but if fishing proves to be the manly hobby you embrace, then there's a flannel shirt in your future. I think you'll enjoy it. It's a hobby where you can drink beer. At least in a canoe. I believe it's frowned upon in motorized boats."

He surprised her and didn't make a lewd comment about another manly hobby he embraced, but got up for another cup of coffee. Before this change in their relationship, he never would have let that opportunity slide.

Never.

## Chapter 21

"I'm meeting someone. She'll ask for Ted."

The hostess nodded and gave him a friendly smile as she grabbed two menus.

The restaurant was crowded and noisy, and he was seated at a table by a window overlooking the street, which wasn't his first choice, but objecting would draw attention to it, so he just smiled at the hostess and sat down.

She wore a blue dress.

He liked it. It looked good on her, when normally she went for frumpy and plain. He'd wondered why once or twice because she really wasn't bad looking, but that wasn't his concern.

She'd flirted with him frequently enough that he'd made a decision, though this one was on the reckless side and he was a methodical man.

This victim could be directly tied back to him much easier than the others.

Maybe if it hadn't been for what he always thought of as "the accident" back when he was in college, *none of any of this would have happened and she wouldn't be sitting there ordering a cosmopolitan with vanilla vodka and cherry liqueur the house called a red sunset.*

*The sun was certainly going to go down on her this night.*

**Jason was eating** a grilled cheese sandwich when Fergusson walked up, and at a glance he could tell that was one unhappy man. Grasso was with him. "I want to see you and MacIntosh in my office in ten minutes."

It was an educated guess. "Let me call it: A murder last night made you think of me."

"Every time I think of you I consider murder, Santiago, but in this case I'm not the one you are unsuccessfully looking for. We have an immediate ID on this one: Regina Juno, elementary schoolteacher."

"Oh Jesus." Suddenly the sandwich didn't have much appeal. "I want to nail this guy to a wall."

"I'll hand you the hammer." Grasso sounded sincere. "She was with a friend. Apparently it was a date and she was nervous about it, and so she'd asked the friend to come to the restaurant in case she needed an excuse for a hasty exit. All seemed to go fine, so no exit needed. She said they were laughing and talking. Now the friend can't get ahold of her and there's a woman of her exact description right down to her dress in a park down by the lake. The cause of death is pretty obvious since she had a plastic bag over her head. That also makes manner of death really easy. She was stabbed first, and probably bleeding out when she was suffocated."

"In a park again. What the hell," he muttered.

Fergusson said, "There was the usual note on her wrist too. It said: *You'll be mine*. This particular killer is on a rampage."

Jason had to fight the chill that went through his entire body. "That's not very comforting. Well shit. I don't want to tell Ellie this."

"Too bad, this is her case too. The media consists of bloodhounds. They are really starting to get going on these cases. It doesn't help that someone leaked information that Grasso's case is linked to these murders. Ten minutes."

Grasso watched the chief detective walk away. "It could have been anyone who saw the vase of tulips sitting on MacIntosh's desk. I'm in the same position you are. At least in my gang murder I know who did it, I just can't get a prosecutor to go for an indictment because everyone is lying left and right. In your case, I have about zero except a bunch of graphs and charts about the likelihood she was murdered. The family of my victim is calling me almost every hour now. I want to promise we're making progress but can't in good conscience lie to them. I repeat that we're working on it like I'm a trained parrot. "

So much for the relaxation of fishing. Jason wasn't at all happy either. "Yeah, we're screwed right now. Can the friend describe this date?"

"Tall, fairly young, she'd guess about thirty, brown hair. Said his name was Ted and claimed to be a financial guy for a company called Nevis Investments. I'm running down the list now of anyone who is named Ted and works for them. I suspect it's a dead end because he wasn't telling the truth, but do you want to hear the kicker?"

Ellie came up then, holding her phone, and immediately her gaze sharpened. "Fergusson just called me. What?"

"Oh, you'll find out." Jason said to Grasso, "I don't know if I do want to know the kicker, but go ahead."

"He signed this one. The Observer."

Ellie went still. "This one? We have *another* body?"

"You have to be kidding me. Okay, okay, I'm taking this all in, keep going. He's really making a name for himself, isn't he?"

Grasso agreed and his voice was grim. "I'm afraid so."

**Ellie didn't need** to be a detective to figure out that this one was bad as they walked down the hall. "I was downstairs getting a file. Clue me in, because while none of us are happy, I'm sure Fergusson and Metzger are taking a lot of heat."

"Yeah, they are." Jason's expression said they were about to inherit that heat themselves. She felt the pressure; that wasn't in question, not just for the victims, but for herself. She couldn't even live in her own home at the moment. If they thought for a minute she wasn't thinking about this every waking second and throw in a few nightmares, they were all wrong.

"Don't even dare say I told you so."

Why did she even bother?

"I told you so."

Ellie wasn't fooled. "What did he write on the victim this time?"

He didn't want to tell her, that much was obvious. "Ever thought about getting a big dog? Maybe like a Rottweiler or German shepherd? Name him Killer or something like that. Feed him raw meat, walk around with him on a leash."

"No. I work long hours, so I can't take proper care of a dog, and I carry a gun. Anyway, I'd be more inclined toward Cuddles or maybe Sweet Pea as a name. Just tell me before we walk in there. What did it say?"

Santiago did have a redeeming quality or two and honesty was one of them. "*You'll be mine*. Kind of like a Valentine theme this time."

"The Observer?"

"That's what Grasso said. You heard him."

"What does that mean?" She thought it over. "Okay, so maybe a voyeur of some kind. We have another blind clue. He could still be talking about you."

He didn't agree at all. "Not one flower on my doorstep. It's you. Maybe we could find you a nice desert island to stay on until we catch him. Wear a bikini and text me pictures please."

"Don't count on that." She wouldn't be human if it wasn't at least a little disturbing, but no way was she going to hide. "We have a solid description of him and I close my curtains when I get dressed, for the record."

"Maybe that's what has him so pissed off. I know I'd be disappointed. Anyway, that description part is true more than ever. A friend of the latest victim saw him clearly, but it is all very circumstantial, even if she could pick him out of a lineup. The other people won't be helpful. Yes, he fits the profile of the helpful jogger and the last person the latest victim was seen with, but unless we have something more to prove he killed anyone, taking someone on a date and jogging through a park are not crimes. We need physical evidence, and he isn't leaving it behind, the bastard."

"It is inconsiderate of him. Maybe when this autopsy comes in, we'll have more."

"More than nothing isn't too much to ask." Santiago didn't look happy. "We have more witnesses than any case I've ever worked, but we can't pin him down. Why?"

"You're the one that keeps telling me he's going to mess up and give us a prime clue."

They stopped outside Fergusson's door, looking at each other. "He will, but he's taking his own time about it. He's leaving you gifts and calling on the phone, writing messages on the victims, showing up at the crime scenes; he's one ballsy guy and it seems to be working for him and not so great for us. This time he stabbed her first, but suffocated her before she died. That's what it looks like, anyway."

She intrinsically knew their job was to make sense of something that didn't make sense, but how, where, and who were more important than why, but sometimes why meant a lot. It made her sick to think about it all, and the day that reaction went away she should just start selling insurance or something.

"The suffocation angle is the key."

"I'm sure we're about to get Fergusson's opinion. I call his style midwestern no-bullshit." Santiago knocked on the door. "After you."

Oh sure, into the lion's den first. Accurate call on the style. Fergusson didn't pull punches. He was nice enough to tell them to have a seat, but then showed no mercy. "Let's recap. You have how many eyewitnesses?"

"Quite a few," Ellie admitted.

"Surveillance installed by the state-of-the-art Milwaukee Police Department on your growingly infamous front porch show nothing, correct? Explain it to me, MacIntosh."

Santiago spoke for her. "Until the black roses picture, we weren't positive anything was connected to the murders. No one shows up on that tape that shouldn't be there. All the regular cars go by, the people in the neighborhood are familiar, and so on. Our surveillance team so far has seen nothing unusual."

He was right. They'd pulled the images on video immediately.

"Then how does he manage it?"

"He turns them off somehow." Ellie had a technician explain it to her carefully. "How he has that password is a mystery to me, but computers get hacked all the time. It goes down for just a few strategic minutes, and then it comes back up. They've tracked it, but can't nail down the source yet."

"Battery backup? Of course."

"He switches that feature off." Santiago was emphatic. "We knew he'd anticipate cameras, but didn't know he was a geek who could rig them and make smoke bombs. He should be in a Bond movie."

"I don't have time to watch those flicks," Fergusson said plainly. "I don't think I've ever heard of a case where he's in such plain sight. When you know his favorite cheese, please inform me. What type of toilet paper he prefers, I'm sure you'll have that information before you have a name. You are supposed to be the homicide division's dream team, but right now you're a nightmare, get it? One more thing before you go: We have an anonymous tip that your partnership gives a whole new meaning to the word. Just so you know."

"Like what?" Ellie was afraid maybe her expression

reflected the truth, but this invasion of her life on all levels was really getting to her.

"I'll let you have this conversation with Metzger," Fergusson just said evenly. "We're done here. Go solve this case."

When they left, Ellie shook her head. "A part of me thinks they expect miracles from us."

"We aren't miracle workers, but in this case we'll deliver."

A good thing he was confident, because she wasn't sure she shared his faith. "A tip about us? Like what kind?"

"I literally have no idea. I was afraid to ask."

**Jason knew how** to play odds; he'd been doing it his whole life. He thought better when he paced, so he walked back and forth, wearing a path in front of Ellie's desk. "Let's change it out. Let's announce we have a clear suspect in the park slayings. I think Metzger would do that for us because he's going to have to give a press conference after this last murder. It isn't original, but there's a reason it's still used: because it works. I don't know about you, but if I'm looking over my shoulder, I want the killer looking over his. My only fear is that he'll run. It might work, but it also might make him move on to another state and start all over again. But then he'd have to give you up, and somehow I doubt he's going to do that."

She didn't like it put that way. It was clearly in her eyes. "Give me up? Stop that."

"Well, it's true, isn't it? Maybe he's ex-military. At the rate he's moving, it's possible. Some of those special forces guys can make themselves invisible.

Otherwise, I swear I'd know it if some asshole was following us around. I'm like really, really paying attention these days." He stopped pacing and stared at the wall where they had a timeline written out on a board and the names of the victims, hands in his pockets.

"Special forces. There's a comforting thought."

"He knows about our relationship not just being professional. How? You can't tell me this 'anonymous tip' didn't come from him."

"We don't even know what it is." Ellie wasn't sure she wanted to find out.

"Maybe you told Lukens, but she's so close-mouthed it's like running into a brick wall if you want information. All your sleazy secrets you've confessed to her are safe, by the way. I keep asking but she just won't give the details."

"There are no sleazy secrets except maybe you." Ellie no doubt was unhappy, but composed. "And Georgia knows about the case, so no, she wouldn't mention it to anyone. If Grasso talks to her about it, I don't mind at all, because on a rare occasion you're right about something and she wouldn't say anything to anyone else. I did mention the occasion was rare, right?"

"And you call *me* a smartass." He came over to drop into a chair. "Huh, look who's talking."

"I've spent too much time with you. I wonder if I could sue the department for character damage and emotional suffering for making you my partner."

"You can take it, so isn't a case. The surveillance team outside your house said there was no delivery of flowers or anything else. Our asshole stabbed the last victim. Why? He's evolving?"

"He varies his pattern to challenge us, we both know that."

"If word gets out that someone is murdering people because he's fixated on one of MPD's detectives, then the press is going to have a field day. Want to rethink Siberia or the desert island?"

The last thing she wanted was officers watching her come and go, intruding on her life, he knew that, but then again someone else was already doing that apparently. "I don't like any of this, but perspective is important. What is really awful is what happened to our victims. I'm a person, and this is obviously affecting my life, but at least I still have it."

"If they can get a solid view, we can show it to the friend of the last victim, and even though we still would be dealing with circumstantial in a big way, given Grasso's case and the tulips and the expert opinion the old lady was killed, it's thin, but if they brought him for questioning, we could take it to the prosecutor. Handwriting analysis—if we had a suspect—might seal the deal."

It might, but it might not.

"Now who is the optimist?" she said.

**Chapter 22**

It was the end of his personal list.

Almost.

Two more people on it. One would be easy. One would be the chance he wasn't positive he should or would take.

Sitting on a fence about how it could be done.

He woke up sweating in the middle of the night thinking about it. What would happen if he did take out Detective Santiago?

Maybe it would be the thrill of a lifetime.

He couldn't move on it for a while, but the itch was there, making him toss and turn. He knew everything he needed to know about the man. Where he lived, his truck right down to the license plate number, even what kind of beer he drank, because one morning he'd gone through Ellie MacIntosh's recycling after she'd brought it out to the curb and left for work.

That was before she'd essentially moved out of the condo.

A few times he'd risked it and watched her leave

*from the police department, but safely across the
street out of range of any cameras, just to get a glimpse
as she pulled away. Santiago was always right behind
her, like a shadow.*

*That would be his weakness.*


**Jason scowled at** the windshield. "Shit. Let's just skip
right to triple shit and not mention double shit. I'm
too tired for this. How many hours did we spend
going over cold case files to see if maybe we are dealing with a repeat offender?"

"A lot."

They had come up with nothing that helped them
really. The closest was an unsolved strangulation and
drowning in a fountain on the University of Wisconsin's campus well over a decade before.

"My mother sent a text to remind me about tonight. I wanted to tell her we don't have the time."

Ellie gazed at him from the passenger seat. "We'll
talk about the case on the way. We don't have any
leads we can really pursue in any other way. I think
sometimes it just helps to go over it again and again.
I know you don't want this, but give it a chance. You
have to eat at some point, why not with them? Man
up. We'll be working all the way there and all the way
back. You can take an hour or so to make your mother
and father happy."

"Man up? Can I point out that making me happy
wasn't on their agenda my entire life?"

"Stop whining. I see you got a haircut."

He muttered, "For Metzger so he'd leave me alone
about it."

She wondered if Georgia would agree it was for

Metzger. She doubted it, since he'd ignored that for quite some now. He was also dressed with more care than usual and looked nice in dark denims and a white shirt. It wasn't like Ellie didn't understand he was in a situation that made him uncomfortable. "Good timing."

"We can turn around."

She could point out he *wanted* to cancel it, but refrained. At the end of the day it was just his decision. She waited. Lights flashed past; the freeway still busy at this time of evening.

"Might as well get it over with." He exhaled. "I'm not five anymore. Or ten, or twenty-nine, or all those other birthdays they missed. Why do they care now? Don't answer that. Let's talk about the case."

"You'd rather talk about murders than your family? Besides, you already know your mother didn't tell your father he even had a child in an effort to keep you from being dragged into the circle of a family connected to organized crime. I am sure she regretted having to make that choice every single day, but I can understand why she did what she did. I doubt she realized that after she walked out, the man you thought was your father would turn into a raging alcoholic. He did adopt you when he married her, so he stood by that." Ellie had thought about it quite a bit. Her childhood had been happy and what she considered to be typical with loving parents, riding bikes down the street, quarreling with her sister but ending up best friends, summer vacations on Lake Superior . . .

The grim reality of becoming a police officer had brought it to light that there was no such thing as typical. Good, bad, and in the middle was the best anyone could do.

"One hundred percent I would prefer to discuss the case, and as far as I know, it could be all the same thing as talking about my father. Murder isn't why he went to prison, but nothing would surprise me." Santiago said it darkly. "I pulled some files besides our cold case research. I have at least one uncle doing time for manslaughter, and that was a plea bargain because they weren't sure they could make conspiracy to commit murder stick."

Ellie chose her words carefully. "So now maybe you see your mother's concerns. Let's talk about the campus cold case murder. It was ten years ago. It was in Milwaukee, and from the descriptions of our possible suspect he'd be about late twenties to early thirties or so now."

"Let's do talk about that. All we know is she left the party at a frat house with a guy. Everyone was pretty drunk, but a few of her friends remember her leaving. Then they remember her dead. No leads. But we have three threads that include alcohol, strangulation until she was unconscious, and then drowning her. She wasn't dating anyone according to the interviews at the time, so no boyfriend."

"We don't have a description either. They said he was tall. Here we go again."

Santiago said, "It isn't much, but maybe something."

She didn't agree. It was nothing. "You're fairly tall. Where were you that night?"

"I can say honestly not at a frat party. No Greek houses in my life until this case."

"One down if I take your word for it. The rest of the men in America are still suspects unless they are short."

At least that lightened him up a little. "Good to be

no longer suspect number one. It all could just mean nothing."

"I don't know." She meant it. "I keep going back to it. I'm wondering if he committed that first murder a good decade ago. Let's talk to the detectives that handled it."

"If we survive dinner, that's a good idea."

**The menu proved** to be some sort of chicken dish with biscuits on top. Very homey and actually delicious. The house itself was modest, probably because his father had an honest job, and being an ex-con didn't make it easy to find work. Jason had the impression from his mother that the man had done a variety of things like construction, road work, and in the winter helped a friend with a private snowplow business.

Sitting across from him was like looking at an older version of himself. The same slightly Roman nose, the same blond hair, though his father's was starting to show threads of silver, but mostly it was the eyes. They were that same color of blue that practically every woman Jason had met commented on sooner or later.

"That was delicious," Ellie said as his mother rose to clear their plates. "Let me help you."

He really wished he hadn't recognized the tablecloth once the plates were gone, but he did. It was hand stitched and stirred childhood memories he didn't even know existed. He'd always wanted to sit near the part with a log cabin with smoke curling out of the chimney and a snowman out front, and maybe it was a calculated move on his mother's part, but that's where he'd ended up tonight.

Jason realized then she had left him behind, but taken that tablecloth. Talk about irony.

He was tempted to comment, but didn't because he had a feeling it would make Ellie uncomfortable.

He was, that was for sure.

"So, Jason." His father was trying to make conversation, though neither of them had been very successful in that regard so far. "What made you decide to become a police officer?"

At least he could answer that one. "I was an MP in the military. I liked it a lot better than getting shot at on a regular basis and sleeping on the ground half the time."

Right then and there he decided he should get a medal for not adding that arresting people who flaunted the law was much more satisfying, but he had the feeling his father was braced for him to say something just like that.

He didn't say it, mostly once again because Ellie would be ticked off at him.

Perhaps he also acknowledged his parents were trying and it was pointless to be angry about something that absolutely could not be changed. They'd made choices, and he wasn't sure if they were right or wrong, but he couldn't alter the past. If nothing else, a sense of inevitability settled over him.

So he gave it a shot. "What about you? Regrets over the decisions?"

"Your mother? No way. Love of my life. On other things, I've obviously made some mistakes." He added, "I've paid."

That was fair enough. Jason nodded. "I understand you did your time."

His father shook his head. "No, not what I meant. All those years I didn't know I had a son. I should be furious with your mother, and I was at first, but have realized she was probably right in the long run. Being in prison was a hard lesson, but if I had known you existed, I would have come for you the minute those gates opened. I also would have told my family, and I doubt you'd have ended up a homicide detective."

The message was clear that he needed to forgive his mother. That wasn't in the immediate future, and he wasn't inclined to take advice from this man, but he was there anyway, having a congenial meal. He opted for saying, "I'll take your word for it."

"Do. I suppose it could be argued I always had a choice, but you know, life wasn't presented to me that way. I thought I didn't. I believe your mother thought the same thing."

His mother bustled up then with two dessert plates laden with some concoction that involved a lot of whipped cream on the top. She asked brightly, "Coffee?"

The strawberry cake was very good as promised, but Jason was relieved when they left. Ellie didn't pull any punches, but then she never did. "How did that deep, dark conversation go?"

The night was starry, the county road bumpy after the winter. He steered around a pothole the size of Kansas. "The bottom line is he wants me to forgive and forget."

"Are you going to?"

"I don't know. He might be under the mistaken impression I'm a lot nicer than I actually am."

Ellie reclined the seat a little and closed her eyes. "I'm going to take a nap since you're driving. And I'd like to say I think you're the one under the mistaken impression you aren't a lot nicer than you actually are."

## Chapter 23

That long-ago accident had planted a seed.

Drunk girl weaving on her feet, and he was more than willing to walk her home and see what might happen next. She was decently nice looking but hardly memorable, except he was pretty sure she had a nice body under those jeans and that sorority sweatshirt.

When she tripped, he really wasn't surprised, and he did try to catch her, but she pitched into the fountain, hitting her head on one of the tiers gushing water into the bottom.

He thought about dragging her out, but then reconsidered. She was still breathing for a minute or two because he could see the bubbles on the surface, and then they stopped.

It was self-preservation to just turn and walk away. That easy.

She meant nothing to him, and why go through all the questions and interviews with the police if he didn't have to deal with it? In the furor that followed—press and campus news, and the fraternity being shut

*down for having the party in the first place—he was
absolutely anonymous.*

*It was an interesting experience.*

**Georgia picked out** cherry cabinets and white quartz for
the counter because she thought it suited the dated
elegance of the house but still preserved the character
of the time it was built, with a waterfall edge on the
counter and travertine for the kitchen floor. She suggested stainless appliances, pendant lights, and a new
picture window for the view into the backyard and
pool.

By the time they walked out of the store to the car,
Carl had spent a small fortune, but he'd asked for her
advice and hadn't blinked an eye at any of her ideas.
She'd also tentatively recommended a contractor who
was married to a friend of hers, and he'd called and
hired him over the phone.

She thought it was going to look stunning, but
hoped the change wouldn't affect him too much emotionally except in a positive way. If there was one
thing she'd learned it was that people were unpredict-
able, and what you saw was not necessarily what you
got. He seemed always collected and confident, but
that might or might not be true.

In her opinion, Carl should have done it a long time
ago, but this new kitchen he wanted to have her help
design was a sign he was finally moving in the right
direction. She couldn't decide if it was just something
he'd been thinking about and never bothered to do,
or if having a relationship pushed him to make other
changes in his life.

It was really starting to be a relationship.

"Successful shopping trip? Are you happy with the choices?" She was careful about probing him over his emotions and refrained from asking if he thought his mother would approve. That was going too far. A grown man might resent that question and might be justified in doing so, but it could be there in the back of his mind. There had never been proper closure.

"Oh, I think so. I'm making you do all the work."

She went for middle road. "I think you will like it at the end of the day, if you've gotten to a place where you're comfortable with the change."

His silver eyes glimmered in the fading afternoon light as he started the car. "If I wasn't, would I have suggested the trip to the hardware store and taken your suggestions? Use logic, Dr. Lukens."

"You were just thinking about this case the whole time."

"I was, and you were thinking about what I was thinking. We have an interesting dynamic."

**"I'll give you** that."

He mused out loud, "I can see shooting someone in an alley somewhere in a drunken dispute. I can even see an escalating emotional situation that gets out of control, but this perpetrator is very hands on."

Good-bye to granite or marble countertops decisions and right back to police work. God only knew what MacIntosh and Santiago were like together.

She intensely disliked that insight but agreed. "He targets victims that he can take absolutely by surprise. That's his thrill. Betraying their trust."

"Why suffocation?"

She wasn't a forensic psychologist, but she did feel his frustration.

"I think unfortunately it is a slower death than most. Stab or shoot someone and it is over quickly, but this is different. You can look into their eyes as it all ends. I've read about cases like that, and then I can't sleep at night. It's about power, but then all murder is about the ultimate power over someone else. You won, and they lost. Contest over. What motivates him? You and I can only speculate. I've dealt with some disturbed people, and so have you in in a different way."

"There will be no rematch if you kill someone, I understand that." He was quiet for a moment. "It's moving pretty fast. I don't like it at all. I went through the FBI database to see if there were other cases like the ones we are suddenly dealing with, and it isn't as unusual as you'd think for the killers to call in tips to law enforcement or to write to them or even contact the media. In this case it appears MacIntosh is being directly targeted, whether it is out of sexual interest or jealousy."

**Georgia looked out** at the street, now glimmering from a light rain that had moved in, and the streetlights reflected on the wet pavement. "None of you have an easy job. Speaking of which, I have a patient who is making some progress and expressed an interest in police work. She's young, rebellious, and that she's considering a discipline like that took me off guard, but she'd like to talk to someone about it. You look too James Bond, but I was thinking about them. Good or bad influence on a developing psyche?"

He pulled into her parking lot and then coasted into the garage, since her condo had two assigned spaces and she only used one. "More your area of expertise, Doctor, but I'd say they would both give it to her straight. Believe or not, Santiago can clean up his language if necessary. Just remind him. It wouldn't hurt. Too James Bond, huh?"

"That's hardly an insult." She unfastened her seat belt as he parked. "Best analogy I could come up with. She'd find your appearance and the title lieutenant to be too much authority oriented. She has issues with her father, and Santiago would not remind her in the least of anyone except someone who might own a motorcycle, which she would think was cool. And trust me, she doesn't think that about many things."

Carl gave a genuine laugh, which didn't happen often enough. "I'm kind of surprised he doesn't have a monster bike."

Georgia was too. "Give him time."

They went up on the elevator to her floor and she flipped on the lights once she'd unlocked the door. It was surprisingly comfortable to say, "You know where the scotch is, so please help yourself. I'm going to change my shoes. Heels look good, but flats feel a lot better."

"I might lose my tie," Carl commented, walking toward the cabinet where she kept the glasses.

"Good idea." She went in and changed shoes, and when she left her bedroom, he had taken off both his jacket and his tie and was on the couch.

It was . . . nice.

She sank down in an opposite chair. "So, you're an experienced investigator. What do you think happens next?"

"With?"

She *had* been vague. "Back to the case. Ellie is a friend of mine."

Carl swirled the ice in his glass. "I'm afraid he's going to go for it. Trap her somehow, take her off guard, but I really think he's going to target Santiago first. I've told her that flat out. But Santiago has the tendency to think he's bulletproof, and we all know that isn't true."

"I believe he's taken three and gotten lucky." She had to point that out.

"Can you count on that luck forever?"

He had a valid point.

"Probably not. Don't say that to me. I'm fond of some of my patients more than others."

**Ellie rolled over** and listened to the soft sound of Jason's breathing in the dark.

One o'clock in the morning.

She got up, slipped on a pair of loose pants and a shirt, and went to the kitchen. She might as well work, since she wasn't going to doze off on her own even at this hour.

The case was why she was still awake.

She was still processing the scene in her head, and that kept her awake when it happened. She wasn't able to get the sight of the victim's face flat and pallid behind the plastic out of her mind, and she had to breathe deeply and consciously let it go. She punched in the elementary school roster to see if anything had been missed about Juno's colleagues.

Nothing.

She checked the notes on the first victims and one thing popped out. Before now it wouldn't have.

Calvin Hanes, the second victim, had worked as a janitor at an elementary school before he got fired and went to work for the storage company where he unloaded trucks. It was just a five-word notation in his profile.

Juno had been an elementary school teacher.

Ellie squared her shoulders and wondered if by chance it was the same school.

It was.

She went into the bedroom and poked Jason in the shoulder. It was late, but he hardly ever slept so she felt guilty, but this might be important.

Instant response. "What the hell?"

"Get this. Juno taught at Parkview Elementary."

Jason sat up. "You are kidding me. We needed this. It might be a lead."

Ellie thought so too. The information was interesting and connected two of the victims, but it could mean nothing more than that the killer lived near the school, or even that maybe he went to the school years ago. That would be like the proverbial needle in a haystack if who they were looking for was close to thirty, because literally thousands of kids would have gone through that school by now, and he certainly wouldn't look the same as a man as he did as a child, but at least it was something.

He got up and wandered into the kitchen behind her. "I'm going to have a cup of coffee, but I'm guessing that doesn't interest you."

"I might never shut my eyes." Ellie pointed at the cup next to her laptop. "Herbal tea. Just the cold hard truth. I'm sure you've already figured out I have my demons too. I don't need anything extra to keep me awake."

It was definitely not new information.

"As far as I can tell, we have the same problem, it is just a matter of degrees. I think Grasso is a vampire." He took a cup out of the cupboard. "Parkview, huh?"

"One of the other victims also worked at an elementary school but was fired years ago. If it happens to be the same one . . . well, it doesn't mean we've got him, but it might mean something to get us there." She picked up her tea and took a sip, thoughtful. "My initial reaction is that means something. Association is real, or so a certain Georgia Lukens tells me. All along I've felt he's sending a message of some kind, daring law enforcement to decipher it. Unfortunately for us, he seems to be fascinated in a very negative way with how we work."

"That isn't an understatement. That school thing makes me wonder if he just lives nearby or maybe went there?"

"Any and all insights are welcome on this cheerful subject."

"How did you figure this out?"

"Background checks and the name popped. If he lives nearby and sees the sign for the school every single day, that might be it, but I'm inclined toward a connection to the school itself. A former janitor and a teacher from the same place is personal. *If* it is the same place. It is difficult when the pieces of the puzzle scatter instead of falling into an order that fits. That is hardly the only school named that in this world, but

I actually see it pretty often. I drive by it on the way to your condo."

"I think it's worth a look anyway."

"I agree." He poured cold coffee from the morning into his cup and stuck it in the microwave. Jason was in some ways the ultimate bachelor and seemed to value simplicity above comfort, or maybe it was his time in the military that made stale reheated coffee acceptable. Ellie had to admit to being more picky than that, and his coffee even when fresh made her shudder.

"It might mean nothing, but it struck me."

"How was your conversation with Grantham? I don't think I knew you still talked to him so often." Jason said it casually, but Ellie took the sudden change in subject to mean it wasn't casual at all. The microwave beeped and he took out his cup and leaned against the counter.

Ellie thought carefully about her response. "It was fine. We're still friends, so we talk. In a way, we're comrades in arms, considering what we went through during the Northwoods case. He didn't send the tulips, but you already know that."

"Is that what I am? A comrade in arms?"

"You would certainly qualify." She wasn't about to have this argument. "Look. If you ever think I'm going to share every facet of my life with you, think again. I don't expect it from you either. If you talked to Kate, it would be fine with me."

"I actually have no desire to talk to Kate." He'd relaxed a little, though. "I'm just not used to giving a shit, and quite frankly I'll be edgy until we catch this guy."

She hated to break it to him, but he was edgy all

the time. She decided to not point that out. "Giving a shit. That's extremely romantic."

"I'm practically Shakespeare."

"I think you might be a little out of touch with reality right there." Ellie went back to her screen. "Come take a look at this."

## Chapter 24

It was starting to get tricky with remote cameras and cops parked outside.

He knew about both, of course.

A new strategy needed to come into play. He'd thought it over, since that was part of the game. It was fine; the risks adjusted.

So could he.

Inventive was his middle name.

So he did figure it out.

No sweat.

He asked if there was no response to deliver to the neighbor, since he knew the wife next door was home. It worked beautifully. Florist van and all.

The police took video. He wasn't in it, just observing. The wife accepted the flowers when Ellie MacIntosh didn't answer her door.

Perfect.

\* \* \*

**The knock came** at about two minutes after they walked
into the condo. Between the surveillance and two
very competent officers parked outside they were
surely safe enough and Ellie needed to get more clean
clothes.

Santiago won the race to the door of course with
longer legs and a head start. It was just Mr. Nichols
from next door with a vase of flowers and a properly
startled look on his face because Santiago had his
sidearm drawn. He stammered, "I saw you were back.
Blackie was over here again yesterday so I went looking for him. Someone tried to deliver these for you
yesterday, but the evening was supposed to be cool so
I didn't want to just set them on the porch. I thought
you might want them safe. My wife thought they were
really pretty. I probably should be more thoughtful
and get some for her soon."

They were. Yellow roses in a glass vase, and there
was a card too.

Oh, Ellie couldn't wait to read that card. *Not*.

"That's nice of you," she assured him as she accepted the flowers. They'd have all that on video, but
the officers had reported what they thought was a legitimate delivery van pull into her driveway. Still, the
flower theme made her wonder. "I don't suppose you
saw who delivered them."

It was a hope.

"I'm afraid not." Mr. Nichols looked like he wanted
to escape as soon as possible and she couldn't blame
him. "I was just looking for the cat. Most of our windows face the back of the house. You know that since
your house is just like ours. My wife spoke to him.
You could ask her. There seem to be some unfamiliar
vehicles parked close by, and I mean all the time. I'll

be blunt and just ask, is everything okay? Since the smoke bomb thing . . ."

She didn't blame him. In this quiet neighborhood, he probably wasn't the only one who had noticed.

"Police officers." She owed him that. "Keeping you safe."

"Oh." He didn't look happy. "So there *is* a problem."

"We don't know if there is or not, so we are being cautious. Just lock your doors, since you should anyway. Thank you."

"No problem." He left and she closed the door and handed Jason the vase. "I know you're going to take this from me anyway. Help yourself."

"We need gloves. It is possible to lift a fingerprint from the envelope or card."

"With gloves we could smudge it."

"Then let's not open the card."

She wanted to wait as well. "The vase is going to have Nichols' prints all over it, and probably those of his wife, now yours and mine and whoever put in the flowers at the shop and the delivery person, so that is kind of a doubtful option. The card might be a possibility, since it isn't opened. He was very careful with the picture of the black roses so we got nothing. Besides, if he called it in, the florist probably printed the message."

"Called it in? No way. He'd never risk a credit card."

That was probably true. Ellie agreed.

"I think we should take it to the lab first and let them deal with it. I want a print from this jerk. I have a feeling that the handwriting is going to be familiar." Jason looked vaguely ridiculous holding a vase of yellow roses with a definite scowl on his face. He hadn't shaved in two days, so that made it more amusing. She could use that twinge of amusement.

She thought the same thing about a viable fingerprint. "It won't help unless we have a suspect, but not a bad idea. Though if he's in the database for a previous crime, we would at least have a name. I bet it isn't Jack or Ted either."

"It will help when we make an arrest."

"You are so much more confident than I am."

"Between you, me, and Grasso? Oh yeah, we'll get him." He carried the flowers to the kitchen and set them on the counter as she followed. "This motherfucker is making me rethink ever giving you flowers in this lifetime."

She headed toward her bedroom. "Can you call him something else? I know you do it on purpose to annoy me."

He didn't even blink. "It's habit. I was on military bases for quite a while. After a few months you come to understand you just say what you mean. With him, I mean it."

"I—" She stopped short and took in a breath in shock. "This I do not like. That bastard."

Sitting on her nightstand was a vase, an antique one that her aunt had given her, with a single red rose in it.

"Shit! He's been inside. How the hell? Don't move." Jason pushed past her. "Who is this guy? Houdini? The Invisible Man? What the hell?"

"I'm starting to think so." She had to reluctantly agree. "He's demonstrating he can still communicate and get to me."

Santiago said almost savagely, "Tomorrow we'll hit Parkview Elementary, since the staff and students will be back from spring break. And then we can interview everyone who lives even remotely nearby. We already have his description, so it probably won't help much, but we can give it a shot. Why couldn't we catch a break and her friend could at least describe his car?"

Woodenly Ellie said, "I'm starting to think Fergusson is right and we will know his favorite kind of cheese before we have a name." The idea someone— especially him—was in her home without her permission or knowledge made her skin crawl. She was hot, and then ice cold and shivering. She struggled to pull it together.

"I don't argue any of that. I think we need to take some photos of the drowning victim along with us to the school. No one has reported anyone matching her description missing yet. Maybe all her relatives live out of town, maybe she doesn't have friends . . . it's disturbing. The ME put her age at maybe fifty to fifty-five. She should be missed by someone; children or husband or coworkers or *someone*. She was definitely not dressed like a street person."

Santiago said unemotionally, "When I got out of the military, no one would have missed me. No family, no job, no girlfriend. Any friends I had from school were used to me being gone. I swear no one would have noticed if I disappeared."

Ellie knew for a fact he wasn't as indifferent about it as he seemed. She said, "Well, that is no longer the case. Metzger would in particular be furious if you didn't show up at your desk on time. He'd try to hunt you down like a Ninja warrior. I get the impression he values you."

Santiago didn't look convinced. "The chief? I think

he'd love to terminate my ass if possible, but I'll take your word for it. We need to bag the vase as evidence."

Jason was a challenge in that he went his own way—but he was a very talented detective. Metzger understood that. Grasso was a skilled investigator who had crossed the line, but he'd had some measure of forgiveness since he did the job. As for the vase, she would never be able to look at it the same way and despised that feeling of personal violation. "Let's stop by and get a picture from the morgue before we head to the school tomorrow."

"Ah jeez, the Underworld again?"

"You're a homicide detective. What did you expect? I know it is probably useless, but we can look at the footage from the flower delivery and at least find out how he paid by a visit to the vendor. We will maybe get another description to match all the others."

"Credit card would be nice. But he wouldn't do that. It's too careless for him. I'm starting to resent that he's at least as smart as me."

That was a conviction Ellie shared. "If he did that, paid in cash, I doubt he brought them himself."

"I think so too, since it sounds just like him. It doesn't hurt to ask, though. The color and make of his car might help out. There's a possible lead."

"You don't believe it will pan out." She folded her arms on the table. "Not for one minute. He paid an old lady to buy flowers and then killed her. He isn't going to ever, ever park close enough to the shop so someone could identify his car." Ellie stared at that single red rose, but didn't really see it. "That first murder . . . he was nervous. He's lightening up now, flexing his muscles. If you were him, what would you do next?"

He was Jason Santiago and unfailingly blunt. "I

don't know. Few people scare me, but he does. I've been a police officer for quite a while and we aren't going to sugarcoat this, Detective MacIntosh. I'm currently your best friend in this world in more ways than one. I want to catch him for myself as much as I do for you. I want someone besides Metzger to care if I disappear. That means my vested interest in your well-being is pretty much a hundred percent."

"What makes you think I'd care?" She was pushing him and she knew it.

"The nights we've spent together?"

Jason was a stranger to commitment. She hadn't fared all that well either in that department.

"Relationships are complicated. They aren't simply about sex."

He rose from where he was crouched down by the nightstand and staring at the vase. "I know. I make love to you. Very different. Maybe I'm starting to really hope you'd care about the difference. That bothers the shit out of me, and yes, I said it just that way to annoy you."

**The next morning** the florist visit gained them nothing. They'd delivered the flowers. No one answered, so they'd gone next door. Yes, the buyer paid in cash, and no, they didn't have cameras.

The bleak landscape of their questioning wasn't heartening, but then again he hadn't expected too much.

Jason walked next to Ellie, and it was his policy to say the truth. "Nothing worthwhile."

"No." She didn't sound disheartened as much as resigned. "He isn't going to make this easy. Nichols has noticed the surveillance team. I'm sure that my neighbors all wish I'd move away. "

"I suspect my neighbors feel the same after the car explosion. I'm thinking about buying a house with a big backyard. Get that ferocious dog I mentioned. No flower delivery on his watch. You want to be my roommate?"

He actually wasn't sure where that came from exactly. Well, that wasn't entirely true. He'd thought about buying a house before, but he was afraid of utter solitude. He was moody enough without throwing an empty house into the mix. At least at his apartment in the summer he could sit on the balcony and watch the kids playing in the pool, hear the shrieks of laughter, in the winter see them in mittens and scarves tossing snowballs at each other as they got off the school bus . . .

Ellie stared at him as they walked back to her car along the wet sidewalk, not saying a word until she sputtered out, "*What?* Are you insane?"

"There are those who think so. But maybe consider it. We could carpool."

He always got sarcastic when something mattered to him. Maybe Lukens needed to help him work through that.

"Oh, now you've made it irresistible." Luckily, Ellie was really used to it. "Carpooling. That will seal the deal. Forget fidelity, undying love and all that drivel, but carpooling will take the day."

She was as bad as he was. It seemed practical to point out, "We pretty much are living together right now. Both of us are throwing money away on rent. I know you tried living with someone before and it didn't work out; I had a similar experience. You could have your own room, your own space. I kind of like the idea. Think about it."

"That idea is so flawed I can't even begin to list the reasons. Not the least of it is if we had the same address, I promise you Metzger would reassign us."

She had a point there, he probably would. If it wasn't apparently obvious how he felt about her, Jason could argue roommates only with his boss, but he'd probably lose that fight. Metzger wouldn't believe him.

"You still have your house up north. Use that address."

"Do you think anyone would believe I commute four hours one way to Milwaukee from there? Look, I appreciate the offer. Let's just pretend you didn't make it."

"It was just a thought." He was reckless from time to time, no doubt about it. His tendency to say what was on his mind had gotten him in trouble before, so she could be exactly right.

"Well, let's think about something else. Can we deal with our very real problem first?"

"So next stop is the friend of the latest victim? Man, I hate saying that. 'Latest' and 'victim' should not be in the same sentence."

Ellie seemed more than willing to change the subject. "Grasso interviewed her, but we both know that maybe she remembers something else now that the initial shock has passed."

"Let's see if she's willing to talk to us. Grasso gave me her number."

She was and she was home since she worked second shift. Marcy Drelling lived in a small house in a neighborhood near downtown. She was midtwenties, tall with long brown hair, and teared up the minute she opened the door. "I should have protected her better. I was there to make sure if the date went wrong she'd have a ride home. He seemed nice. He *looked* nice. Please come in."

Her living room was small but tidy, with a couch and two chairs around a polished table. They both perched on the couch side by side since she chose a chair. "We know Lieutenant Grasso already asked you some questions, but if you could run through it again, we'd appreciate it. We are the detectives actively investigating this case."

Ellie always assumed a reasonable and calm demeanor. He didn't have that same ability to reassure. He probably would have said something very frank like: *Can you just repeat your story?*

Nonetheless, he listened carefully as Ms. Drelling recounted being backup. "She was nervous, so she asked me to go along. Not with them, but in case he was a frog and not a prince, you know. Like I told the other officer I could see them and could tell she was enjoying herself."

If it was him, definitely worse than a frog, but at this point they were just speculating. Ellie asked, "Was there nothing about him that raised any red flags? He didn't seem nervous or preoccupied? What did she know about him?"

Marcy was emotional. "He said he was employed in finance, but he'd once thought about being a teacher because he loved kids, and so they really hit it off. Maybe it wasn't him. Maybe she was abducted when he dropped her off."

Jason wasn't nearly as sure. "Describe him for us please?"

"He was tall, light brown hair, a great smile, casually dressed but nicely." She plucked a tissue out of a box. "Sorry, I've been crying just so much. This doesn't happen. Not to someone I know. This is just on the evening news or something."

It wasn't just on the evening news. Ellie asked, "Did he pay for the drinks?"

She sniffled. "I think so. I saw him put some bills on the table after she gave me the signal all was well and they left."

"He never mentioned exactly where he lived?"

"Maybe to her, but if he did, she didn't mention it."

"Do you know where they were headed? Was it back to her house or to a restaurant? Did she text you?" The cameras in the bar told them nothing, and both he and Ellie agreed their quarry was too savvy to make the mistake of sitting in full view.

"It seemed to be going so well I would guess out to dinner, but I don't know. I know you're going to ask but no, I didn't see his car. I arrived first, actually."

But her friend could no longer tell them. Dead end there in a very real sense. "We'll take anything that will help us. You don't have a last name, but can you tell us anything else you noticed about him? We understand you wanted to be off his radar, but what did he wear? Did he have anything distinguishing about him? A scar? An earring maybe?"

In court that would be leading a witness, but this wasn't court. "Yes, he did have an earring. I didn't see it, but Regina mentioned it. She thought it was sexy. He looked so professional, but then had an earring."

Ellie was as usual composed, but Jason could sense her reaction. "That's very interesting to us. Is there anything else you can add?"

"I don't think so. He had a beer and she had what looked like a cosmopolitan."

Jason hated to ask this, but in good conscience had to do it. "Do you think he saw Regina give you the thumbs-up signal? Is there a chance she might have told him about you being there for the 'just in case' scenario?"

Marcy was a fairly quick study. She paled. "You think he might try to hurt me?"

"If he knows you were there and could identify him because you clearly saw his face." Ellie said it evenly. "If he saw her gesture and asked about it and she explained, anything is possible. This suspect has done it before, and he really fits the description of who we are looking for. Can you go stay with someone? I don't want to scare you, and if she didn't give him your full name it would be hard for him to find you. But on the off chance she did, you'd be safer not to stay at your own address until we make an arrest."

"Oh God." She put a trembling hand up to her cheek.

"If you see him anywhere, near your work for instance, call 911 right away. We can't know the kind of questions he asked her." Jason didn't add that once Regina realized she was in danger of losing her life, she might have told him anything he wanted to know. The initial report said she was strangled to unconsciousness before the bag was put over her head. With someone's hands around your throat, you'd probably talk.

Marcy nodded jerkily. "I have a friend from work. That way we can drive together." She took in a shuddering breath. "This just keeps getting more awful."

Jason couldn't agree more.

## Chapter 25

*The move was a hard call, but he'd been trapped in the urgent desire to do something.*

*Anything.*

*In many ways it was the story of his life.*

*So he'd slipped on gloves.*

*He'd taken worse chances, and the jealousy was eating him alive. He couldn't get anywhere close to her. Not sleeping and not eating were both counterproductive to his ultimate goal.*

*So no return address and he'd driven over to a very specific spot to mail his special delivery.*

*It should arrive in a day or two.*

*Then he assumed all hell would break loose.*

**Ellie walked down** to the forensics lab with the card in an evidence bag and handed it over. She'd spent two days with that card sitting on her desk but made Jason keep those flowers. Rob, the technician, who was an icon in the Milwaukee Police Department and the only one she wanted to deal with this, lifted his bushy brows. He was past middle-aged, white haired, wore suspenders every day, and was an absolute wizard at his job. If anyone was going to handle evidence, it needed to be him, but he'd been off for the weekend. He asked, "What are we looking for here? Fingerprints?"

"And a handwriting match. I haven't opened it, so for all I know it's printed, but I somehow doubt it. I brought photos from the victims' bodies so you can compare. Santiago is bringing you a vase of flowers."

"That's thoughtful of him. I have always liked that boy despite his brash sense of humor and that he has a full head of hair."

"He can grow on you, and brash is being kind."

Rob chuckled. "He doesn't pull a punch, I'll give you that."

"The vase is probably going to have all kinds of different prints on it, but I have hopes for the card. I really want one to show up in the database, but I think this perp is homegrown and a Milwaukee pioneer. I doubt he'll be in there, but one never knows."

"I'll run it. Park Bench case?"

"You got that right."

"Then flowers for you. Word gets around here." Rob nodded. "Orders have trickled down to give it priority. I'll get on this. Speak of the devil, here he comes."

Santiago sauntered into the lab and deposited the vase in front of Rob. "Here you go, old man. A gift for you as a token of my affection. It will probably involve a lot of trouble on your part with no results for us, but we don't want you to be bored and I think I forgot you on Valentine's Day."

"What a nice a gesture. You know you're like the son I never had."

"I thought you had three or something like that." Santiago furrowed his brow.

"I have four, but none of them are like you, for which I thank the powers above, or below, whatever you choose."

They always interacted this way, which was why Ellie decided to leave. "I'm going to spend some much-needed time on my computer and you two can continue insulting each other without me."

Grasso was at his desk, so she stopped and told him about their interview with Marcy Drelling. "We now have an eyewitness I think we can count on for an absolute positive identification. All we need is someone we can bring in for questioning and a lineup."

He was dressed as usual like he'd be at home at a cocktail party in Manhattan. "Is that all we need? That seems to be harder than it should be. By the way, Georgia has a favor to ask of you for one of her patients if you can find the time. It's a troubled young girl who is slowly turning around and might want to be a police officer one day. I'm sure she'll call you herself, but I thought I'd mention it. She wonders if you and Santiago might sit down with her patient and let her ask a few questions."

"I talk to her frequently."

"But you are working a tough case. She knows that. This isn't life or death, this is just a favor."

That sounded like Georgia. "I'm kind of dubious I'd recommend this job right now because this case is so elusive I'm going to lose my mind. He's out there. We know what he looks like. I've heard his voice. He's been to my house—been *in* my house—and leaves us notes. Why can't we catch him?"

"Oh, I understand. I'll never catch who shot that street gang kid. I know it and I think his parents know it too. I've tried. Hopefully they know that as well."

"This looks like a cheerful conversation." Jason walked up. "Let me guess, NFL draft picks?"

"Some of us have more sophisticated interests," Grasso said caustically. "We were talking about ballet and whether or not we enjoyed the movie *The Turning Point*."

He astounded them both. "Anne Bancroft, right?" He turned to Ellie. "Let's go to Parkview Elementary now that school is back in session this morning and we can actually talk to someone who knows what they're doing and see if they can do anything to push this investigation forward. I picked up the pictures. Let's get there before lunch. Have I ever mentioned cafeteria ladies scare me?"

She slanted him a glance. "Is there anything that doesn't scare you? Spiders and cafeteria ladies are on the list. What else?'

"It's pretty long. Metzger when he's pissed off is on it. Let's go try and make him happy. Let's not forget this wacko killing people and sending you flowers scares me. I believe I've already admitted that."

She didn't disagree on that one.

The school was a newer building and the sign out front announced that grandparents' day would be on the fourteenth and all visitors needed to sign in. They both did so and went to the office, and when they produced their badges were given more badges to clip to their jackets before they could see the principal. She was on the phone but waved them into her office and got off the line promptly. Middle-aged and with a somber expression, Principal Albert said, "I'm absolutely heartsick to do this interview. Please have a seat. Counselors are dealing with the children. You have no idea how students become attached to their teachers, and to have one murdered . . . we are devastated. I have no words. How can I help?"

Ellie said, "We are looking for a link and maybe the school is part of it. We need access to employment records, and we were wondering if you could help us identify this victim. I'm sorry that the pictures aren't more pleasant, but no one has come forward to help us figure out who she is."

She handed over the photographs from the morgue. The principal immediately shut her eyes and handed them back before she opened them again. "That's Patricia. Patricia Stine. She was a secretary here for a while. She retired because her husband had cancer. They had no children."

Ellie was sympathetic, but she had a feeling they'd just made a strong connection that couldn't be ignored. "Those records are really important. We have another person that might be tied to the school. If he is, our search can narrow."

Santiago backed her up. "We don't know how the school might be involved, but it looks like it is. Let's find out. Can you look up Calvin Hanes?"

"I don't have to. I remember Calvin. In 2006 when he was fired for too many absences I felt bad, but it was what it was, a violation of policy."

That confirmed Ellie's research.

He said to Ellie, "Oh jeez, three people. We're on to something."

"I wish it didn't involve the school." Principal Albert

really meant it, her pale blue eyes alarmed. "Do you think it does?"

Ellie gave her the other names. "Five murders. The young woman and the young man might have been students here, but you have a teacher, a janitor, and a secretary. We'll look into it, but there's an older lady we think is connected to the crimes. I know this is time consuming, but can you look at these names also and get back to us? We don't think all of them are tied into the school, but for all we know maybe they are. We do know the older lady is the victim of the same killer, or at least believe she is. If anyone has information you think might be remotely helpful, I'm going to give you both my e-mail and phone number."

"We take security very seriously here," the principal said. "I'll have a staff meeting and warn them that on a private level they should also be very careful. Like any school, we've had our share of problem students and even disgruntled employees, but no one comes to mind immediately that would do anything remotely like this." Her face was troubled. "I've been here for fifteen years and I do pay attention."

Ellie believed her. "If you think of anything, let us know. We appreciate your time."

"I appreciate yours." She was already reaching for the phone.

"No lunch ladies," she said to Santiago as they walked outside.

"Yeah, dodged a bullet there, but I've seen the inside of a principal's office a few times too many, so that didn't give me warm fuzzy memories. What next? Back to the Bat Cave to call the families and find out if the two younger victims ever went to the school? How come I have a feeling they did?"

"Then what is his tie?"

"He's young. Maybe he went there too."

The day was hazy, smelled like spring, and the lilac bushes in the landscaping had leaves and even buds on them. They got into her car and drove back as Ellie thought long and hard about how the evidence piled up, but they were still getting nowhere. "This is insane. We have him. Witnesses, the school, the flowers . . . we *have* him."

Santiago agreed. "That break just isn't coming. He's made a lot of risky moves, but not the ones we need. I'd wipe out Las Vegas on betting that there are no prints on that card. A handwriting match, yes, but no prints."

She had the sinking sensation he was exactly right. "I wonder what that card says. I have a feeling I don't want to know."

"It doesn't matter. He's going down."

**He was starting** to feel it. A sense maybe they were closing in but still just sniffing around, and it was hard not to let it get to him. Jason could read the signs and they had a handle on this, but it was tenuous. If this guy decided to lay low, they might never find him.

Ellie walked up and laid the card on his desk. "No prints. Rob scanned it and sent it off to the FBI for handwriting analysis, but he said though that isn't his specialty, he'd say it matches the handwriting on the victims. He went into all the swoops and so forth in the letters, but I'm just going to take his word for it."

He picked it up.

*I've watched you sleep.*

There was no denying his entire body went tense,

and he wasn't exactly relaxed before. "I'm so tired of this that the desert island idea is really starting to appeal to me. I'll join you. Is it okay if I wear a Speedo the entire time?"

Ellie said emphatically, "No."

"That's not kind."

"I wasn't trying to be kind." She pointed at the note. "If he hadn't obviously been inside my home, I would think he was just trying to be theatrical and scare me, but we know he has been in there. The idea of being asleep and someone coming in who thinks we are playing some sort of macabre game makes my skin crawl. How could we not find him on the video?" Her phone beeped and she checked it. "It's one of the cold case detectives. I'll let you know if he can help us out." She was already talking when she walked toward her desk.

Jason picked up the note and walked purposely down the hall and was in luck, because the chief wasn't in a meeting or on one of his endless successions of phone calls. Jason knocked and poked his head in the door. "Can I have a minute or two?"

Metzger nodded and pointed a finger at a chair. "This saves me a trip down the hall. Funny thing, I want to talk to *you*."

Oh great. That was never good.

Jason sat down, glad he had taken the time to get that haircut now. Metzger didn't look any too cheerful, but then again, he rarely did.

"You go first," the chief ordered, leaning back. "This had better be good news."

What the hell had he done now, Jason wondered, but he had been the one to initiate a conversation, so he leaned forward and handed over the note. "This is just back from forensics. We firmly believe it is from our friendly Park Bench Killer, and Rob says the handwriting matches the notes on the victims, but we are having that confirmed. It was delivered to MacIntosh's door along with more flowers. I think we need more manpower. Officers in her house maybe besides the ones outside . . . I've suggested she leave town, and she wants no part of it. I was not joking. Maybe you could order her to go on leave."

Metzger scanned it and looked even less happy than before. "Okay, done. I agree that it would be a wise move to put some officers inside. I was thinking about doing that already. Just imagine the media firestorm if this maniac killed one of the detectives investigating the case, not to mention I'd lose a competent police officer who usually has the sense God gave a goat, unlike some of the others I can think of."

Well, mission accomplished, but Jason felt a frisson of foreboding at the glower on his boss's face. "Why do I think I am lumped somehow into the nongoat group you just mentioned?"

"Oh yeah, you are the leader right now." Metzger looked at him very directly. "You want to know why?"

He suddenly wasn't sure he did. "I get the feeling you'll tell me whether I do or not." He added, "sir." He always did when he was in trouble and wasn't positive if it helped or not, but it couldn't hurt.

Metzger opened his main desk drawer and extracted a photo. He pushed it across the desk. "Take a look."

Despite the trepidation that he wasn't going to like what he saw, Jason really didn't have much choice, so he picked it up. Involuntarily, he said, "Holy shit."

"That was my reaction too," Metzger said grimly. "I completely believe the note is accurate."

Honestly, he stared at the picture and felt violated.

Ellie was turned away from him, her face peaceful, and thankfully the sheet was tugged up enough her breasts weren't exposed, but it was clear enough they were both naked since his bare chest was entirely visible, and no doubt obvious what they'd been doing, since they were in the same bed together, rumpled sheets and all.

*Well hell.*

"Santiago, what the hell were you both thinking?"

He couldn't speak for a long moment because his throat had tightened so much in anger. He finally managed, "I don't believe there was a lot of thinking going on."

"I agree." Metzger was not just brusque, he was furious. "I don't need this shit."

There was absolutely no point in trying to get out of it.

At least he could say with complete honesty, "If this helps, when you last asked if we were sleeping together, Ellie told the truth. We weren't. She wouldn't lie to you."

"When I last asked? Let's not talk about that for now, but we will address it later." The chief put away the photo and snapped the drawer shut.

*Wait a minute. Back the truck up.* Jason said, "Can I see that picture again?"

"Want to revisit the moment?"

"I just want to look at it again."

Metzger huffed out a breath and got it back out. Jason studied it, thoughtful and disturbed. "This isn't right. This is at her house. It's been altered. I can tell you with all honesty that we didn't do anything the night this was taken. I was worried that sleeping on her couch I would be too far away from her if he chose to break a window. She was wearing pajamas. In this she isn't. There's a hidden camera and this guy is pretty tech savvy. He's gotten in and out under our noses. Maybe we can lift a print off the camera. It has to be in the ceiling somewhere."

"I'll send in for a sweep. Tell me, Detective Santiago, what does 'we didn't do anything the night this was taken' mean?" Metzger was direct, but he always was, so no surprise.

Jason wasn't at all sure what to say.

Best to just keep his mouth shut. It had only taken thirty-plus years to learn that lesson.

Metzger leaned on the desk. "There is a hard decision for me ahead, but for now, the two of you are still a team. Stay at your place or a hotel. I'm not even sure what to tell you. I've never had a detective targeted this way, and you are obviously the best person to protect her; that goes without saying, apparently. I thought she had better taste but I've been wrong before. I have an ex-wife to prove it. This stalker is very active. He's hunting and focused. I expect you to solve this series of crimes as soon as possible and get it all out of my face. No more press conferences. I hate those, and I particularly hate them when they involve my detectives, got it? He could post that same picture on social media and quite frankly, God knows what else. With or without you in the game, he's probably been taking pictures of her undressing. What's more, he obviously has broken in. Keep her away from there."

The picture was certainly a nightmare Jason hadn't expected.

"Guess what, lover boy, you get to tell her, because my job is hard enough and I have no desire to tread that path with everything else I have to do. So you get to tell MacIntosh about the picture, you get to tell her about the camera, and I'm making this all your problem. I'm guessing it won't be the easiest conversation you've ever had. Now get the hell out of here."

Jason left the office with a deep breath.

Metzger was right. Ellie was going to be mortified and really ticked off. Not at him—she wasn't unfair—but she was *not* going to be happy someone took a picture of them in bed together.

He still couldn't believe it.

It happened, he knew it did, and with the technology out there, it was all too possible and you didn't have to be a genius either to pull it off. That the killer could get in and out of her house was not just frightening, but petrifying.

Thankfully she was still safe and sound at her desk, working away with a faint frown of concentration on her face. She glanced up. "How'd that go?"

# Chapter 26

He sat and thought it over.

It had occurred to him that Ellie had a sister.

The sister had children. Vulnerability all around. He wouldn't kill a child—he wasn't a monster—but just hinting at it would be enough, he suspected.

Maybe he was a monster. The idea of it stopped him cold, but then again, it didn't last for long. No, the people he'd killed were the monsters in their own singular way, and all he'd done was get his point across.

He was cleaning his closets.

Ellie was like him. She was a slayer. Sword out and unafraid.

Maybe she didn't have to be afraid.

But Jason Santiago certainly did.

**Four o'clock. Cindy** was always on time since her father brought her and sat in the waiting room during the appointment. On cue the light went on signaling a patient arrival.

This time, when Georgia went to open the door, Mr. Helt came in with his daughter. He'd never done that before and Georgia had to admit she was startled, but then again this wasn't a usual session.

He was midforties or so, a hint of silver in his dark hair. He was a civil engineer so the suit was no surprise. He said in a very moderate tone that spoke volumes about possible dissention over this decision, "My wife and I discussed it and agreed maybe I should sit in on this session. If Cindy is truly interested in a career in law enforcement, that is not at all my area of expertise, so I would like to hear what the officers have to say about it."

Not to Georgia's surprise, Cindy looked resentful about the intrusion. Since their lack of communication had been the source of a lot of the family's problems in her opinion, Georgia however was pleased to see Cindy was wearing again the worn jeans and wasn't spilling out of her top. Instead she had on a high school T-shirt that said Go Falcons, which was certainly more appropriate for her age. Her makeup didn't look like she was an extra in a vampire movie either. She said, "Of course. The detectives should be here in fifteen minutes. Please have a seat."

They did and Mr. Helt looked about as comfortable as his daughter, which wasn't very encouraging.

"How did the history test go?"

Cindy made a face. "I got a C. I didn't study."

It wasn't hard to tell that it cost Mr. Helt not to comment on that, but he did have the sense to keep his mouth shut. It wasn't like Georgia didn't agree Cindy was bright enough to be a straight-A student, but the desire had to be there, and that was just life. Some of his daughter's behavior stemmed from his high expectations and rigid rules, but he did seem to genuinely care; they just didn't understand each other very well. That was hardly a new story in the history of mankind, but he was trying. Georgia was certain that one day Cindy would get it and she would appreciate him as a parent.

Different personalities and different goals were an issue. Children didn't come to order.

Georgia wished he'd chosen to stay away from the conversation, but understood his position. When the light went on signaling Ellie and Jason had arrived, she rose to open the door, hoping their presence would lighten the tense atmosphere at least a little.

Jason Santiago, as usual, looked not the part of a staid detective, but instead like he should be signing pictures for groupies after a rock concert in jeans and a collarless shirt under his jacket. Ellie was more polished in slacks and a light sweater, her blond hair smooth to her shoulders, but there was some definite tension going on Georgia could sense right away. She had brought in several more chairs for this discussion, and she made the introductions. "This is Detective Ellie MacIntosh and Detective Jason Santiago and they are here for a short while to answer your questions, Cindy."

She specifically excluded Mr. Helt because she felt strongly his daughter wouldn't want him to be part of the conversation or she wouldn't benefit from it nearly as much, and truthfully, both Santiago and Ellie were doing her a favor. If he wanted to listen, fine, it was his child.

Surprisingly he was the first one to speak up briskly. "Just how dangerous is your profession?"

Ellie was the one to answer because she would, of

course, be diplomatic compared to her partner. Almost anyone would. "It has some risks, but so does driving a car. We deal with people who break the law. It doesn't mean they are all necessarily dangerous, but some are. It isn't a given that every situation will be safe, but they do train us on how to deal with it if it isn't."

"Do you really carry a gun?" That was Cindy, not looking at her father.

"Yep." Jason moved aside his jacket to show his holstered weapon. "We do. But don't get the wrong idea. It isn't glamorous. There's a lot of responsibility that is involved, and the department hammers that into you, as does the job. The definition of a police officer is to protect the safety of the general public, even if it means risking your life. That is a fairly strong commitment."

For him, that was diplomatic.

Ellie spoke with a hint of dryness. "He likes to walk into bullets, but most police officers do not ever come under fire. If you do choose this path, don't go down it thinking anyone will thank you. It means taking a lot of heat, dealing with not-so-nice people, and you do see a lot of things you'd like to forget. On the other hand, it is rewarding in that you are truly helping people. Some appreciate it, and some don't. It can be hard to live with the ones that don't, but I tend to just put that out of my mind. I like what I do. That's what's important."

It summed it up well. Even Cindy's father nodded.

"You've been shot?" Cindy's eyes widened, and it was obvious Jason had risen to hero status.

"Yeah, and I have to say I'm not interested in going there again, but like Detective MacIntosh said, it really doesn't happen to most officers." He turned to Ellie, "Come to think of it, you've been shot too."

"I was running around in the woods after a really bad guy." She shrugged. "Flesh wound, no big deal, but like you, I'd just as soon skip repeating the experience." She looked at Cindy's father. "Since we are homicide detectives we deal with some people who have already done some pretty bad things and are desperate not to get caught. There are all kinds of different divisions in the police department. I honestly think it is more dangerous to be a convenience store clerk."

Cindy's father said in his formal way, "I have the greatest admiration for your profession."

"Do I have to get a degree in criminal justice?" Cindy asked it eagerly.

Georgia did a mental high five. Cindy was really considering it and had thought it over.

Jason shook his head. "I went military first. When I became an MP, it seemed to work for me, so when my time was up, I became a police officer."

"I have a college degree. You can get in without it, but it doesn't hurt." Ellie was straightforward. "There's an awful lot of paperwork involved, so learning to write papers and study notes is pretty valuable."

"Don't remind me about the fourteen or so open files I have on my computer right now," Jason said gloomily. "I think I'd rather get shot at again than finish those reports, so she's right, some of it can be darned boring. Listen to her and do college first. I'm like an arthritic turtle or something when it comes to writing those things. She's a lot better at it."

Cindy laughed, and it was actually animated, so that was a positive response, and even her father smiled, probably more for the recommendation about getting a degree than for the humor, but it was a good thing.

Then Jason did the unthinkable and started to stare at Cindy's chest. She was certainly well endowed already in that department, but as straightforward as he was, Santiago would never do anything like that, not ever, and certainly not in front of the girl's father. He said urgently, "Cindy, where do you go to school?"

She looked down at her shirt, which thankfully Georgia realized seemed the real focus of his attention. "Fairmont High School. Why?"

"I assume a lot of students wear shirts like that, but how about faculty?"

"Well, yeah. To football games and stuff like that, I guess so."

MacIntosh also seemed suddenly interested. "Wings. An educational institution?"

Jason looked at her and she looked right back.

"Cindy, can I take a picture of your shirt on my phone? We're interested to see if someone might recognize it."

Cindy shrugged. "Sure, I don't care."

Georgia had to admit she wondered what was going on, but was glad Cindy's father was sitting right there and didn't object, but looked as puzzled as she probably did.

"You might have just really helped us out," Jason said as both of them got up and headed straight for the door like something was on fire.

Nonplussed because that was an unexpected moment, Georgia had to regroup. She asked Cindy, "Um, what do you think now? Was that helpful to you?"

"That was pretty cool, actually. If I bring my grades up enough, next year I can take a class at the community college in criminal justice and see if I like it even though I'm still in high school."

"That sounds very reasonable and mature to me."

"What about to you?" Cindy asked her father, and Georgia thought he might topple from his chair he was so visibly startled she wanted his opinion. "If I bring up my grades will you pay for the class? I know someone in the grade above me who is doing it now."

"Uh . . . of course. Absolutely."

He was about to say something else and Georgia quickly intervened because she was sure it was to the effect that he and his wife always wanted Cindy to bring up her grades because they knew she was capable of it. This was not, in her professional opinion, the time to say anything remotely like that. "I'm glad that the positives and negatives from the detectives were helpful. You are at an interesting time in your life when you have to make decisions, and I don't know anyone who would disagree they aren't all that easy. What do you think?"

They talked for a while, and when they went to leave, as Cindy walked out, her father lingered for a second. "I wasn't at all sure this therapy thing would work. Her mother talked me into it."

Georgia lifted her brows.

"But it seems to be helping. Thank you."

That was something anyway, she thought.

"I have to admit, I wouldn't mind knowing someday why my daughter's shirt sent two homicide detectives flying out of here at top speed."

Georgia had to be honest. "I wouldn't mind knowing that either. I'll see what I can do."

\* \* \*

**Carl parked his** car and got out and realized at once something was wrong. He never left his garage light on. It was on a timer actually, and switched off after a few minutes, so why it would be on now . . .

He was an imperfect person—who wasn't?—but he was a very good cop. Prickles ran along his skin as he turned around and barely managed to reflexively deflect the blow aimed for his head as pain exploded in his arm. He went down on the garage floor in disbelief, and then wasn't able to even draw his weapon because he was fairly sure his right arm was broken. He rolled away instinctively, which hurt more than expected, and struck out with his feet, catching the assailant solidly in the ankles. The man went down with an audible thud.

He was the last person who would be unaware something like this could happen, but Carl really was taken by surprise.

Luckily, he still had his keys in his left hand and apparently had hit a button as he fell, because the car alarm had started to go off, blaring away. Whoever had attacked him staggered up and did it again, going for his head, but he twisted and the assailant got his shoulder instead. He heard—and felt—the bone crack.

Salvation came in the form of what he later realized was a UPS delivery truck pulling into his driveway. The man attacking him muttered something and apparently decided to run for it.

The noise of the alarm was appalling, but it was supposed to be.

For a minute he lay there, not a very happy person since he couldn't use either arm without excruciating pain, but somehow managed to get his phone from his pocket. He pressed the first button he could find. Just lifting it up so he could speak into it was an extremely unpleasant experience.

Santiago had been the last person he'd called and he thankfully answered, but with the usual lack of grace. "Santiago. What?"

Carl rasped out, "My house. Now."

"What the hell? Why? I can hear an alarm."

"I'm in the garage. Get here. It isn't good." He said it through gritted teeth. "I'm guessing a hospital is in my future."

"No shit. Ambulance needed?"

"No. Don't want one."

"You sure? You sound . . . well, not like you."

It wasn't necessary. "No, thanks. Hurt but not dying. I have no idea what just happened, but I think I have a broken arm and that someone doesn't like me very much. If I was sure I didn't also have at least a cracked collarbone as well, I'd just drive myself. I need someone here who can drive and shoot a gun."

"MacIntosh and I are on our way."

Carl got to his feet, but it wasn't easy and involved using his vehicle for leverage.

Opening the door into the house wasn't even a remote possibility. He rested against the car and tried to shut off the alarm, but couldn't manage it physically because it involved unlocking the door or the trunk, and so he endured the noise and took in a long breath. The arm was enough, but the shoulder was even worse.

He would have called Georgia, but what if the attacker was still out there? No. At least MacIntosh and Santiago could defend themselves, though he was fairly sure Georgia could handle a tough situation, but why risk her if he had backup.

His arm was aching badly already, but his shoulder hurt worse. Back one million years ago when he'd been in grade school a kid had nailed him with a killer tackle during a friendly football game and he'd broken his clavicle. It had hurt like pure hell. This was certainly the same kind of experience.

Why the assault?

He couldn't imagine it wasn't tied to the murders. His very expensive set of golf clubs sat untouched in the corner, or maybe if it was a thief, he just didn't understand how much they cost because he didn't play golf.

He certainly knew how to use a baseball bat, though.

"Mister, are you all right?"

He found himself looking into the broad face of a young burly delivery driver peering into the garage. Carl admitted in a thick voice, "No."

"You don't look too good," the man confirmed anxiously. "And between the alarm going off and the guy running past me as I came to drop off the package I thought maybe I should just at least look anyway. Want me to call the police?"

"I am the police," Carl informed him wryly. "Lieutenant Carl Grasso of the Milwaukee Police Department. I think that's part of the problem. They are on the way. I also think you just saved my life, so thanks. I just had a close encounter of the bad kind with a baseball bat."

"Oh jeez." The young man's eyes widened.

"Would you mind doing me another favor and unlocking the trunk so the alarm turns off? I'm getting a headache from the noise and it really is trivial compared to everything else, but I'd appreciate it. Those are the keys right there on the floor. I can't pick them up."

"Sure. Of course." The young man hastily scooped up the keys and thankfully a few moments later the alarm stopped blaring. He said lamely, "Nice ride, man."

"Thanks." Carl could feel the swelling was well under way from his injuries. "Did you happen to get a good look at the man who ran past you?"

"I don't know if good would be the right word." He paused and thought about it. "He was really hoofing it and through the lawn, not right past me."

Well, that was disappointing, but how would this young man know it was important to pay attention? Most people didn't. Carl's phone started ringing and he ignored it, since using either arm wasn't much of a cheerful option and was getting worse by the moment. "They'll have to call me back. I'm not really able to get that."

"Um, hey, my route is almost done," the young man told him earnestly. "I think I'll stay here until the police arrive, if that's okay with you. I kinda think if whoever worked you over comes back, there wouldn't be a lot you could do about it if you can't pick up keys or answer a phone."

Carl thought the same thing. He eyed the young man's considerable bulk and agreed that was a very nice offer. "I really appreciate that."

## Chapter 27

*He was taking too many risks.*

*It had gone all wrong and he still wasn't sure why he'd done it. Well, that wasn't true. Killing the old lady might have been a grave error, so now he was backtracking and second-guessing himself.*

*He needed to acknowledge that he was off center, but he also was resentful that Lieutenant Carl Grasso was investigating that murder instead of Ellie MacIntosh. He'd seen the news coverage. She should have been given the case; should have been the one to know it was him.*

*He'd never failed before.*

*Grasso hadn't been taken enough by surprise.*

**"I'm positively infuriated."**

Ellie thought Georgia looked it too.

"We don't know it was the Park Bench Killer."

That Grasso had to have an orthopedic surgeon on call come and put a pin in his arm and was still in recovery didn't make Ellie happy either. No one liked hospital waiting rooms, but in this case it was necessary.

Jason would sit down for about five seconds and then get up and walk around. "Hell yes, we do. Ellie, in that press conference that aired across the state, Metzger didn't mention you or me, but he did say he had his best detectives on the case, including Lieutenant Carl Grasso, who was investigating a suspicious death linked to the other crimes. I don't think you have to be a genius to make the connection."

She wasn't going to argue the point he'd just made, but there was no proof at all. That was the problem. "Whoever he was, that was not playing nice."

"He got lucky," Santiago said emphatically.

"I think Carl will agree once he's not zoned out on painkillers." Georgia was resolute, but at least it was nice to know she was *there*. Grasso didn't have anyone else. "We're remodeling the house anyway. I can stay there for a while with him."

"They" were? Well, in Ellie's opinion that wasn't a bad thing, but she wasn't aware it was so serious between them.

Georgia correctly read her expression. "He asked me to help pick out the finishes. I said yes."

"You might want to use that fancy alarm system he has," Jason suggested, skirting around decorating since it was absolutely not his favorite topic. "He's out of commission in the protection department right now. Luckily, you know how to fire a gun."

Georgia was pretty accurate with a firearm. Ellie knew that to be true. She said, "Metzger won't ignore this."

"He'd better not."

"Want us to stay with you?" Ellie didn't particularly wish to do it, but she certainly would.

"No." Georgia finally smiled even if it was a little halfhearted. "I will use the alarm system as suggested and you're right, I can fire a gun. Did Cindy really help with the case in some way?"

Ellie was the one who answered. "We think so. As per this entire case, it is still circumstantial, but she finally narrowed the playing field for suspects." They had been sitting in the living room of the sweet older couple who found the first victim, showing the picture of a shirt with wings to the wife, when the call came in about Grasso's attack. The woman had been decisive enough that she recognized it that it was worth pursuing.

Parkview Elementary. Fairmont High School.

**"I never admit** I'm hungry until I'm too hungry," Jason told her as they left the hospital. "At that point I'm not functional. I need to be part of a sitcom when I walk through the door and shout out, 'Honey, I'm home,' and someone in a dress has already set the table and I can smell roast beef."

"Well, I'm not her."

"Got that one figured out." He punched up a number on his phone. He ordered two pizzas, and she looked at him like he was crazy, but when they got to his apartment building after picking up the food she understood after they went up the stairs. He said, "This will take two seconds."

He stopped and knocked on a door just down from his. An older lady answered and he said, "For you and Dylan, Mrs. Landry. Have a nice night."

"Thank you so much." She reached out and touched his hand. "You know Dylan will be one happy boy."

They continued on and Santiago unlocked the door, planted the pizza box on the table, grabbed two plates, and ripped off two paper towels for napkins. He asked if she wanted a glass of wine as he got out a beer. She did, and when they sat down she looked at him inquiringly. Ellie just couldn't help it. "That should be on a commercial. You do that often?"

"What?"

"Be a pizza delivery guy."

"Oh, well, she doesn't have much money and her grandkid lives with her. Dylan likes pizza, and I like pizza, so we get along. He's a nice little guy. I can't enjoy eating pizza knowing he would love to have some, so I do it for myself, really. It's a selfish gesture. If you buy one, you can get the second for half price. There you go. Lukens could probably explain it. Anyway, we got nothing from the UPS guy that really helps other than Grasso didn't get beaten to death, so I give him credit there. Where do we go from here?"

There had been times she didn't like him, but there were times Ellie liked him too much.

"That's nice. Not what happened to Grasso, but the pizza thing."

"Ellie, we are talking about the case and just go ahead and cave that it is really good pizza. I think it's the crust. So what do you think happened tonight?"

She did refocus. "I'm trying to make sense of it but not having much luck. Certainly he can't expect to kill off every police officer investigating the murders."

"I sure as hell hope not, because we'd be leading the list. To think Grasso told *me* to watch my back."

"Something set him off."

"Or in that fancy neighborhood someone broke in and it has nothing to do with the case at all. He surprised them and they attacked him."

"He doesn't own a baseball bat." Grasso had clearly pointed that out on the way to the hospital. "So it isn't like the intruder picked something at random; he'd brought it. And the alarm system into the house hadn't been breached, just the garage side door, which isn't wired in. He was waiting for him."

While the subject matter wasn't pleasant, the pizza was really very good. Santiago was easily on his fourth slice. "Maybe," he said thoughtfully, "it was a show of power. From the beginning he's been taunting us, daring us to catch him, and if he could kill an experienced police officer like Grasso who is working with you, how impressed would you be by that? Trying to figure how these wackos think makes my brain hurt, but I'm wondering if the minute Metzger mentioned Grasso's name in the media, our friend out there decided to go for it."

It was a tangible theory, or at least made as much sense as anything else. "I suppose if you are crazy enough for the rest of it, maybe it is possible."

Jason used his makeshift napkin and set it on the plate, evidently finished. "I've got something to tell you and I was going to earlier, but we had that appointment for Lukens and I sure didn't want to tell you before that, and then the call from Grasso got in the way. I have to say ahead of time you aren't going to like it at all. For that matter, I don't like it much either. Wait, let me correct that. I don't like it in any way, shape, or form."

Serious Santiago replacing his usual wisecracking, irreverent style didn't bode well. She said slowly, "Okay, go ahead. It can't be worse than the rest of this after-noon."

"It sure as hell isn't going to improve your day." He sighed and ran his hand through his hair, never a good sign. "Someone mailed Metzger a picture."

"Of?" A very real twinge of apprehension curled in the pit of her stomach.

"Us. Let's say he really won't be asking you if we are sleeping together again because he doesn't need to ask. It was taken at your house."

She couldn't believe it, but the look on his face said it was the truth. Whatever she expected him to say, that certainly wasn't it. "What?" she asked incredulously.

Tact wasn't one of his gifts and Jason didn't deny that, so he just laid it plainly in front of her. "We aren't doing anything, we're just sleeping, but it's damning, I guess. He altered it so it looks like you aren't wear-ing anything. Don't worry, it isn't like Metzger has now seen you naked. I'm happy to say I'm not ex-posed in all my glory either, but there's a lot more of me than you. We definitely appear to have been doing something we did not do that particular evening."

A lot of women—maybe most women—might have a meltdown, but luckily Ellie wasn't one of them. She just sat there with undoubtedly a stricken look on her face and then composed herself. "Okay, yeah, that doesn't improve my day at all. Metzger aside and the fact there will be repercussions from this that will af-fect us both, he had to get that picture somehow. We have hidden cameras watching for him. That means he must too."

"The chief is having your place swept for devices tomorrow. They are going to do my apartment too. He suggested a motel for tonight."

"Metzger suggested you and I go to a motel together and he has a picture of us in bed? I've really never been so mortified in my life."

"He did suggest it. Not a bad idea either. I figure he now knows that ship has sailed, so he's more interested in keeping the situation under control. He pretty much ordered me to keep you in my line of vision at all times. I intended to anyway, so no hardship here."

"I'm so angry, I—I—don't know what to say. I—"

She really was fuming mad.

He interrupted her sputtering. "Ellie, do you want this dangerous man to film you changing your clothes, walking out of the shower, or even brushing your teeth? I don't know about you, but I'd like to be able to use the bathroom and not have a snapshot of it out there for generations to enjoy. I don't see any signs anyone has been in here, but then again, you didn't either at your place until he left that rose in your bedroom. I just think maybe a motel is a good idea. He got to Grasso of all people."

A very valid argument. Carl looked like he stepped out of a magazine shoot all the time, but he was one tough and competent cop.

"Let's just go," he said. "We can sit and talk about it. This thing with Grasso has me really on edge."

He eyed her slender frame and didn't add that the thought of someone coming after her with a baseball bat would give him nightmares for the next decade. At the least a decade and maybe a lot longer than that would be accurate. "I'll grab you a shirt to sleep in, though I'd kind of prefer you without it."

"That hasn't worked out so well for us so far," she

shot back, standing to whisk her plate off the table and take it into the kitchen.

There was a hard argument to make, so he let it go. He was also worried about what Metzger might do.

He had the urge to apologize but he wasn't sure what for. Ellie was a consenting adult and he hadn't made the decision alone. He was going to worry about it later, because right now they had bigger problems.

"I don't normally do this, but we'll leave the dishes in the sink. I'll be back in two seconds."

It was disconcerting to have to wonder if he was somehow being watched as he grabbed his bag and emptied it, tossing in some clean clothes and an extra T-shirt and his shaving kit. He remembered he had an unwrapped toothbrush in the drawer from his recent visit to the dentist, so he took that and put it in as well for Ellie.

The simple act of walking out to the truck made him nervous, and he wasn't someone who got nervous easily. Ellie hid it pretty well, but he could tell she was also on the jittery side, but luckily the vehicle started smoothly and they pulled away safely. He said, "It's my job to drive and your job to make sure we aren't being followed."

"You do realize someone capable of putting in a hidden camera knows how to use a tracking device on a vehicle, right?" Her voice was somber. "Why do I think that now that a police officer was attacked Metzger is going to ask the state or the FBI for help? I wish Grasso had seen him more clearly, because that would be one very reliable witness."

"He was getting the shit beat out of him," Jason pointed out. "And the guy did it right too, making it impossible for him to draw his weapon. He must have a pad somewhere with a note jotted down that says *When assaulting a police officer, break both his arms so you don't get shot.* I'd love to see the rest of his notes."

"Maybe you wouldn't." Ellie was paying careful attention to her side mirror. "The purpose of that picture sent to Metzger . . . was it just to show me he'd been there?"

"I'm not Lukens, and right now don't want to be her, because she's with a badly injured cop who is probably really pissed off because I know I would be, but I think he's just taking control of your life, Ellie. He wants you to be aware of him, 24/7."

"I'm not a psychologist either, but he's winning if that's the game. I'm not seeing any of the same cars behind us."

Jason said caustically, "Well, he's had a busy day. Maybe he's taking time off and unwinding with a cocktail or something."

"I hope he chokes on it. A rogue olive goes down his throat and ends all our problems."

He braked for a light and just in the nick of time, because some distracted asshole ran it and nearly caused a collision with a red van. "But then while justice might be done, we would never know who he is, and that is our main problem. I don't want him to get hit by a car when crossing against the light or anything like that. I want to know he's no longer out there because we put him away in a small, dark cell."

"I suppose there's validity to that."

"I don't know about you, but he isn't adding to my quality of life. Do you have a motel preference?"

"Let's shoot for someplace newer that might have security cameras. That's about it. Clean sheets and decent bathroom and I'll be fine. I'd say what I really want is my own bed, but I doubt I'd sleep very well there right now. I'm going to call Georgia and see how Grasso is doing."

He didn't have any choice but to listen to her end of the call since he was sitting right there, and he got the impression that as long as Grasso didn't drive, since he was on painkillers, the hospital was going to release him at his insistence. That didn't surprise him at all. When she was finished, his comment was, "I'd be happier out of there myself, and there is no given he's safer with all the people coming and going."

She tucked away her phone. "You've been watching too much television. The risks the killer takes are very calculated. He wouldn't do something like that in my opinion. He likes to take us by surprise."

"It seems like it. Let's stay aware of that."

He picked out a generic chain hotel several stories high so they didn't have a ground-floor room. They checked in and got the room keys. One secure door and an inaccessible window facing a city view. He dumped his bag on the floor and dropped on the bed, shutting his eyes. "I'm so insomniac that they could put up a poster of me, but I swear I could go to sleep right now in my clothes. I think you might be a good influence."

"If I don't, through no fault of my own, get you killed."

"There is that," he acknowledged. "If you promise to shoot him if he breaks in, I think I can get in a few winks, and you're right, it isn't your fault."

Ellie said emphatically, "After today? Oh, I promise if anyone tries to come through that door, he's a goner."

Jason said, "God, I love your pillow talk."

## Chapter 28

*It was clear his options were slim.*

*He carefully thought it over while watching a second news broadcast, furious there was no comment on the attack on a veteran police officer.*

*He'd tried to develop a strategy to target Santiago and had come up with a few ideas, but none seemed like they would work. The man wasn't vulnerable through friends or family. He was also vigilant and street smart, so he had to strike directly.*

*Ellie just couldn't get involved with anyone like a commodities broker or a garage mechanic, because he could handle them easily, he thought with resentment; it had to be another cop.*

*What happened next was essentially going to be her fault.*

**The killer had** called her again.

Ellie was using the hotel's free Internet to check

her e-mail, wearing Santiago's shirt, drinking a com-
plimentary bottle of water when her phone beeped.

Unknown number.

She took a moment before she answered. "Mac-
Intosh."

"How's the lieutenant? Where are you? At your
house up north?"

The sibilant whisper didn't make her happy at all
and made her wonder if the theory that he was trying
to disguise his voice was because she knew him wasn't
exactly right. She said shortly, "Why did you do it?"

"He shouldn't get the glory. It belongs to you."

"What does that mean?"

Then he really wrecked her already awful evening.
"How's your sister?"

He hung up. Ellie stared at the phone, more shaken
than ever, because there was no denying that Grasso
had been attacked because of her, and just the mention of Jody turned her body to ice. The chance it had
been some random thug intent on a robbery was out
the window, not that she'd really believed that anyway. Jason sat up and pushed his hair back. Even
with the haircut it was a shade too long. "I heard most
of that. Him?"

She swiveled in the chair. "Yes."

He swore softly, "Shit. What did he say?"

"I have to make a call." Her hands were so unsteady
she almost couldn't manage it, but she pulled up her
sister from her contacts. To her relief, Jody answered
fairly quickly for her, since she didn't cart her phone
around with her all the time. Ellie did her best to
sound composed, but her voice cracked. "I . . . I need
to say something I don't want to say . . . but, look . . .

you aren't safe right now. No one in our family is safe. You need to tell your husband to put your kids and the dog in the car and all of you have to leave."

"Ellie!" It was a gasp.

"Don't trust anyone, Jody. I mean it. Just tell me you'll do it. I don't care where you go, but go."

"You're scaring me." Her sister's voice was small.

"You need to be scared." Ellie's voice wobbled. "Go. We can talk tomorrow."

Jason took the phone from her trembling hand and set it down on the desk. He crouched down by the chair, resting his forearms on his knees. "Well, I don't think I need to ask again what he said, do I?"

"He wanted to know about Grasso. I asked why he did it and he said Grasso shouldn't get the glory which I assume means news coverage on the cases. Then he asked about my sister. "

It was nice when Jason put his arms around her, because she needed to hold on to something. "Ellie, you aren't doing this to your family, he is. That rat bastard. He'd better hope I don't find him in a place where there are no witnesses." Jason's face was grim. "An eye for an eye has a nice ring to it. I think we have a real lead, Ellie. Take a breath. On the authority of one observant older lady, he was very likely wearing a T-shirt from a specific high school."

She rested against him for a minute and then pulled away and looked blankly out the window. Her voice was bleak. "My mother's cancer was absolutely not my fault. This is. I keep wondering how I got his un-wanted attention in the first place. I mean our last se-rial case was more about you than me."

He followed her. "You sustained the most injuries and are a lot prettier than I am. I wonder if it was that article in the paper about you figuring out the cold case. Unfortunately, considering the circulation area is huge, that wouldn't narrow it down for us. Same thing for the brief interview we did for local TV. Maybe he caught it and took one look at you and decided you were his dream girl. I know that happened to me, and apparently to Grantham too . . . ever considered growing a few warts?"

It was nice of him to at least attempt to make her laugh. "You do know your questionable sense of humor surfaces at all the wrong times." The parking lot below was full of cars, most of them not Wisconsin plates. She stood there, thinking hard. "He really works to disguise his voice. The first few calls I thought he was just being creepy, but I'm starting to *really* buy into the theory I know him somehow. I think he's doing his best to make sure I don't recognize who I'm talking to when he calls. He doesn't have an accent, which means he's probably from Wisconsin or Minnesota, or maybe even Iowa, which doesn't narrow it down too much, but a little anyway."

"Let's not forget South and North Dakota." Santiago's voice was wry. "I think we all sound pretty much the same. So he isn't from New York or Savannah or Sacramento. We are still wandering around in the dark."

That was distressingly true. "He knew I wasn't home tonight. Maybe surveillance will hand us something. He has to know after that picture and the rose we are aware he broke into my house."

She didn't even want to think about that picture, but she had to consider it. If Metzger had it tested for prints, and she would guess he had, then her personal life was not so personal. Rob might keep his mouth shut, but if a different technician handled it, that wasn't a given. If everyone knew, Metzger had no choice but to reassign them.

There was a conversation she didn't want to have in her future. Maybe he'd pair her up with Grasso instead, but the lieutenant usually worked cases alone or gave assistance on difficult investigations. Except he was out of commission right now, and there was a killer out there who really frightened her.

She'd just have to worry later about all that upcoming upheaval in her career. Santiago said, "Maybe he'll figure it out, but maybe he'll slip up. Once the sweep is done, we'll have a better handle on it."

She wasn't quite as confident. "How did he not trip the security system?"

With narrowed eyes, Santiago replied, "I've been thinking about that. Who installed it? Male technician, tall and with brown hair?"

That had crossed her mind as well. "I have no idea. It was there already when I rented the condo. I just made a phone call to change the code and went to the office and signed a different agreement. It's worth looking into, except I assume any of the technicians handling those systems could disable it and then turn it back on."

"The same five-state dilemma again. It's so broad. I assume the company screens carefully: Are you a serial killer/stalker? It could be part of the background check, but for some reason, I doubt they ask it."

She chose to ignore the sarcasm, which was the best way to handle him. They were both under pressure and more than a little stressed. "It can't hurt to look into it. We know this can be hit and miss."

"We've been missing a lot. He hasn't. He's cautious. He's careful, but I still swear he'll trip up."

"So you keep saying, and your personal foibles aside, I think you're a decent detective, so I'm willing to believe. However, I want *us* to be the bump in his road." She was starting to rally a little, trying to get her anxiety under control. Between Grasso and the overt threat to her family, not to mention the damn picture, this really was getting to her.

"Foibles? Like what?" Jason demanded, but she knew he was doing his best to lighten the mood. "And just decent? I'm getting kind of insulted here."

She tried too and waved a hand. "We don't have time to go into that extensive foible list. Can we stay on topic, please?"

"Well yeah, that list might take up the next decade or so." He grinned, but it faded fast. "It wouldn't be the first asshole we've invited to run over us. Ellie, why don't you come to bed? It's getting late. I'm not suggesting anything other than sleep, if you can believe that. *I'm* having a hard time wrapping my mind around it. You have to be at least as tired as I am. Maybe twice as much. And I'm tired."

She was tired, but she was also wound up. "I just talked to *him* on the phone."

"You need all the pistons firing if we are going to get him. Take it from someone who rarely indulges in it, sleep is pretty fantastic to help clear your head."

It was probably good advice. She switched off the lamp. True to his word, when she lay down next to him, he didn't move to touch her. She said, "I'm really thinking about this. Despite his best efforts, I think I recognized his voice. I just can't place it. Maybe if I just stare at the ceiling long enough it will come to me. I'm searching for it and I have to figure it out. It feels like I'm playing a game and I know the answer, but it isn't right there on the tip of my tongue."

"Been there and done that." Santiago did turn so he faced her. "If I think about something else, it usually comes to me."

That wasn't bad advice.

"How did he know we were gone? That is really bothering me. He just asked if I was 'up north.' "

"I know you don't want to hear this, but maybe he has your place wired for more than just a camera and overheard or recorded something. Not to mention it would make sense to me if I was examining your life with a microscope that you'd go there."

He was right, because she didn't want to hear that at all. He was also right because she was bone tired and maybe could drift off.


**Jason had a** bagel for breakfast and watched the sun come up. He'd brought up some orange juice and a croissant for Ellie, but she was still sleeping, and he figured she needed it.

He would send Grasso a message about the phone call, but he figured the man was probably strung out on pain meds and it was still pretty early.

So he sat and thought it all over.

The murders linked now to the school, the phone calls, the obvious obsession . . .

It first came to him as just a random thought. A glimmer of light like the glow on the horizon dawned on him as he sipped a cup of coffee from the lobby and reviewed the facts and wondered if he'd made a connection.

*About time.*

He went down and got a second cup of coffee and thought about it some more when he got back to the room. It made sense. Maybe it made too much sense.

He waited until Ellie stirred and rolled over and he thought she looked more than delicious in just his shirt as she got out of bed, but that was beside the point. He offered, "I can go get you coffee or there's orange juice. Jody sent me a text since you didn't answer her. They're fine."

Ellie hugged him. "Thank God. That's how I want to start my day. I gave her your number awhile ago in case she couldn't reach me. She asked for it. I hope you don't mind."

She could probably walk on him in stiletto heels and he wouldn't mind. "Nope."

"Orange juice is fine. I usually want coffee, but I really slept."

She went into the bathroom and he got the orange juice from the minifridge and steadied himself for this conversation. Maybe he was out of his mind, but maybe he wasn't.

No, he wasn't. He was sure of it, but then Ellie was better at this part than he was, and they had different angles at how they approached an investigation.

He let her eat half her croissant before he said, "I think we might have a viable suspect."

"What? Like with a name?" She stared at him, poised to take another bite.

"I don't know. You tell me. I've been awake all night. I want you to look at your messages." He didn't mention how much he'd wanted to wake her up, but held back, sorting it all out.

She did and scanned the list. "Oh shit!"

Girl after his own heart. "Nichols? That's the high

school he teaches at? Fairmont?" She didn't need all night. She sat there, just staring at the faculty list he'd brought up and texted to her. "He fits the physical profile. No wonder he flies under the radar of the surveillance team. He lives next door to me and has every reason to be right there."

"My thinking too. I'm not quite as quick as you. I thought we could use him, see if anyone on the teaching staff came to his mind as someone who ran and might fit the description, but I realized that he can watch you and no one would notice. There's also that he doesn't like me."

"Irrefutable proof right there." She kept scrolling through the list, the orange juice forgotten.

He ignored the derision. "I'm pretty serious here. Guys can tell, and he's polite and all, but he has to work at it."

"I am going mention now that when I first met you I didn't like you either." Her brows went up. "No wonder he speaks in that voice that makes me want to go hide in a closet. I *do* know him."

"He sent that picture because he's jealous. I bet if we look he cut a hole in your attics that share a wall and put in that camera, so no, he didn't set off the alarm system, and the most damning is that when I was standing outside waiting for you to come out, I asked him to watch out for anyone nearby your condo but said there were going to be officers in the area. *That*'s how he knew. I also think we both remember him in person delivering those flowers. I bet he got a special thrill out of that one, being able to hand them straight to you. Ellie, he fits the description."

Her eyes were shadowed. "He's married and has two kids."

"When did you become so naive? He *seems* nice. I looked him up online while you were asleep. He's also the track coach at the high school. I bet he does a lot of jogging."

Young and personable plus the right build and coloring . . . he really did fit.

"I'm blind or an idiot. If it wasn't for Cindy's shirt . . ." She rubbed her forehead. "Wait, he doesn't have an earring."

Jason had considered that too. "You don't have to wear it all the time. If I was a teacher, I wouldn't wear it to school. I had one for a while when I got out of the military, but when I applied to join the force, I took it out and just never really wore it again, but I could have off duty. I've literally been thinking this over all night."

"Why is it I'm not surprised? I can't believe you don't have a tattoo." She started to pull on yesterday's clothes.

"I don't like needles." That was the truth. "I'm glad you've looked me over."

She said pragmatically, "Stop that. Surveillance isn't going to do a thing to catch him, if Nichols is the one. He has every right to be there. What perfect cover. And if he is the 'Observer,' he has a chance to do it every single day. I wonder if he has a connection to Parkview. We can certainly check my attic, but think about it. If someone got into my neighbor's house and went up there to cut a hole and put a camera in, a good lawyer could argue the point. I have no idea if they use their security system or not."

"Ellie, think about how many eyewitnesses we have."

"This is starting to come together." Her blond hair

brushed her shoulders as she shook her head. "He could easily also argue that he's a track coach so he runs, and of course a park trail is a good place to do it. Even if someone identified him, it doesn't constitute proof of anything. I would think it would support his defense. The bodies are found in parks and that's where he runs. But we have the friend. I'm so glad we told her to go somewhere safe. Nichols is a married man. If he made that date, it's another piece of evidence. It doesn't make him a murderer, but it adds another layer to this. Let's talk to her again."

**Chapter 29**

*S*omeone had gone through the pictures.

*They were out of their usual order. He kept them meticulously hidden and stacked in just a certain way.*

It wasn't like he didn't know who was responsible for the infringement on his privacy. If there had been a police search with a legal warrant, his wife would have called him hysterically over it, so he was still safe in that regard, but now she knew.

He'd met her right after the drowning incident with that other girl when he was in college, and then they'd crossed paths again when they were both student teaching. His parents had liked her, which was a miracle, because as far as he could tell, his father didn't really like him very much. So he'd married her.

He'd settled for what he didn't really want to please someone else, and he was tired of it.

\* \* \*

**It wasn't familiar** for a moment, and when Carl tried to roll over he realized he really couldn't and didn't at once know where he was exactly.

Not his own bed, that was for sure.

He was somewhat hazy on the details of coming to Georgia's condo. He'd opted out on pain meds for his collarbone, but they'd definitely had to use some for the surgery on his arm. He felt like a beached whale trying to get out of bed. There was just no leverage and he made a note to himself never to take sitting up for granted again. Three attempts and a true groan of pain and he managed it.

A look in the bathroom mirror didn't help matters. He was bandaged and casted on one side, had a sling on the other arm, and in his opinion, maybe a little old for this kind of collateral damage. He was lucky in that the tip of the bat had caught his lower jaw but not broken it, but the bruise, he'd been told by a prosaic and weary emergency department physician, was going to be quite a sight to see.

Spot on. The young doctor had known what he was talking about. Half of Carl's face was purple, cheekbone all the way down to his throat, and not a light purple, but the kind on a Victorian settee cloaked in velvet in an old parlor. Shaving on that side was out of the question right now, and being only half shaven seemed ridiculous, so he decided just to forget it, even though he hadn't skipped that since he was fifteen. He also had to sit down like a woman on the toilet to relieve himself, and just the simple act of using the lever to flush it made him break out in a sweat. Washing his hands was even worse.

When he went out to the kitchen, Georgia looked up from the paper and got up quickly. "Good morning. This might not make you happy, but I ran to the corner and got you an iced coffee with a straw. I thought holding a mug might be a challenge."

That was thoughtful of her. "Splash some whiskey in it and I'll drink sewer water. I hate those pain pills. Whiskey and I are old friends."

"You self-medicate too much."

"Absolutely. No argument here."

"Police officers. Aren't they always supposed to be on the alert?"

He gingerly took a stool and managed it pretty well. "Well, not always apparently, or did I imagine you there at the hospital after I wasn't on the alert and I hadn't had a drop but was looking forward to it."

"No, you didn't imagine it." She looked at him with real sympathy—to him anyway—in her beautiful eyes. "But I also heard from the medical staff it might have been a lot worse."

He didn't disagree. "Whoever came after me wasn't fooling around. He made sure I couldn't draw my weapon."

"I hope you don't mind, but I called a locksmith to go repair the side garage door at your house. He just called. Whoever it was used a drill on the lock. He said he'd drop off the keys to the new one at my office."

He grimaced as he noticed from a clock on the wall it was past eleven. "I'm sorry if you missed appointments for me."

"No, no problem, everyone rescheduled. People want to talk to me, but they don't usually die if they can't." She made a face. "Not always true. No suicidal patients on for today. A man who believes his parents were foreign spies and three different patients battling

marital problems that need to hash it out with someone who won't condemn them if they decide to just
stay or do the alternative, and one patient who is very
afraid maybe he is gay but has yet to say it out loud.
He and I aren't working on his sexual orientation—I
wouldn't even pretend to be able to help him with
that, he is who he is—but he needs to be able to say it
to me first apparently before he tells his family. I'm the
dry run. He's probably relieved to put it off, so you
did him a favor."

"I'll tell him to inform the man with the bat he did
a good deed then."

"The coffee?"

"With whiskey, please. I'm not going to take more
pills, and since I can't even scratch my chin, it is clear
I won't be driving anywhere."

"You haven't eaten anything." She moved to the refrigerator.

"I'll have a piece of toast or something. I'm not sure
I can chew anything else. I keep trying to decide what
hurts the most, my face or my shoulder or my arm.
Not complaining, just making an observation that
there seems to be a hung jury on the winner."

"I'll kiss you in effort to make it all better."

She set down the cup and fulfilled the promise, and
if it wasn't all better, it was certainly some better. He
wasn't used to sharing with anyone—not his personal
space and not his feelings—and especially not used
to being dependent like this. In the course of his
career he'd never been really injured, and it was a
good thing, since no one would have stepped into the
breach.

That was a wakeup call.

"I'm going to have to owe Santiago for introducing

me to you." Carl said it and expelled a breath. "And I've never wanted to thank him for anything."

Georgia said, "Not true. I really think that if Chief Metzger of the Milwaukee Police Department didn't think both Santiago and MacIntosh needed your level of experience to help them along, he would never have sent you back to homicide, where you've always belonged. Ellie is smart and intuitive, and Santiago could run with the bulls in a street in Spain. However, you balance them. He's also always wanted you there."

She could be right. He was transferred to vice for a while after the Internal Affairs investigation couldn't prove anything, but he'd known Metzger had done it because he felt like he had to send out a message to everyone.

Carl smiled, which he learned hurt his face quite a lot. "Psych 101?"

She smiled back. "I'm thinking at least a sophomore course. Give me some credit."


**The sharp knock** on the condo door came when Ellie was changing. Even though she'd showered at the hotel, wearing the same clothes for two days made her feel like she'd pulled an all-nighter at the library studying for a college test. Those days were over, and she was happy to have left them behind.

Jason was in her living room, so she'd just let him answer it, since it was probably the sweep team. She actually had chosen the walk-in closet to change, as-suming whoever had done it with the camera just targeted the bedroom and wouldn't film her picking out what she going to wear in the morning. She felt beyond outraged and vulnerable if she really thought about it, so she tried to ignore the thought and plucked a shirt at random off a hanger.

"Ellie."

She was still slipping on her blouse when Jason came into the bedroom. She said hurriedly, "I know the sweep team is here. I'm going as fast as possible so we can get out of their way."

Santiago's voice sounded not at all normal. "Um, no, not them. I checked and they'll be here soon. But there is someone to see you and I can't wait to hear this conversation."

That seemed like a strange thing for him to say coupled with the look on his face. She swiftly buttoned her blouse. "Who is it?"

"Mrs. Nichols. She asked me if I was aware you were having an affair with her husband. Apparently she believes I'm your boyfriend. She isn't a happy camper at the moment."

"Interesting. Why on this earth would she think *that*?"

"Let's find out."

This was not a blip she saw coming on the horizon, so Ellie said under her breath, "I meant that you were my boyfriend."

"I'm not?"

"We'll discuss that later."

"She's pretty upset."

He was right there.

The woman looked . . . distraught when Ellie walked into the living room. The word applied. Her eyes were red like she'd been crying and her mouth pressed into a very firm line. Ellie certainly didn't need this in her day, but it might prove helpful. "I would say something polite but I don't get the impression this is a neighborly visit. Why on earth do you think I'm having an affair with your husband?"

Mrs. Nichols' gaze was accusatory. "What are these?" She tossed a stack of pictures on the coffee table.

Ellie looked at the top several and reminded herself she was a police officer and to hold steady. "I don't know."

"He has more naked pictures of you. I found them yesterday after he left the receipt for the roses in his pocket. I was doing the laundry and found the bill and realized he was lying to me because *he* bought the flowers. So, yes, I'm not going to deny it. I went looking around. The bottom of a sock drawer really showed me quite a lot. Of you."

This didn't get better, it just got worse and worse. Ellie was the one who had to stand and gather her breath to look into angry eyes, when she was the one who was the injured party. They both were victims if Nichols was guilty. "I'll be concise. Those pictures were taken without my consent and there is no affair. A crime scene crew is going to arrive any minute to sweep my home for a hidden camera, and I wish I could promise that will be the end of it, but I can't. We are now officially investigating him."

"I don't believe you."

"Does it look for a minute like I'm posing for those pictures? Is the camera shot at eye level, or maybe taken from above?"

"You had to be posing. How else would he have them?"

"Think it over." Ellie had to balance her job and her personal sense of outrage. "You wouldn't be standing in front of me if you didn't think he was capable of violating your trust."

Mrs. Nichols' voice went from angry to small. Her hands dropped from being planted on her hips to limp at her sides. "Oh God." All the color left her face and she dropped her head. "What else did he do?"

It would be unfortunate to mention the possible murder charges at this crucial moment. This new development was starting to win her over to the theory that Nichols was responsible for a lot more than buying some flowers, and this woman might be able to help; maybe not in court, but with the investigation. Ellie couldn't whitewash it. "He's in big trouble. At the very least breaking and entering, plus the varying charges that go along with voyeurism and that I can launch a civil suit against him as well. He's destroyed personal property, and we think we can prove your husband attacked and injured a police officer. Other crimes might also be involved."

Alissa Nichols asked on a whisper, "Like what? Murder? I found a lot more than just those pictures. Some driver's licenses. I watch the news . . . I recognized the names. Why would he have those?"

Evidence. At last. It was the one thing they really lacked. "Please tell me you kept them." Ellie couldn't help it. "If you ever thought murder was possible, why wouldn't you say something?"

"You have to ask me that?" The young woman turned away, sobbing. "We have two children! I can't have married a monster."

That was the understatement of the year. "I'm here, a homicide detective, right next door."

"If he killed me, they'd be left with *him*. I couldn't confront him."

"What about him makes you so afraid?" Ellie tried out her best Lukens impersonation, but it wasn't her area. "Has he hurt you?"

"He's not stable."

An answer, but a nonanswer.

During all of this Jason stayed quiet, leaning against the living room wall. At least he was right *there*. "Please answer Detective MacIntosh, ma'am. Has he?"

If she had an answer to the question that would help them, they didn't get a chance to hear it.

"Hello." Nichols strolled in at that moment, interrupting, just absolutely walking in the back door without permission. Ellie wasn't armed either, because she'd just barely managed to finish dressing before her first visitor arrived. "Why do I have the feeling I should be part of this discussion? By the way, the two officers outside won't be joining us."

Being caught unaware was the theme of this investigation, at least for her.

Their visitor looked absurdly normal in pleated tan slacks and a pressed pale blue shirt, his hair neatly combed. But there were white lines of anger around his mouth.

The new arrival's wife was so pale now she looked like she would fall on the floor. "Why? What did you do to them? Why are you home so early and why would you just come in here and not knock?"

"Early release day for standardized testing. I saw you walking over here. Where are the kids? More important, are those even my kids? I've always wondered. They sure as hell don't look like me." His voice was hard and he seemed to completely disregard that Detective Jason Santiago was even in the room. Ellie wasn't positive it even registered, but on the other hand, she was afraid it did. They'd been underestimating this man all along, both his intelligence and his deranged behavior.

Maybe they were hitting pay dirt all of a sudden, but Ellie wasn't sure it was good to be part of the equation. Still she edged closer to Alissa. "Let her go. She's not part of this."

Nichols ignored her. "You know, Alissa, I've forgiven all your affairs, I think you can allow me mine."

Jason said harshly, "Listen—"

Ellie had to get control of the situation somehow. "We are *not* having an affair."

He rebuffed that statement in a soft and very chilling voice, "Oh yes, we are. It might not be physical yet, but it will be."

Her gun was on the dresser in her bedroom. All she needed was a chance to get there.

Jason moved forward, his tone lethal. "Is that a physical threat of some sort, Mr. Nichols?"

"It's a promise."

"You're out of your mind," Alissa said in a choked voice, showing some true backbone. "What have you done? I knew after I thought about it that the smoke bomb was you, but I couldn't think of a single reason why. I guess I should be happy you didn't just kill us all to get her attention."

"Not too late."

Three things happened at once. Nichols lunged toward his wife, Ellie was ready to bolt for the bedroom to get her weapon, and Santiago was right there. All he said was, "Oh hell, I've been waiting for this."

And then he went for it.

Typical Santiago style. He tackled Nichols about

two seconds before the man could get his hands on his wife and Ellie had her opportunity, so while they were wrestling around her living room floor, she ran to get her gun, yelling frantically at a paralyzed Alissa Nichols, "Get outside. Get outside. Run!"

If there was one thing she didn't want it was a hysterical wife around to add to the melee so she couldn't get off a shot if necessary.

Luckily for her, Santiago had brawled a time or two. It didn't surprise her he'd won the fight, because she'd seen him in action before, but she expected that picture sent to Metzger had motivated some interesting emotions Georgia would have to help him sort out. When she rushed back out, weapon drawn, Jason was already on his feet, blood running from his nose, but he wasn't the one unconscious. Nichols wasn't going anywhere soon, but at least it seemed like he was still breathing.

She lowered her weapon.

Jason wiped the blood off his upper lip with the back of his hand. "He really has pissed me off lately. I could have shot him, but she was standing between me and him. This was far more satisfying."

"I can tell." At least her heart rate was already slowing. Nichols was also bleeding all over the floor and a rug she really liked that would probably never be the same.

"Ah man, I can see another IA investigation for excessive force in my future." Santiago went over to the kitchen and wet a paper towel and ran it over his face. "I hate that kind of thing. We need to go check on the surveillance team."

Someone was pounding on the front door. Ellie said, "I think his wife might back you up. I'm just hoping out of gratitude she'll give me those pictures so I can burn them so they aren't evidence."

"Don't do that, I'd like to have them."

"Dream on, cowboy."

# Chapter 30

"I'm not going to lie, I've talked to the district attorney and this is going to be one of those trials where they have to turn people away." Metzger was as frank as always. "It will be a media zoo. Tell me about the Parkview connection."

"Nichols went there and his kids go there now." Ellie had spent hours and hours trying to figure it out. "I've consulted with Dr. Lukens, and she speculates that he had some bad experience there, maybe bullying that made him distrustful and insecure. Murder is a show of power, and he was taking revenge on people he associated with not protecting him. His first victim was maybe random. She might have just reminded him of someone. The same with the young man he hung . . . Lukens thinks they ran into each other and there was a memory flash that also reminded him of someone and he decided to kill him. The others were people he knew as a child."

Santiago spoke up. "The staff of the school where he works was not as surprised as we thought by a possible murder charge. He's a classic sociopath. One teacher told us that when he was caught eating the chicken salad she'd brought for lunch, he didn't even really apologize and just ate the rest of it in front of her."

"A stolen sandwich isn't—"

"Hold on. When she got home later that day she found someone had strangled her cat and left it on the front porch. I realize it is quite a step from that to murder of a human being, but it still shows a lack of remorse that is consistent with his type of behavior. That's just a small example. He apparently frequently referred to his wife as a bitch or worse, so his marital problems weren't a secret. She was—and is—afraid of him."

Ellie said, "He made people uncomfortable. Me too, looking back. I never addressed him by his first name. I always kept a distance by calling him Mr. Nichols. I certainly called his wife Alissa. We are taught as officers to address people in a proper fashion, and he never invited me to do otherwise, even though we were neighbors."

Metzger rubbed his jaw. "Without Mrs. Nichols you wouldn't have a viable case. Luckily for you both, she seems to be more than ready to talk. Finding the hidden camera helps. It doesn't prove anything, but it doesn't hurt."

"We have enough eyewitnesses that we can make it stick." Jason settled his hands on his knees. "The driver's licenses alone will put him in jail for life."

"Internal Affairs wants me to suspend you for excessive force," Metzger said.

Ellie had seen that one coming, but so had he. "Sir, you have my report—"

"I do. Be quiet."

Santiago didn't blink. "Fine, I know I went for him hard. In my defense, I think it can be confirmed he had just threatened to kill his wife because Ellie and I both heard him say it. I saw him moving toward her. You were once a patrol officer. Time to choose exists. She was in danger. Really, what would you do? Let him kill her?"

Metzger didn't argue. "I'll put that in the paperwork with everything else in an effort to support that you went overboard but had adequate motivation. I think all three of us here know you had some personal motivation as well."

"He threatened Ellie in a very personal and sexual way right in front of me. What would you do?"

Metzger pressed his fingers to his forehead. "I see the argument, Santiago, I just don't want to participate in it. You could have just cuffed him. Broken nose? Fractured jaw?"

"I wasn't the only one in that fight. He went for me too. Do you know how many people he's killed? Ask his wife. He was going to strangle her. He said it."

"Yes. Believe it or not, I read every single report."

Oh, here it came. Ellie had been more than dreading this moment. "Sir, about that picture he sent you."

What was she even going to say? It was altered but damning.

Metzger solved the dilemma in an unexpected way by stopping her. "What picture?" He just looked bland.

"Well, I'd really prefer if it wasn't admitted into evidence."

"Detective MacIntosh, I have no idea even remotely what you are talking about." He leaned forward deliberately. "Care to clarify?"

Ellie had to admit she blinked, but in a second Jason grabbed her arm and pulled her from her chair. "No, she doesn't. Are we all done here, Chief?"

"Done. You are officially suspended with pay until there is a decision made about your conduct, Detective Santiago, and this better be the last time I have to stick up for you."

Being dragged out into the hallway wasn't fun, and she yanked her arm free as soon as possible. "Was that necessary?"

He looked unrepentant. "Yes. I know you. You might have clarified, and he didn't want you to say another word about it. Look, if he's choosing to overlook it, let's take it as a gift. We both just dodged a bullet."

She really didn't think they had. Metzger wasn't their only problem. "You just got suspended." The press, IA, her family being disrupted—she wasn't going to look at the condo the same ever again—there was a long casualty list.

"With pay, which means he thinks I'll be cleared. I sure should be. I know I wasn't gentle, but he was a lot worse with his victims and he tried to give as good as he got. I was just more ticked off."

"I need to get away now that he's in custody," she told him impulsively. "How about that fishing trip in say . . . an hour? I have some calls to make, letting the families know we got him. The trial will be painful, but they deserve to know right away where we stand. I have to talk to Jody too."

"So where are we going?" Jason checked the straps on the carrier, but this was not his area of expertise so he wasn't insulted when Ellie checked them again as if she knew what she was doing. He could load a tank onto a transport ship, but buckling down a canoe was not something he'd done before.

"Glen Lake. Close by and pretty deep, so there are some big fish in there, and it has public access since it isn't entirely private, but as far as I can tell, it isn't used much. I prefer the experience to be as solitary as possible."

"I suppose I can see that."

The paddles and poles went into the back of the car, and while he was still amused by her determination, he was willing to fly with Ellie's desire to take him fishing. He hadn't had that growing up, so he just wasn't used to it. The closest he'd come was when his math teacher, who was also the football coach, had asked if he'd ever thought about trying out for the team. He hadn't. He did think it over, and went ahead and did it. Surprise, surprise, he'd made it.

Yes, he'd screwed it up, but hell, he'd been seventeen with virtually no guidance his entire life. It had been good while it lasted; he'd been the star running back. It had also given him some insight on discipline and teamwork.

Lesson learned.

He'd even voluntarily called his mother to thank her for their dinner together. She had been surprised, but effusive.

Now that was real progress.

The lake was as pretty as promised, the banks crowded with trees, and a great blue heron took off as they arrived, winging past like a low-flying plane. Ellie commented, "They come back pretty early. You can see them as soon as there's clear water." She added with a straight face as she parked the car, "That's about the time the spiders migrate back this way."

"Spiders migrate? I'm going to tell you that I'd stand between you and Bigfoot, but I'll toss you between me and that spider as a shield."

"My hero. Bigfoot? Really?"

"Hey, I'm a believer. I watch TV. If it's on there, it must be true." He admired how the length of her lashes sent shadows on her cheekbones, which told him he was hopeless, but he had been for some time.

"And yet you doubted me about the spiders."

"Yeah, well. Stop telling me stuff like that, please."

She wore a flannel shirt but it was patterned in pink and light green, and jeans just as faded as his. He was really admiring the view. Ellie went on. "Who knew you'd be so susceptible? I thought you were a tough soldier turned cop. Have you ever heard of the Gilman? He's this creature that lives in the lakes around here and supposedly crawls out of the water—"

"Uh, I think that's enough, Detective MacIntosh. I appreciate your sense of humor, though. I'm going to skip the Gilman story unless you want to hear some of mine, which are not for the faint of heart."

She declined. "No thanks. Isn't this a beautiful morning?"

It was. It had been a beautiful evening too, though they'd arrived late. Her house was rustic and there was a lot of wood and stone, but he found he liked it, and it fit the fishing theme of their trip.

She handed him the paddles. "Hop in."

Hop? He would have ended up in the water. Getting into a canoe wasn't as easy as it sounded. As he carefully stepped in it moved from side to side. He could swim, but he wasn't good at it. She was also right, the lake was beautiful, but it was dark and deserted.

"Like this." She got in much more gracefully and handed him a rod before pointing at a tackle box. "Pick a lure, tie it on, and pay attention. Do this with your reel and cast it into the water and slowly draw it back in. It's called trolling. I'll paddle us out."

She demonstrated and it didn't look too hard, but he had the feeling that was a skill that required some practice. Still, the setting was great, the closest freeway noise was about thirty miles away, and other than birds flying here and there, there was no one around.

He dug into the tackle box and chose this orange lure with black spots that didn't look remotely like a meal for a fish to him, but someone evidently thought so, and fastened it on.

First cast was an embarrassment, but the second one was a lot better. On about the fifth try, he actually got a strike.

He panicked. Just a little. "Hey, something is pulling on my line. Now what?"

To her credit Ellie didn't laugh at him, but there was amusement in her eyes. "You need to play the fish if it is big, because otherwise you can't land it without snapping your line. Wear him out. Let him take off and then bring him back slowly. He's like a suspect; you've got him, but just no proof it's going to come to anything. So work it. If you push too hard, he'll run and you'll lose him."

That was a way to put it he could understand.

It ended up not being all that big, but was still over

a foot long. She informed him it was a walleye as she deftly took it off the lure and gently lowered it into the water.

Maybe he would take this up and forget Everest.

At the end of it all, she caught the biggest fish, and it was a beauty, a northern pike about twenty-five inches long, but he did like the quiet, and maybe the wilderness lifestyle wasn't so bad.

MacIntosh was definitely catch and release, so they put every fish back, watched it swim away, and decided to go back to her house for lunch.

His phone rang just as they were walking inside. Jason answered immediately, since Metzger didn't bother with calls that weren't important. "Santiago."

"Internal Affairs has decided you aren't worth it. I've always wondered about that myself, so good call on their part. With so many murder indictments on Nichols, the statements from his wife and MacIntosh, and the attack on Grasso, you are clear. Can we please never have this conversation again? The suspension is over, so enjoy the rest of your involuntary vacation because it's done. I expect you back on the job."

Jason had to admit he was relieved. He told Ellie, "Internal Affairs is backing away."

She didn't look surprised. "I thought they might."

"I thought they might not."

"You do take a risk now and then."

"In a good cause." He meant her.

And she knew it.

# Epilogue

"I need for us to make a stop."

Santiago was his usual self. "Okay . . . sure, that's fine. What for?"

"Not saying." Ellie was hesitant about this whole thing anyway. "If you can't do it, don't worry about it. I can just drive myself. Just take me home."

"Did I say I can't do it?"

"Never mind. Just drop me off and I'll get my car."

"Ellie, really?"

"Two o'clock."

"Where?"

She looked at the time on her phone. She could go it alone, but he'd know anyway, and it was now a decision she'd made, and for that matter, it really had never been a decision.

This was a difficult road to walk.

The last case had been hell, and she was fatigued for more than apparently one reason.

It wasn't entirely his fault.

He owned a good deal of it, however. So did she. She gave him the address.

"Are you sick or something?" he asked as he parked his truck in front of a doctor's office. "Flu?"

Wasn't the man a detective? It was so irritating to even have to go through with this, but at the moment all men fell into the stupid category. Ellie said, "Not exactly. I do not have the flu."

"You've seemed awfully tired, but I just chalked it up to that last case."

"I *am* tired."

He figured it out in about two seconds when they walked through the door and he took in the waiting room. He caught her wrist, his blue eyes intense. "Are you shitting me?"

There were multiple physicians in the practice, so the waiting room was full and it was quiet. Or it had been until they arrived.

"I was kind of counting on you to behave for this experience, so clean it up, please."

"You're . . . pregnant?"

"Unless all three of those tests are wrong and medical science has lost its edge. Let's let them tell us if it's true. We'll still have to deal with Metzger."

It was a good and bad thing he looked like he'd just hit the lottery instead of being horrified. "A baby?"

She couldn't do this. She could not have a baby with Detective Jason Santiago. This wasn't what she'd envisioned for her future . . . she needed a stockbroker who loved meat loaf or something, instead of someone who'd been suspended from duty for winning a fistfight with a stalker and killer. "I'm going to go sign in. That is if you'll let go of me."

Jody had been the one she'd called first, not sure whether she should laugh or cry. Her sister had informed her she had the most interesting life in the world and it beat the hell out of watching cartoons and using bottle brushes, which is what she had to do for a good deal of the day.

Forget the stockbroker.

She didn't picture the stockbroker getting up in the middle of the night, and yet she was fairly sure Jason would cradle a baby in the wee hours so she could catch some sleep. He'd probably have a holstered weapon and be watching women's beach volleyball, but as long as he did it, that would help.

"We all got here somehow."

"I'm kinda off guard here. We were careful."

"If you will cast back, we weren't careful every single time. Guess what happens now and then?"

"You told me not to worry about it."

"I meant it. At that moment I wasn't worried about it either."

"We made love. I'm not the one who won't give into that."

*Everyone* was listening to them.

He had a legitimate point. "You aren't the one who might have a baby."

"Marry me."

"What?" She'd never been so taken aback in her life.

"For the smartest woman I know, you are so obtuse. Why don't we get married? We practically live together anyway."

"That started to avoid a murderer. You'd consider that a proposal?"

This had now escalated to perhaps a contender for most unusual waiting room conversation ever. She felt like a soap opera star.

"Is that a no?"

"I'm not sure." She was emotional and it showed, so she just said it. "Then we can't work together."

"That's the objection? Oh shit, this kid is doomed. You'd say no because of that?"

There was a solid point. "You have a lot of flaws."

"Oh, your perfection isn't in question? Ellie, help me out here. I love you. What else is it you want?"

She couldn't really ask for more. They'd never have a romance novel kind of life, but it wasn't like she was a stranger to the twists and turns.

The nurse saved her. "Eleanor?"

To his credit, Santiago asked, "Can I come with you? I assume you want that, otherwise I wouldn't be here."

"I guess." She shrugged, but the truth was, she didn't want to do this alone. "I might need someone to hold my hand."

"Right. You need someone to hold your hand? Haven't you shot serial killers?"

He *had* to say that out loud. No one even pretended to be reading their magazines any longer.

"So have you. Can you keep your voice down?"

The women were staring at them, and that was *everyone*. Ellie blamed Georgia for this conversation. Since she knew him, Ellie had actually asked how to break the news, and Georgia had suggested that simply taking him to the appointment might be the easiest since he'd insist on going anyway.

He, of course, didn't pay any attention. "I've only shot a few. This I haven't done before."

She was so grateful when they were guided down the corridor to the exam room.

The doctor was older, but she'd been seeing him since she moved to the city for annual routine exams, so at least he was familiar. The man took one look at Santiago and said, "Father?"

"I sure will be." He sounded like he meant it.

The physician said, "Let's listen to the heartbeat. From the timeline you gave my nurse when you made this appointment, we should be able to get one."

# TOR

## Award-winning authors
## Compelling stories

Please join us at the website
below for more information
about this author and other great
Tor selections, and to sign up for
our monthly newsletter!